DOUBLE DARE

Dare to Dream

Linda Rakos

LINDA RAKOS

Double Dare
Copyright © 2019 by Linda Rakos

Tellwell Talent
www.tellwell.ca

ISBN
978-0-2288-1810-6 (Hardcover)
978-0-2288-1808-3 (Paperback)
978-0-2288-1809-0 (eBook)

Dedicated to Leona

My twin

My best friend

CHAPTER ONE

The band Double Dare, featuring identical twins Laney and Raven Dare, was the newest phenomenon to hit the music scene in the last decade. Their lyrics showcased their distinct talent and their combined vocals harmonized beautifully. The twins were the centerpiece of the band and for them their future was bright. Laney and Raven were an exquisitely matched pair. Mirror images. They were physically striking. Ebony hair cascaded down their backs and framed flawless faces accented by smoldering gray eyes and warm seductive smiles.

It was Independence Day. The warm summer air was filled with an electric, contagious excitement and the crowd was super hyped as they waited for the show to start. The screams were deafening when the twins stepped onto the stage. It was like seeing double and the crowd loved them. Both girls were immediately caught up by the enthusiasm that swept through the crowd. They loved performing and the crowd loved them.

Tonight there was no holding back. From start to finish their show was full of excitement and emotion. They were completely in accord with each other, knowing how the other would follow a lead. When they finished their last set Laney, usually the lead singer, took the microphone. Smiling, she acknowledged the exuberant crowd. "What an amazing night this has been. We absolutely have the best fans and all of us in the band want to thank everyone for your love and support. Tonight was our last tour date and of course we saved the best for last." Cheers again erupted from the crowd.

Double Dare's tour across North America was awesome. They'd been performing non-stop throughout the States from coast to coast and border to border. The band had received rave reviews from the media but after tonight's show they were taking a well-deserved break for the summer. The girls were flying to England in the morning and would be spending the summer visiting their grandmother and sight-seeing. They were tired and both were looking forward to some time off and relaxing for a few weeks.

Raven watched in awe as Laney worked the crowd and she could understand why Laney was such a big star. Her twin had charisma and charm to spare. The fans were all cheering by the time Laney said, with an unexpected break in her voice, "In closing, Raven and I want to leave you with the first performance of our newly released single, Dare to be Alone." The crowd went wild but calmed when Laney handed the microphone to Raven.

Raven stepped forward. The spotlight encircled her as she started to sing. Her voice, clear and pure, hushed the crowd. By the time Laney joined in, the crowd was captivated and awestruck. Every person there knew how personal this song was.

Even alone, we're never apart,
Together forever, you're in my heart;
Double dare, pinkie swear,
Think of me and I'll be there.

At the end of the song, Laney wiped the tears from the cheeks of her twin sister. The audience remained spellbound for they knew they had just shared an experience between two kindred spirits that exists beyond mortality. The twins were like two people with one soul. Hand in hand, Raven and Laney walked off the stage. The lights dimmed and finally went out.

In the back the two girls were spent. Usually on a high at the end of a show, tonight was different. The new song was personal to both, symbolic of the changes that lay ahead. Laney's own eyes were bright with unshed tears. "That was quite the finale. Are you all right?"

"I'll be fine. I don't know why I cried." They both knew that part of it was that, for now, this was the end of their performing together. For the first time in their lives they were going to go their separate ways. Independent of each other.

"How am I going to continue without you? We've never been apart." Laney couldn't imagine what her life would be like without her twin.

Desiree, for she was only Raven on stage, reassured her sister, "Don't be silly. That's what our new song is all about. We'll never be alone. It doesn't matter if we're here together or living independently in different parts of the world, we're still connected. Our souls, our spirit, our very essence was united the day we were born."

Desiree's expression remained serious. "Performing is your dream, Laney, not mine. For you, it's exciting to meet new people every night. You love the bright lights and the attention. I know your need, your desire for fame, just like it was with Dad."

Laney couldn't deny it. She thought of their father and his failed dreams. Johnny Dare never quite made it in the music industry so she felt she had something to prove. She knew this was what she wanted and she wanted it more than anything else. Laney had to admit that Desiree didn't have that same drive and intensity. She also had to admit that she knew this for a long time and now had to appreciate Desiree's commitment to her.

Desiree's words were sincere and heartfelt when she declared, "You're the star when we're on stage. The fans will hardly miss me. Cash would love to duo with you and you have great chemistry. He always has a special look in his eyes when he looks at you and I didn't notice any objections when he kissed you back stage the other night."

Laney's cheeks colored. "It was just a kiss. It didn't mean anything."

Desiree wrapped her arms around her sister. "I'm looking forward to this new direction in my life. We each have our destiny to follow. For now, this is mine, Laney."

"I do understand, Des. You know me, I'm just being selfish."

Both girls had a natural gift of laughter and were the first to make fun of themselves. Laney released her infectious giggle. "If we were really famous the gossip columnists would have a field day with this. You'd either be in rehab somewhere or we hate each other and can't perform together any more so we had to break up. They'd probably put the blame on me."

"One of us has to be the evil twin. You're different, stay that way. You're open and alive. You love to be on stage and share yourself with everyone. People want to be around you because you bring them joy. You're that free spirit that shines and everyone is drawn to you like a moth to the flame."

"You're different, too. You always present an aura of mystery. Other than me, you don't allow anyone get too close."

"We may look alike but it's okay that we're different. I'm just more serious than you."

Laney blinked in surprise. "Not always." It was fun for Laney to watch the change in her twin as she transitioned from Desiree to Raven. "Sometimes, even I'm taken aback by your fierce, audacious attitude that you can possess on stage."

Desiree smiled knowingly. It came from within because she'd always taken on the role of protector since the girls were little.

Laney giggled, "Whereas, I'm susceptible to a whim and game to do anything without thinking. You must admit we've had some wonderful experiences. Do you remember the summer we played at the Golf Course in Phoenix and we borrowed the golf carts and raced around the course after the show? I'm surprised we didn't end up in jail more than once." Both girls laughed out loud.

Desiree sobered first. Her voice was quiet but utterly determined, "Our adventures will continue. The time has come for us to have new ones on our own."

"Was that our last performance together, Des?" Silent tears fell without warning.

Desiree brushed the tears from her sister's cheeks. "For now. We need to cut the strings and see what the future brings. I know this hasn't been easy for you." When Laney looked up Desiree calmly stated, "We've talked about this before. You and I both have the same zest for life. But as much as we're the same we're that much different. Together, we found our wings after Mom and Dad died. It's okay if we fly solo for awhile. So, my little chickadee, you're going to fly home after our vacation to a life you love. You are a rising star that is just beginning to shine. You'll become famous and the whole world will know who you are. And I'm going to stay and find out who I am starting with our family tree. I want to know more about our parents and our grandmother. I want to explore their world. Mom's mother is our only remaining family so that's my beginning."

Together, they allowed themselves to drift back to their childhood. Their parents, Johnny and Phoebe Dare, had left England as soon as they turned eighteen to fulfill Johnny's dream of becoming a singing star. It was a romantic fantasy of course. The odds of him rising to stardom were gigantic but he believed he had a God-given talent.

Phoebe loved Johnny and she loved his enthusiasm. She shared his belief that singing was his gift and he had to share it with the world. His dreams were big but his successes weren't. After the first year Johnny formed a band and they gave up their apartment and began living a very nomadic lifestyle. When Phoebe found out she was pregnant with the twins Johnny was ecstatic but he was still chasing his dream. Phoebe knew that she wanted the family to stay together so the travelling lifestyle continued. Other kids called them gypsies growing up. The twins accepted the ignorance of others. There was no need for friends because they had each other. They were inseparable companions who were all and everything to each other.

Due to their transient lifestyle the girls were home schooled by their mother. Phoebe worked hard to build a good life for herself and her children with the resources she'd been given. Sometimes their education came with great planning and sometimes it was the result of a whim. The only constant in their lives was the endless love from both parents. How unfair that both of them had already died. Their mom had passed just after they turned fifteen and their dad a few years later.

Like their dad, Desiree and Delaney loved music. It wasn't long before they were back-up musicians playing drums and guitars, a far cry from the two little girls who played tambourines alongside their daddy. Johnny enjoyed having the twins on stage. Sometimes they'd sing with him and on rare occasions he'd highlight them and they'd perform a duet. It never ceased to amaze Johnny how the girls could captivate an audience. They had something special, that something he'd searched for all of his life.

Over the years, the twins had matured into stunning young ladies. Johnny was supportive of everything his girls did and he couldn't have been prouder of their talent and accomplishments. Just before they turned twenty Johnny died. They now only had each other and all they knew was music so they decided to form their own band. They had no difficulty in agreeing on the band name, Double Dare.

With strong belief, Laney declared, "It's just you and me now. There are no parents to please or answer to. This is the beginning of our band and I think we need to be distinctive and edgy. If we wear wigs, outlandish makeup and amazing outfits it'll disguise who we are on stage. We can maintain our anonymity and keep our private and performing lives separate."

The last comment caught Desiree's attention but she quickly dismissed it. "The uniqueness we offer is our looks and the fact that we truly mirror each other. That's something we should never change. We can still be edgy without any gimmicks."

"You're right. Like usual, I got carried away. I guess we need to think this out if it's really going to happen." She switched gears again, "You need to change your name."

A look of bewilderment crossed Desiree's face. "What's wrong with Desiree?"

Laney had always been outspoken, "Nothing. But you should have something unique."

"I like my name. Change yours."

"Mine is already unique. Des or Desi could be a guy's name and Desiree is too sweet. You need something that will fit our image. I've got it. Your stage name has to be Raven. Your long black hair shines like a raven's wing. The name sounds beautiful and mysterious at the same time. It'll help give you that distinguished quality as a performer."

Desiree wasn't sure if she wanted to play a role, pretending to be someone she wasn't, but she reluctantly agreed, "Fine, but only on stage."

Laney hooked her little finger around her sister's finger. "Double dare, pinkie swear."

"Double dare, pinkie swear," Desiree repeated. As always they followed it with a hug.

Once they found the right band members their concept of Double Dare took form. That's when the hard work began. Double Dare had to get their music heard. Neither Delaney nor Desiree were diverted from their set path. They learned everything about how the music business worked. They didn't know what the rules were and as a result there were times the girls were known to be head-strong. The girls were relentless when looking for gigs despite the magnitude of the challenge.

Laney was fearless and was never one to be discouraged by anyone let alone by any rules. "If you don't ask, you don't get. Besides, we have nothing to lose."

"Be prepared for a lot of no's," Desiree said practically.

To which Laney countered back, "It only takes one yes."

"You're incorrigible. It's a long way to the top."

"Less, after you climb the first step. Besides, we've never avoided a challenge."

Both became skilled at networking and marketing. Their persistence paid off and it wasn't long before they became the popular band they were today.

The first year was a challenge but everyone was driven and had the motivation to work hard. The members had their weird idiosyncrasies but they bonded just the same. It was a lifestyle the twins enjoyed, relishing their success with both amusement and pride.

Laney brought them back to the present. "It was like we lost Mom twice. Why did Dad let her parents take her ashes back to England? She should be here with us."

"Dad said that was what Mom wanted. We were always unsettled as a family and even though she lived here in America it was never her home. Dad loved Mom more than anything, so as hard as it was he honored her wishes. That's part of why I need to go to England." The girls were silent for a moment. "You're so much like Dad. You know you were his favorite. I wasn't jealous," she added hastily. "I know he loved us both but you were his golden child because your drive was as passionate as his."

"And you always had Mom. I have to be honest, I was jealous. She named you Desiree because she said it meant the desired one. She always wanted a girl."

"Yes, she did. And she also said heaven blessed her and that having twin girls doubled her joy. You know she loved us both; we were her world outside of Dad's. She always said we were brought by her guardian angel and when she left she gifted us with angelic voices." Both girls burst out laughing. They knew this was the only thing angelic about either one of them.

The sound of fireworks outside reminded them how late it was. Hand in hand, they exited the building. They had a special relationship like no other.

The next morning the sky was gray and stormy and heavy rain was forecast by afternoon. When it was time to leave for the airport the weather was oppressive as the rain poured down. A terrifying feeling of uncertainty enveloped Laney, causing her to say, "The sky is like a cloak of doom. Maybe this is a bad omen. Are you sure you don't want to change your mind?"

"Are you just doing this for me?" Desiree asked, with a look of shock. "It's not too late to change your mind."

"At first I was," Laney admitted honestly. She quickly reassured Desiree, "Now I'm doing it for us. This time together will be priceless."

Desiree had to admit to herself that for the last few months she'd become increasingly restless. It was time for a change and she was too honest to maintain the delusion. There was a great deal to learn about their parents and going to England was the beginning. The relationship with their grandparents had always been on a formal basis due to the estrangement throughout the years. The disengagement was not due to distance alone.

Desiree said lovingly, "We'll always be best friends no matter where we are. You know there's no better friend than a sister."

"Okay, bestie. Tally ho, driver. To the airport."

Both girls giggled as they climbed into the back seat. The taxi driver looked at his passengers in his rear view mirror and caught a brief glimpse of their faces. Like everyone else, he couldn't believe how much these two young ladies looked alike. They were still laughing when they pulled away from the curb. The girls chatted away.

"According to her address, Constance Malone, our matriarch, lives in a hotel in London. Who has a grandmother named Constance? She's probably horribly prim and proper. What do you think?"

Desiree refused to take the bait, "I wonder what she'll think of us. It's been years since she's seen us. After Mom's ashes were taken back to England Dad basically cut our ties with her family. It's sad that we don't know more about her."

"Well, I hope she's not too uppity. We've all heard about the British reserve. And the fact that they drink too much and the food is terrible."

"Lighten up, Laney. We're going to have a good time and you'll enjoy yourself."

Laney was never one to give in too easily. "Okay, I'll give you the benefit of the doubt. We'll probably have to share a bed like we did when we were little."

Desiree grabbed her twin's hand and squeezed it tight. "That would be okay. Remember all the fun we had when we were younger. We'd whisper and giggle, share confidences and fears. You and I would lay there and dream out loud long into the night. You were never afraid to dream, Laney. Don't change."

"I'm relieved it's summer. I always think of England as damp and cold. Mind you, today doesn't feel much like summer here," Laney added as she shivered.

Intentionally changing the subject, Desiree said, "There are so many fascinating historical sites. I think we should book one of those Hop-On, Hop-Off bus tours. We'll be able to see iconic landmarks as we tour around London. We can decide which ones we want to go back and see on our own and spend as much time as we want exploring them in detail."

Excitement grabbed hold and Laney added, "And a river tour on the Thames River. Imagine seeing London's skyline as we float down the river at night. It'll be amazing. You're right. We're going to have a marvelous holiday. What's a must see for you, Des?"

"We know Mom loved the arts so I think we need to go to the ballet and the theatre, tour art galleries and of course there are lots of famous castles. Outside of London, I really want to take a bus tour to Stonehenge. I want to walk around the Stone Circle, which history says is a spiritual place and a source of inspiration." Her voice broke with emotion, "I want to walk in the footsteps of our ancestors."

Laney quickly interjected, "And of course there's the famous London Bridge." Instantaneously, they broke out singing, "London Bridge is falling down, falling down, falling down." This was followed by a fit of giggles.

Both girls lapsed into silence and were soon lost in their own thoughts unaware that the rain had worsened. They were forced back to the present when the taxi swerved violently. They both screamed as the taxi skidded off the road and over the steep embankment, slamming into several trees. Shattered glass peppered them as the taxi rolled before coming to rest at the bottom of the coulee with a bone-jarring stop. Only then did the screaming cease.

The twins looked at each other in horror, both fully aware of the severity of the accident. The taxi driver's lifeless body was slumped over the wheel. Blood covered both girls; neither knew if it was their own. It soon became evident and fear was reflected in their eyes. One twin leaned over and cradled her sister twin as the life blood trickled from her. A young life was ending before it had a chance to be lived. As the sirens drew closer, they looked at each other one last time. For one twin, life ended. For the other twin, the nightmare began. The lone survivor again began to scream and then the world went black.

The still form in the bed moaned as she stirred. Her eyelids felt incredibly heavy as she struggled to open them. The bright lights made her squint. She moved her eyes slowly around the sterile room and came to rest on a woman in uniform. The movement caused her head to throb and for a moment the room spun around her. With effort, she attempted to focus. Every limb of her body hurt. Experimenting, she moved her legs and wiggled her toes and was relieved to find they worked. Although her body ached all over it appeared to be okay.

The nurse smiled, "Well, well. Look who's finally awake."

"Where am I?" Her mouth was so dry that her voice was barely a whisper. It sounded far away to her own ears.

The nurse walked over and raised the head of the bed so she could give her patient a sip of water. "You're in the hospital."

When the nurse started to hold the glass to her patient's lips, the young girl took it from her. "I can hold it," she assured the nurse. Weakness and tension caused her hand to shake as she took the glass. She swallowed and with a creaky whisper asked, "Why am I here? Have I been here long?" Exhausted from the simple acts of drinking and speaking, she closed her eyes.

"Three days. You've been through a terrible ordeal, Miss Dare."

The girl's eyes flew open as a blank look came across her face and her mind filled with sudden panic. Her eyes darkened with confusion. "Who is Miss Dare?" She tried to sit up but a searing pain shot through her head and she sank back onto the pillow. The young girl was so confused by what had just happened she lay there trembling. She couldn't understand what had happened to her. Nor could she shake the feeling that something was wrong. Terribly, terribly wrong. Why didn't she know who she was? Trying to push away the jab of pain that slowed her thoughts she came up with nothing. She closed her eyes. *This is just a dream, a horrible dream.*

As the walls began to close in around her she vaguely heard the nurse say, "I'll get the doctor." Without another word the nurse turned and left the room.

When the nurse returned with the doctor the patient stared at the two of them, her mind paralyzed, refusing to function. "I don't know my name. Why don't I know my name?" The hysterical shock was evident in her voice, as well as on her face, as fear sent chills racing up and down her spine. She looked frantically at the doctor. "What's wrong with me?" she dared to ask in a feeble whisper.

After Dr. Jonas Hahn introduced himself, he said, "Don't panic on us, young lady. I'm sure it's temporary. You've suffered a hard blow to your head as a result of a car accident." He bent over her to examine her head. "You were unconscious when you arrived at the hospital and slipped into a coma," he added as he beamed a tiny light at each of her pupils. He paused for a moment as if to make certain she was following the conversation.

She continued to look at him with blank eyes, unable to make sense out of what was happening. Her mind refused to understand. The doctor handed his patient a mirror hoping it would release a memory. There was a heavy silence as she looked at the doctor and back to the nurse. Her hand shook as she took the mirror and held it close. A pale lifeless face was staring at her, a stranger's face. She dropped the mirror in shock. The terror was back. She turned and stared back at them, her eyes brimming with unshed tears. She swiped at them furiously when they fell. She opened her mouth but words failed her.

Dr. Hahn had been observing her expressions closely. "I'm going to have the nurse give you a sedative. It'll relax you and help you sleep. We'll see what tomorrow brings." He left to schedule tests for his patient. He also had a very difficult call to make.

The young girl lay still subconsciously knowing something terrible had happened and she was fighting desperately to remember what it was. Her mind again began to fill with panic as she blinked back tears. *Maybe if I concentrate really hard.* She closed her eyes tight and a lone tear escaped. The sedative took hold and she slipped into a void, a dark empty place.

Constance Malone, who was the epitome of a successful and powerful woman, and her godson, Rowan Le Baron, were sitting in her parlour. Constance was an attractive widow who had aged gracefully. Regal looking with a natural dignity, she was a lady who possessed inherent poise. She lived a quiet life but one that suited her. Her conservative demeanor often made her appear aloof.

Oliver Malone, Constance's husband, and Preston Le Baron, Rowan's grandfather, had been successful business partners as well as friends. Together, Oliver and Preston had invested in both residential architecture and land development throughout the United Kingdom. Small investments paid off and provided monies for larger investments. The one that meant the most to them was the purchase of the hotel that Constance Malone and Rowan Le Baron now lived in. The two men named it after their wives, Constance and Lynette, and it became the Conlyn Grand Hotel. The hotel was Victorian in architecture and was located on a quiet street in one of London's more desirable areas. It was perfectly situated for shopping, theatres and was within walking distance to several famous sites.

Preston Le Baron had been a Baron of considerable lineage and estate. He'd been both father and mentor to his grandson, Rowan, who sadly had lost his parents when he was merely a lad. Rowan Le Baron, like his grandfather, carried the aristocratic look that went along with his title. He had inherited his status and wealth but remained successful due to hard work. His power was legendary. Today, Rowan Le Baron was one of the most eligible bachelors in London, a prime target who remained elusive.

As usual, Rowan was focused on business. "I'm planning on going up to our hotel in Manchester this week. There appears to be a few management issues that need to be addressed. Our other properties are fine but this one needs my attention right away."

"You already work too hard, Rowan," scolded Constance. When he shook his head she asked, "Will you be away long?"

Rowan's face wore a serious expression but he managed to smile at his godmother. She worried too much about him. "Just a couple of days. Of course, that can change after I get there." To anyone who knew him, Rowan always appeared to be in control.

They were interrupted when the phone rang. "Rowan, you're close. Will you answer it? It might be the girls. Last time we talked they thought they'd be here by the end of the week." Constance was longing for their arrival so she could get to know her granddaughters. They had reached out to her after their father had died and time was slowly bridging the gap that was created years ago.

Constance became anxious because the conversation was very one-sided and as Rowan listened his face was bleak. There was an odd expression in his eyes that Constance didn't understand. When Rowan did speak there was grimness in his voice, "Very well, you can leave the arrangements to me." Rowan put down the receiver and went and sat down next to her.

The seriousness in her godson's voice told her the matter was of importance. "What's wrong, Rowan. Is it the girls? Aren't they coming?"

There was no way to prepare his godmother for the devastating news so there was a long painful silence as he struggled to find his words. His voice took on a grave tone, "I'm sorry, Connie. Your granddaughters were in a serious accident on the way to the airport. The police found your name and phone number in one of their handbags."

"Dear God!" Constance whispered as she collapsed against the back of the settee. She dared to ask, "The twins?" His eyes were so serious it frightened her.

There was no way Rowan could soften the blow of what he had to tell her. When he spoke again his voice was even softer as he took her hands and said, "It was a bad accident, Connie. Both the taxi driver and one of the twins were pronounced dead at the scene." There was a long moment of silence while Rowan gave her time to absorb the horrifying news. "They took the surviving twin to the hospital. She took a blow to her head and has been in a coma for the last few days. The most they've been able to determine is that she's definitely one of the twins. But at this time, they can't verify the identity of their patient."

Because she was frightened, her voice was sharp, "How can they not know which one, Rowan? She can tell them."

"When your granddaughter woke up she had no recollection of the accident or who she is. She has no memory of her past. The details at the scene were no help. Your granddaughters' passports and other identification were in their handbags that were thrown from the taxi. Physically, they are identical and their blood type is the same. All they know is that she is either Delany or Desiree Dare. For now they call her Dee, as this is the initial of her first name."

At Constance's questioning look he continued, "It was her doctor that I was talking to. Dr. Jonas Hahn believes your granddaughter has traumatic amnesia. This type of amnesia is usually triggered by an event that the person's mind is unable to cope with. They think she may have seen her twin sister die in the accident. In most cases the memory comes back but he can't say how long it may take. It could be weeks. Months. Even years. He also said that the memory of the shocking event may never come back completely."

"For some that may be a good thing," Constance whispered in a dazed voice. She was almost afraid to ask, "Is she okay otherwise?"

"Other than scrapes and bruises, she's fine. That's another issue. There's nothing else they can do for her medically so they want to release her. Until your granddaughter regains her memory, as her only living relative you've been assigned as her legal guardian."

Constance was devastated. Her voice sounded sad and distant, "The poor child has no family left. Both parents are gone. The twins only had each other. She's all alone now and it's my duty to see that she's protected. We'll bring her here and this will be her home."

Rowan's eyes filled with genuine concern as he anxiously observed his godmother whose face was pale and drawn. It was evident that the poor woman was numbed by the horror of what happened but he knew that there was no way he could persuade her to change her mind. "That could become complicated and she won't know who you are."

Not for a moment did Constance question her decision. "Life is complicated. My granddaughter will be safe and that will be enough to start with," she stated candidly.

Rowan's jaw tightened as he and Constance shared an anguished glance. "Dr. Hahn said that reality orientation may help if surrounded by familiar objects or smells. Even sounds like music can stir a memory." With a troubled note that Constance didn't miss, he stated, "This can be a very complex situation. Some never recover lost memories due to the severity and scope of the amnesia and even mild amnesia can take a toll on daily activities and quality of life."

Constance sat still and spoke not a word. The silence between them was heavy.

Rowan quickly added, "You must understand that if you're going to take over the responsibility of looking out for your granddaughter you need to know what you may be up against. Connie, her amnesia can be permanent. Episodes of amnesia are usually temporary but in severe cases the memory never returns. You must be prepared for that." The troubled note was again evident.

"I understand that." Constance remained preoccupied, completely tormented by the news. It was impossible to believe. Her eyes filled with tears but she forced herself to maintain control. She would weep for her loss later. With a heavy sigh of determination she turned to her godson. "The big question is how to find the trigger that will release her memories. When that happens, we'll help her together and deal with whatever is."

Rowan knew that no matter what else he said it would be useless. Constance Malone was a remarkable woman. She had made up her mind and there would be no changing it. Rowan respected her decision but was concerned about the future for both grandmother and granddaughter. The impact of events was felt and Rowan agonized over this woman's dilemma.

Constance Malone was a proud woman. Rowan couldn't resist the silent plea in her eyes. He knew she was grateful when he said, "It's going to be all right. I'll call and book the corporate jet and make the necessary arrangements to bring your granddaughter here." He gave her a reassuring smile but his mind was already turning to the difficult task ahead of him.

Rowan left and made several calls which included researching the credentials of Dr. Jonas Hahn. He was relieved to hear that he was recognized as one of the leading neurological specialists in this field. He returned to find Constance sitting and staring out the window. She glanced up when she heard him.

"I could use a stiff drink," Rowan announced from the side bar against the wall. "Will you join me?" Constance nodded and accepted the glass of brandy Rowan handed her. He took a long swallow of his drink before speaking again. "I've rearranged my schedule and will be leaving in the morning. Are you going to be okay if I leave you?"

Constance didn't comment; she simply nodded.

"I'm so sorry for what's happened. I'll call you as soon as I've met with both your granddaughter and her doctor."

"She only has you and me to help her. Thank you, Rowan." After Rowan left, Constance sat for a long time in deep thought trying to analyze this strange twist of fate. She closed her eyes and prayed silently for her deceased granddaughter. Then she prayed for the strength to face the task that lay before her and for her remaining granddaughter. Only then, did she allow the tears to flow.

When the young patient woke she wasn't alone. An intern was standing at the foot of her bed reading her chart. Unable to free herself from the effects of the drugs she closed her eyes and drifted off. A persistent voice coaxed her back to the present. "Miss Dare, I'm sorry to wake you but we have to take you downstairs." And so it began. The day was filled with continuous tests and questions. It was a long and stressful day. Dee was exhausted as she waited for Dr. Hahn. She found herself gripping the sides of the bed when she heard his voice.

Large, solemn eyes under surprisingly long lashes looked up at him as he came over to stand by her bed. Dr. Hahn took her hand and got right to the point. "We did a CT scan of your brain looking for damage or abnormalities. It confirmed that there is no bleeding. We also took images of your brain while you were performing cognitive thinking. All of the tests and x-rays today rule out any other possible cause of memory loss. You have amnesia due to the blow to your head from the accident."

"That all sounds positive. When will I get my memory back?"

Dr. Hahn replied cautiously, "I'm sorry, Dee. I don't know. I'm confident it will return but none of the tests can tell how long it will take. When you're ready your brain will release the block that is keeping your memories locked away."

Tears of frustration blurred her vision. "Do I just stay here until it comes back?"

"Fortunately, in the majority of cases amnesia resolves itself. You require no additional treatment for other injuries. We've done everything we can. There's no reason for you to remain in the hospital." Dr. Hahn stopped abruptly as he recognized the impact of his words.

"I see," Dee said, controlling her panic with great effort. But she didn't. Not in the least. She paused and took a quivering breath as fear set in. "Will somebody come and get me? I don't know where to go," she whispered, once again feeling anguished and frightened.

"The police found contact information in your purse. There was an airline ticket to England and an envelope with the name and address of a woman named Constance Malone." There was no sign of recognition when the doctor said the name. "I've contacted her and she's your maternal grandmother. She's sending her godson, Rowan Le Baron, to come here and take you to stay with her in England. He'll be here in a day or two."

Dee's eyes filled with confusion. She gazed at him with troubled eyes. "I'm afraid I don't understand. Where am I now?"

"You're in Los Angeles in the United States." Dr. Hahn watched her expression. His patient's eyes remained vacant.

Nothing he said was making sense. "I'm trying to remember, Dr. Hahn. I remembered your name. Maybe by tomorrow my memory will come back and I'll remember mine."

The doctor's response was gentle. "That would be wonderful and definitely what we're hoping for. But there's no further treatment we can do here. We must discharge you."

His patient was dismayed and she stared at him with disbelief. She drew a shocked breath as she fought to keep her voice steady, "Why do I have to go to England?"

"I'm sorry, Dee," he said painfully. "You have no choice. I have discussed your release in great detail with Mr. Le Baron and that's what your grandmother has arranged for you."

The frightened girl opened her mouth to speak but suddenly realized there was nothing she could say.

"When Mr. Le Baron arrives you'll be discharged into his care. He's a very generous man. Not only will he pay all of your expenses, he'll take care of all of the legal documents required to allow you to leave our country under the circumstances."

Dee's distress visibly increased. "Please don't make me go," she pleaded, not bothering to hide the panic in her voice. The questions continued to pour out of the frightened girl, "Why can't I stay here? There must be someone here who can help me. Why has nobody come to get me?" Dee felt as though she was suffocating in her own fear. Nothing seemed real.

"That is something Mr. Le Baron will have to tell you. I'm sorry but I've done all I can for you." The doctor turned and left.

The frightened young woman lay for a long time staring at nothing while trying to absorb what was happening. She felt battered, twisted and knotted inside. Her anguish visibly increased knowing she would be going out into a strange world. It was terrifying. She knew nothing except that she hated the stranger she hadn't met with an intensity she hadn't expected. She prayed for a miracle, hoping for some answers but there was only a deep foreboding silence. Unchecked tears ran down her face as heightened fear washed through her in waves.

As arranged, Rowan Le Baron met with Dr. Hahn as soon as he arrived at the hospital. They needed to discuss the patient as well as the procedures required to release her to his care.

"There has been no change in Miss Dare since we last spoke, Mr. Le Baron. Her memory loss is due to the hard blow to her head and she hasn't been able to recall any memories since she woke up. Knowing that the young girl that was killed at the scene was her twin sister, and that Dee may have watched her die, we feel that she suffers more from hysterical amnesia. Like Dee, patients forget not only their past but their very identify. When Dee woke up she didn't know who she was and when she looked in the mirror she didn't recognize her own reflection. The person in the mirror was a stranger to her."

Rowan Le Baron's expression was skeptical. "Is there any way she can be faking?"

"We've done neurological testing over the last few days plus spinal taps and blood tests. Staff have been observing her continuously. We're positive that she has amnesia. Dee can remember everything that she does and what she sees and hears since the accident. She's a very intelligent young lady who has complete recall of general knowledge but she has no recollection at all of her life prior to the accident. She's a very frightened young lady, Mr. Le Baron. She keeps asking questions that we had no answers to. So be prepared."

Rowan asked a few more questions concerning medications and follow-up treatments. After being provided this information and finalizing Dee's release, he asked, "May I go see her now?" Not knowing what to expect, Rowan was surprised at how apprehensive he felt.

"Of course."

Rowan took a deep breath and followed the doctor. At first he thought they were in the wrong room for the patient in the bed appeared to be a child. He was stunned by how young she looked. He studied the delicate planes of her face while she lay motionless and his heart ached for her. Her face was as white as the sterile pillowcase her head rested on.

They were joined by her nurse. "She just lies there," she declared sadly.

Hearing voices, the young girl opened her eyes. The eyes were hollow; the face impassive. *Another stranger, another doctor who wants to probe and ask more questions looking for answers that aren't there. I wish everyone would leave me alone.*

Rowan Le Baron surveyed her while the doctor introduced him and then took his leave. Fear was evident in the solemn eyes that glared back at him.

Dee sat up and studied him closely. Rowan stood there, his expression somber as she looked him up and down. The man was dark haired, tall and definitely handsome. There was something about him that commanded attention. She recognized the understated authority in his face and there was definite power in his stance. His expensive attire suggested that he was a sophisticated gentleman. He smiled at her, showing even white teeth. After a long moment, Dee turned her head and closed her eyes to shut him out.

Rowan's dark eyes filled with genuine concern. He could understand how the idea of leaving the hospital and going out into a strange world would be terrifying to the young girl and it showed. His voice, when he spoke, was deep and had a distinct accent. "I'm aware of how difficult this must be for you but you don't have to be afraid."

His show of concern had an unexpected effect. Her eyes angrily snapped open and she met his gaze with defiance. "There may be a lot of things in life that I'm going to have to do and not like. But this isn't one of them. You can't make me go to England. Find someone here who knows me. I am not going to leave this hospital until you do." Folding her thin arms across her chest in a futile act of defiance, her expression remained set and hostile.

Rowan was caught completely off guard. She had appeared to be so docile and indifferent. It put him on the defensive. "I'm sure you've already been told that there is no one here who can help you. Legally you have no other option."

Dee looked at his angry face and knew that she was being unreasonable. She continued to fight back; it was easier being angry than being terrified. "You imply that I have no say whatsoever. Well, I'll find some way around this." Unshed tears burned her eyes but her inner pride surfaced. *I will not cry. Not in front of this despicable man.* She looked away from his direct gaze and bit back further words of protest.

Rowan was not only challenged by the situation but also by this slip of a child who kept glaring at him. He'd never seen someone go through so many emotions in such a short time. From fear to fury, from fury to frost. Consequently, his own reaction was harsher than he intended. It was evident that he was angry. "You seem determined to believe you have a choice in this matter and that simply is not the case. We both must obey your grandmother's wishes. Whether you like it or not those are the facts."

Her finely arched brows drew together as she continued to stare angrily at him. "You just want to get back to England with your obligation fulfilled." She knew it was an unfair accusation but she didn't care.

The look on Rowan's face was cold and uncompromising. His voice remained insensitive as he wanted to make his position clear, "Your grandmother entrusted me with your care. It doesn't matter if either of us likes this duty or not. I'm your temporary guardian and you'll do as I say. This isn't personal, it's just that I've had to rearrange important business meetings to come over here to get you and play guardian. Not to mention the legal hoops required to be able to take you to England. I'll be back for you tomorrow." Rowan added a hard glare so she would understand he meant what he said.

Dee hadn't missed the firmness in his voice. Speechless, she could only glare at him. Her rage was replaced by a far deeper emotion. The fear inside was suffocating her. Their gaze held for a long minute before Dee finally accepted defeat and turned away.

Rowan's voice matched the coldness in his eyes. "Be ready by noon." With an air of finality, he turned and left. Outside her room, Rowan took a deep breath and shook his head. That did not go as expected.

Dee couldn't believe what had just transpired. She was terrified by the fierceness of the man that just left. She felt like she'd been attacked by a grizzly bear. Released tears flowed as a wave of depression washed over her. How she hated this man who could make her cry.

When Rowan returned to his hotel, he called his godmother as promised. They talked for a long time. On closing, he said, "We'll have to be careful with what we reveal to her about her past. Dr. Hahn reiterated that it would be better if she recovers her memories on her own."

"How will that happen?" Constance asked in a mournful tone.

"Your granddaughter may have brief glimpses of memory that will remind her of her past. Or there will be a trigger that releases the dam and all of her memories will come flooding back. It may be a phrase, a smell, a voice, a song. We'll just have to wait and see." Rowan continued, his voice drained, "Tomorrow I'll arrange for their belongings to be packed up and shipped. For now, all your granddaughter has is a small suitcase."

Constance drew a deep breath. "Don't worry, Rowan. She'll have everything she needs when she gets here." After another thank you the line went dead.

Rowan went and lay on his bed reflecting on the events of the last few days. From the beginning he had remained intent on his mission. Hours were spent speaking to several agencies to obtain the legal documents for his passenger to leave the United States under such extraordinary and unusual circumstances. He was also able to reach Cash Bentley, one of the band members, and set up an appointment to discuss the turn of events. After dealing with the initial shock, Cash was quick to offer his help in any way and Rowan was indebted. Because the band was on hiatus for the summer, they wouldn't have to explain the sudden disappearance of the twins. If necessary, their go to response would be 'no comment'. They agreed to meet in the morning so they could pack up the twins personal belongings. Only the items that would have belonged to either Delaney or Desiree Dare would be packed into a small trunk. All other items that related to a set of twins and their life and career together would be packed into a larger trunk. That trunk would be stored away until the poor girl regained her memory. Rowan sighed heavily. Such an unjustified loss that affected so many lives. And a young girl oblivious to any of it.

Rowan felt the weight of his mission as his thoughts changed direction. He had to admit that he felt sorry for both Constance Malone and Dee Dare. The whole situation was incredibly sad. His thoughts remained on the young girl with the huge eyes veiled with misery. He had to admit that she was tougher than she looked but it didn't ease his conscience. He could deal with her feisty anger but her tears were another matter. She was also a complication that he didn't want to take on. This was getting more complicated by the minute. He acknowledged that he purposely hadn't shared her reaction to him and her situation with Constance. There was no need to upset his godmother any further. Grandmother and granddaughter would have to form their own opinions of each other, unbiased by his observations of today. Rowan was soon frustrated with his train of thoughts but he couldn't let them go. The vulnerable image of Dee Dare lying in that hospital bed popped into his mind only to be replaced by her defiant look when he left her. Tomorrow was going to be a challenging day.

Dee had been awake throughout the night thinking about the unknown future that lay ahead of her. A lot of her waking hours were spent cursing Rowan Le Baron as she replayed their conversation over and over in her mind. It made her miserable. She tried to eat her breakfast but the food seemed to get caught by the lump of fear in her throat. In frustration, she pushed the tray aside and went to shower. Dee took her time and allowed the hot water to wash away some of her tension. She was glad to see that most of the bruising on her body had faded. Sadly the dark shadows under her eyes remained.

The morning passed all too quickly because she dreaded the return of the 'Bear'. Dee had unconsciously named Rowan Le Baron this the minute she realized who he was. It was just before noon when the nurse walked in and she knew it was time to get ready. "It's a big day for you, Dee. You get to go home today," she said cheerfully.

Dee snapped at her, "I don't have a home. I'm going to a strange country with a stranger to meet more strangers. Forgive me if I don't share your enthusiasm." The young nurse cowered and took a step back.

Blinking back tears, Dee apologized. "I'm sorry. I didn't mean for it to come out like that. I do appreciate that I'm well enough to leave." The severity of the situation caused her voice to break, "I don't think I can do this." It was all Dee could do to keep her legs steady.

The nurse's eyes were sympathetic. "You're going to be fine." She went over to the closet and pulled out the girl's suitcase and placed it on the bed. It was all that the paramedics had brought with the patient. "Do you need some help getting dressed?"

Dee shook her head, not trusting herself to speak. What she really wanted to do was scream in frustration. This had all been a living nightmare from the moment she woke up in the hospital. Her life had fallen to pieces and there was nothing she could do about it.

"If you need me I'll be at the nurse's station."

Dee slowly unzipped the suitcase and opened it up. There wasn't much and she recognized nothing. She selected a pair of jeans and a white peasant blouse from the clothes inside. Also inside was a worn denim jacket. Dee took it out and held it to her chest, then smelled it up close. The scent was comforting. When she put it on it felt like a suit of armor protecting her from the future. Or was it protecting her from the past? She looked at her image in the mirror. All she saw was the pale face of a stranger everyone called Dee. Frightened eyes stared back at her.

Dee sat in the chair, watching the door waiting for the man who was going to take her away. Fear clutched at her with icy fingers, making her shiver. She sat motionless. Dee was sure she'd never been this frightened in her life. She couldn't help but think about the nightmare she was engulfed in. She had to wonder how she was going to regain her memory in another country half way across the world where nothing would be familiar. Her thoughts turned. Was she going to learn some terrible thing that had happened in her past? She was growing more frantic with each passing minute. She could feel her heart pounding in her chest as she watched the clock crawl slowly from minute to minute.

Because she had allowed her thoughts to drift, she was unaware of Rowan Le Baron's presence until she blinked and saw him standing in the doorway watching her. She had prayed that her memory would return before he came back to get her. Dee jumped involuntarily and tears began to slide down her cheeks as her hopes vanished. She could no longer ignore the gruesome reality from crashing around her. Her nerves were so frayed that she felt sick but she managed to swallow the nausea. She stared at him with eyes that were sharp and aware. They were also wide and filled with fear.

The trail of tears did not go unnoticed and increased Rowan's concern, taking away some of his annoyance. Her pale face was make-up free and again Rowan thought she looked like a child. He knew she was terrified but he also knew better than to address it. He'd already been on the receiving end of one of her attacks. He deliberately softened his voice, "I'm sorry, I didn't mean to startle you. Are you ready?" He waited for her outrage.

Instead, Dee rose at once and nodded in icy silence. *I have no choice.* She hated him. She loathed him. She followed.

CHAPTER TWO

Rowan led Dee onto his private plane; they were the only passengers. As soon as they were buckled in she heard the roar of the engines. Within minutes they were airborne. Dee was acutely conscious of the man across the aisle from her. She could feel his piercing eyes on her while she sat mute and still. To avoid eye contact as much as possible Dee shifted and turned further into the window. With firmly set lips she maintained her resolute silence.

Rowan was fully aware of her distress. She was obviously frightened of the unknown and it was his duty to help her get over her fear. "It's a long flight and we're going to have to endure each other's company," Rowan said suddenly, after miles of silence.

Dee made no acknowledgment that she even heard him.

Rowan looked at Dee with a hint of compassion. She was a striking young girl in spite of the constant look of panic and the frown that often altered her face. His voice was gentle when he spoke again, "I realize this is difficult for you."

Dee turned and glared at him. *Ignorant man, he has no idea,* she thought, with freshly fueled anger. With eyes blazing and lips trembling, she whispered, "I would prefer it if you would leave me alone."

Her rudeness was wearing on him. Rowan was going to say more until he saw the tears in her eyes. Nothing else would have stopped him.

Dee sat back, withdrawn and sullen, lost in her thoughts. Her feelings changed by the hour, but more than anything, she was frightened. Turning back to the window, Dee released a heavy sigh, her tense shoulders dropping as she rubbed her aching temples. She wondered what her grandmother was like and how she would receive her new house guest. She also wondered how well the Bear knew her grandmother. *Why didn't she come herself? Is she old and frail? Maybe she's an invalid. Maybe I'm being taken there to be a nursemaid?* Dee didn't care for the negative direction her thoughts were taking her. Sadly, she couldn't stop them anymore than she could replace them with old memories. Unaware, she wiped a tear from her cheek. She felt like she was in purgatory and she would spend eternity wondering who she was. Her unwanted thoughts persisted. There were questions, so many questions. *Why don't I know who I am? Why can't I get my memory back? Why are they doing this to me? Why? Why? Why?* Dee stopped herself for she had no answers and she asked none of her questions out loud because she was terrified of the man next to her.

Rowan looked over with sympathy and studied her. Her frigid attitude continued. He accepted her silence as he, too, remained silent and thoughtful. His passenger wasn't the only one wondering what the future held in store.

The flight was long but uneventful. As mile after mile disappeared, Dee's panic died down, leaving only a dull resignation in its place. Off and on, she drifted into a light sleep. She was jarred fully awake when the plane touched down. She anxiously sank back in her seat, shut her eyes and took a deep breath. She was in England and this was real. But where and what was here? A sudden wave of unbearable pain engulfed her but it wasn't physical. Scary what fear can do to a body. She had been plunged into uncertainty, vulnerable and at the mercy of others.

Rowan, equally guarded, watched her with hooded eyes. The drawn look on Dee's face revealed how overwrought and tired she was. Without thinking, he reached over and pressed her hand, "I have a car waiting for us at the gate. We'll go directly to your grandmother's."

Dee flinched as if his touch was offensive. Rowan frowned and released his hold. Her hands were shaking as she disengaged her seat belt.

The sky was gray when they stepped off the plane. She wondered if this was a bad omen or just a reminder that there was no longer any sunlight in her life. A shiny black limousine was parked close by. Once settled, they headed toward the city of London.

Dee remained silent, ignoring Rowan as she stared out the window seeing nothing. She shifted restlessly trying to alleviate herself of her unease.

Rowan noticed her discomfort. "Are you in pain?"

Dee's retort was both swift and annoyed, "No." She was nervous but she regained her control and sat very still while remaining guarded and reserved. The drive continued in silence.

It was mid-afternoon when the limousine turned into the circular drive and pulled up to the curb in front of a grand hotel in central London. "We're here," Rowan announced.

Dee's eyes were dark with distrust as she turned to him. "You said we were going straight to my grandmother's?"

Rowan's guilt resurfaced. He had forgotten that she had no recollection of the plans she had made before her accident. It was a reality check of the awkwardness that lay ahead. This situation was definitely going to be complex. "Your grandmother lives here at the Conlyn Grand Hotel. She has a private suite on the top floor." He didn't miss the look of relief in Dee's eyes.

As Dee stepped out of the limousine she took another deep breath to control her nerves. It didn't help. Her legs were trembling and she felt as though her knees might dissolve under her. *God, give me strength.* When Rowan took her arm she was grateful for the support, while at the same time she resented it.

Dee failed to notice the grandeur of the main foyer as they walked through to the private lift. Neither Rowan nor Dee had spoken a word since they entered the hotel.

A formidable manservant dressed in black trousers and black waistcoat opened the door to the suite. His craggy face remained expressionless. "Good day, Boris." Rowan handed him Dee's suitcase. Dee stood there terrified not knowing what to say or do. She forced herself to show none of the frightening emotions within her but her face had lost what little color it had.

"Madam is in the parlour; she's been waiting."

"Rowan, is that you?" an anxious voice called out.

"Yes Connie, it's us." Dee forced her unsteady legs to move as Rowan took her elbow and guided her along. It was as though she had no will of her own anymore.

The suite was exquisite, impeccable and elegant and bespoke an undeniable air of wealth. It was evident that Constance Malone lived in fine style. The room they entered was large, comfortable floral settees and chairs were situated close to the fireplace.

Constance and Dee stared at each other without speaking. Here stood a young woman who remembered nothing of her grandmother and a grandmother who remembered everything about her granddaughter. The atmosphere in the room was tense.

For Dee, there wasn't the faintest flicker of recognition. All Dee saw was a stranger. But there was something in the sharp blue eyes of the old woman that comforted her.

For Constance, it was as though the mere sight of her granddaughter erased the years that had separated this woman from her daughter. The resemblance to Phoebe was uncanny. Constance's eyes misted over. Without hesitation the elderly woman stepped forward and took the girl into her arms and hugged her close. "Welcome, my dear. I had Boris prepare a room for you. I hope you'll find it comfortable. He'll show you the way and you can freshen up before dinner." Her tone was warm and her smile was welcoming.

Boris led Dee into a spacious bedroom beautifully decorated in soft, subtle shades of white. Her surveillance of the room was slow. In appearance everything was perfect. Centered in the room was a magnificent canopied bed covered with a thick quilted comforter. Added for effect was an assortment of pillows in a variety of shapes and sizes. Across the room there was a welcoming window seat with gold brocade cushions and a velour throw lying at one end. The room had a peaceful feel to it. The beauty of her surroundings dispelled her fear for the moment. There was a large bouquet of fresh flowers on the table. A warm feeling emerged for she appreciated the kind gesture. Dee noticed that her suitcase had been placed next to the bed.

Boris informed her, "Dinner is at eight o'clock sharp. The attire is semi-formal. No trousers or denim."

This man terrified Dee with his curtness and gruff tone. Feeling ill at ease, she stated, "I don't know if I have anything appropriate to wear."

His manner remained polite, "What you're wearing will be acceptable for this evening. Madam has arranged to have some clothes sent here tomorrow for your approval. Would you like me to unpack for you?"

All Dee wanted was to be alone. "No, I'll do it." *I have nothing else to do but wait.*

"If there is anything you need, let me know. Madam wants to make your stay pleasant." Abruptly, Boris turned and left leaving Dee standing with a bleak look on her face. She looked around feeling forlorn and unsure. It was difficult to believe that this was now her home.

Dee entered the shared bathroom that was connected to a third bedroom. Next to the pedestal sink thick, rich towels hung on a heated brass towel rack. Dee indulged in a long, relaxing bath in the gorgeous claw foot bathtub. Feeling refreshed, she dressed in a simple dress she found when she unpacked. The sun had yet to set so the room was filled with natural light. She wandered over to the window and gazed out, taking in the beautifully manicured gardens below. It was a vast private garden surrounded by flower borders and shrubbery. Perhaps tomorrow she would go for a stroll around the gardens and explore the beauty up close. She opened the window and let the gentle breeze blow across her face. The air coming through the open window was sweet with the scent of summer. *Maybe the wind will blow away the cobwebs that are suppressing me from my past.*

Dee sat down on the window seat. Through a veil of tears, she spent the next few hours staring out longing desperately for something she couldn't put a name to. The gathering darkness outside reflected her mood. The isolation and darkness felt as though they were seeping into her soul. When the clock on the nightstand told her she couldn't stall any longer she took a last look in the mirror. The reflective image looked scared to death. Fear had been her constant companion since the day she woke up a stranger to herself.

Dee returned to the parlour. It was unoccupied so she took a moment to inspect the room. It was such a welcoming room. Her eyes were drawn to a grand piano in the far corner. It brought an instant feeling of pleasure and a look of joy came into her eyes. But a moment later it was gone and once again there was only the vacant stare.

Dee could hear the faint murmur of voices which led her to the formal dining room. Feeling awkward, she paused at the doorway, not knowing what to do. Constance sensed her presence and turned to greet her. Although her granddaughter had changed and pulled her hair neatly back, the dark blue smudges beneath her eyes were still evident against her pale skin. "There you are and looking very pretty."

Dee wanted to say something but the words couldn't get past the lump of fear in her throat. She noticed the table was formally set for three so was not surprised when Constance announced, "Rowan is joining us for dinner." Dee heard the affection in her voice and saw it as well when Constance gave a smiling glance to the man beside her.

Rowan stood beside Constance, posture unyielding, expression stern.

Dee struggled to maintain her composure. *Can things get any worse?*

Constance turned back to Dee, "Boris has prepared a traditional English dinner in your honor. I hope you found everything to your satisfaction."

"Yes, thank you. The bedroom is lovely," Dee replied cordially, in a voice taut with exhaustion and anxiety. She discreetly surveyed the formal dining room. Rich embossed wallpaper enhanced the room with understated elegance. The classic oak table and high back chairs sat on an exquisite Persian rug in the middle of the room. A rich woven runner ran end to end on the sideboard featuring sterling silver candlesticks at each end. The lit tapered candles offered subdued lighting that added traditional ambiance to the room. Like the rest of the house, Dee had to appreciate both the décor and the elegance. "You have a beautiful home."

"Thank you. Have you settled in all right?" Constance could tell by her granddaughter's rigid posture how frightened she was.

Dee simply nodded as she stood there reserved and guarded.

"Come sit down next to me, my dear." Constance took her seat at the head of the table.

With a feeling of nervousness, Dee obeyed. She gripped her hands together in a nervous gesture, completely uncomfortable with her situation.

Constance and Rowan chatted easily throughout the evening meal and both tried to include Dee and put her at ease. But Dee made no effort to contribute to any conversation. She had nothing to share, no memories to talk about. Recognizing that Rowan took Dee's continued silence as a note of disrespect, Constance quickly shook her head at him. She felt extremely protective of her granddaughter.

Boris had served up a wonderful meal but Dee's stomach was tied in knots and she could barely swallow anything. The entire day had been an ordeal and now mealtime was worse. She endured the meal with a great deal of effort as she sat there feeling like an outsider.

"You haven't eaten much. Would you like something else?"

Dee nervously twisted her napkin as she switched her gaze away from Rowan, who she found to be extremely intimidating. "It was fine, Ma'am." Dee tried to smile normally but knew she failed miserably.

Rowan and Constance shared a look. Rowan frowned, but remained silent. Constance decided to ignore the formality for now knowing the girl was terrified. In an attempt to ease the tension in the room, Constance rang for Boris to bring coffee and dessert. She turned to Dee, "How do you like your coffee?"

There was an agonizing moment of silence as Dee sat there shocked. *For God's sake, I don't even know how I like my coffee.* Dee's voice was shaky, "Black, I guess."

Dee's tone shook Constance. It was so filled with terror that she understood for the first time how tormented the child was. She could see that Dee was visibly panicked. "I'm so sorry, Dee. I know how distressing this must be. You've been through a lot in the last few days. Why don't you retire and try to get some sleep."

Dee's cracked composure crumbled. She looked at the strangers seated at the table as they stared back at her. "You don't know anything about me. Nobody does. Not even me." She looked over to Rowan and her voice turned to anger. "You drag me here against my will and then expect me to be thankful and just accept everything. You both sit there enjoying the familiarity around you while I sit here terrified. Your world is the same as it always was. You're not sitting there with a blank slate praying for anything familiar so you can have your life back. When you look at me, the look of pity is evident on your faces. You have no idea whatsoever how much courage this day has taken." Dee burst out sobbing and ran to her room.

When Dee reached the haven of her bedroom she closed the door behind her with relief. She sagged against the door, knowing the familiar feeling of panic followed her in. Tears ran down her cheeks. She knew the evening hadn't gone well. Dinner had been a nerve-racking ordeal. She was unable to participate in meaningful conversation. She could share nothing at all about herself, not even her likes or dislikes. She was a stranger who was now living among strangers. Then reality hit her with the force of a tidal wave. She was a stranger to herself. *Your past is what makes you who you are. I have no past. I am nobody.*

Dee got up and flung herself on her bed and wept. The long journey from the past to the threshold of her future had taken its toll. Everything around her was strange. Her grandmother's stories of family didn't comfort her. She was unable to relate to them or to her. Dee ached with loneliness as she gave in to self-pity. She suddenly realized how tired she was and she began to feel the familiar pain in her head. She climbed into the unfamiliar bed and closed her eyes terrified of sleep and the dreams that would come with it. She lay still, surrounded by a feeling of total unreality. *I don't belong here. But I don't know where I belong?* She wondered again what lay ahead for her. Dee felt like she was locked in her own head and prayed it wouldn't be a life sentence.

No sooner had Dee fallen asleep and she awakened in a cold sweat. For a moment she didn't know where she was. Ever since the accident, the nightmares were endless and it was often the same dream. It was as if she was outside her body looking in. There were spirits in white floating around her. Her body lay still while her soul drifted upwards. Then the world would spin around faster and faster, preventing her soul from returning to her body. She was lost in her own nightmare. Dee struggled to shake the frightening images away but the menacing dreams would not leave her.

Dee turned on the bedside lamp. Shivering, she told herself it was just a dream. There was nothing to read into the disturbing images. She forced the nightmare back into the dark corners of her mind. Sighing heavily, she closed her eyes and prayed that the nightmare wouldn't return. The soft light gave the room a comforting glow which offered her a sense of protection. It burned softly throughout the night as she drifted in and out of sleep.

Meanwhile, downstairs Constance and Rowan had withdrawn to the parlour. Rowan poured two glasses of brandy, passing one to Constance. She shook her head at Rowan's rigid expression and sighed, "It was too much, too soon. The poor child was terrified. Right now Dee doesn't know who she is and she doesn't remember who she was. I'd be scared too."

Rowan had been infuriated by the girl's disrespect to her grandmother. He aired his grievance in a clipped, no-nonsense tone, "I find her to be insolent. She lets loose of her tongue without any self-restraint."

The sudden anger in his tone upset Constance and she wondered where it was coming from. "Please try to see past this, Rowan. Give the child a chance and don't judge her so harshly or so quickly. It's not all Dee's fault. This was all too much for her but I just wanted her to feel welcomed. We'll have to allow Dee time to adjust."

Rowan understood what Constance was saying but it didn't excuse rudeness. Constance was providing Dee a life with family and security which the child so desperately needed. He walked away in frustration and poured himself another brandy. It took all of his effort to keep his temper under control. What really bothered him was the fact that he didn't understand why he was so upset.

"Right now she's angry because she's frightened. I'll have to find a way to reach her." The frantic despair in her voice was evident. Constance realized that the first thing she'd have to do would be to establish a level of trust. Only then could she begin to knock down the wall of fear surrounding Dee. Constance had anticipated that there would be difficulties that she'd have to face and she thought she was ready to deal with anything. But she hadn't anticipated this open anger. She had experienced it at times with Phoebe. All she ever wanted was for her daughter to be happy. Now she would do whatever she could to see this in her granddaughter, not this empty shell with no spark of life.

Rowan watched his godmother closely for a moment. He had studied up further on amnesia during the flight but he hadn't found anything different than what Dr. Hahn had told him. Anything could trigger her memory or it could remain wiped clean. "There's no guarantee anything will change."

"It already has," Constance stated solemnly.

Rowan turned his full attention to his host. "I've upset you. I'm sorry. Like everyone else I'm tired. I believe I'll call it a night." It was he who had taken the blunt of Dee's suffering, anxiety and unleashed anger.

After Rowan left, Constance sat for a long time contemplating the upcoming changes to her own life. Nothing would be the same for any of them.

Despite the fact that she'd slept poorly, Dee woke early. For a moment she blinked in puzzlement. Then she remembered yesterday. This was all new. Just as Dee Dare was new and she didn't know how she'd fit into this life that would be hers here in England. Knowing that she had behaved badly last night, Dee was somewhat uneasy when she went to join her grandmother for breakfast. She was relieved that it was only the two of them and even more relieved that her grandmother didn't bring up last night.

"Good morning, Dee." Constance didn't ask her how she had slept. She knew, for neither had slept much. The girl was deathly pale except for the dark shadows under her eyes.

Dee's only response was, "Good morning."

Throughout breakfast, Constance endeavored to encourage Dee to talk but her responses were constrained. Aware that the conversation was mostly one-sided Constance decided to take matters into hand and addressed the situation by coming right to the point, "This is going to be a period of adjustment for both of us. Today we'll simply get to know each other as new acquaintances who hopefully in time will become friends. If I upset you because of assumptions I may make, I apologize now. But this will only be easier if you make an effort as well. I can only know how you feel, when you remember something or what you remember, if you tell me. So, for now, dear, we move forward together." She smiled with encouragement. "I like a beginning. Everything that follows has such possibilities."

Dee took no offence to Constance's straightforwardness. Her grandmother was direct. Yet there was something in her grandmother's manner that was reassuring. She nodded in agreement and, though it was weak, managed her first smile.

Throughout the morning Dee found that her grandmother had a very sympathetic and comforting style. This helped to put Dee at ease. Constance successfully drew her granddaughter into conversation. She slowly began to bring down the wall between them which allowed Dee to confess, "I'm sorry about last night. I wasn't trying to be rude. I just didn't know what to say. It's frightening when you've forgotten everything about yourself. Not having any recollection of one's past is extremely unsettling. And there's always the underlying fear that I may never get my memory back."

For a moment they sat in silence before Constance declared, "I can understand that this situation is difficult but we can't change it. You have every reason to feel the way you do but I'm not your enemy. Neither is Rowan. Just know that I'm always here for you and you're never alone."

Dee was grateful to hear it. Through a cloud of despair, Dee confessed, "I realize I've been dropped on you and it's put you in an awkward position. This can't be easy for you either."

Constance took this statement as a positive even while clearly hearing the unhappiness in her granddaughter's voice. Dee had taken someone else's circumstances into account due to her situation. "Don't worry about that. I'll admit that we've found ourselves in a position that is both strange and uncomfortable. But never question that I'm not pleased that you're here. You were actually coming here to visit me. You were on your way to the airport when your taxi was involved in a single rollover."

"Is that why I had to come here when I had to leave the hospital?"

"Partly. I'm your legal guardian so you have to be here until you regain your memory."

"Why are you my guardian?"

"Dee, this whole situation is complicated. Your doctor said to let your memories return naturally. I'm afraid if I give you too much information it may do you more harm than good. So, no more questions today. Take time to adjust and accept the next few days for whatever it brings." Constance Malone offered no more details as she put up her own wall of defense.

Dee felt that her grandmother was being evasive and that she didn't want her asking any more questions at all.

Once the conversation changed direction Dee relaxed and her protective armor slowly peeled away. It allowed Dee to share her fears. "It's so frightening not knowing. I don't know any of my past as to who I am and now I'm here. I don't know how to move forward to get through this. I don't know what's expected of me or what I'm to do. How do I answer people's questions about why I'm here or, worse yet, about my past?"

"You answer how you want to and you don't owe anybody any explanations."

Dee felt that this was what her grandmother had effectively done with her.

"It's going to be all right," Constance promised.

For some reason Dee believed her.

They were chatting away when Boris announced that the delivery had arrived. "Have them take everything to Dee's room." She turned to her granddaughter. "I requested the store to send a range of sizes and styles. Why don't you go and try things on and don't be sparing when deciding. You'll require a full assortment of clothing as it will be weeks before your other belongings arrive from the States. Keep in mind that your wardrobe must be versatile."

Dee was impressed with the assortment of clothes hanging on display racks in her room. She had to acknowledge that Constance Malone was a very thoughtful and generous person. Her grandmother had thought of everything including trays of accessories from jewelry to scarves. Dee was conservative and chose pieces that she could mix and match and complimented her delicate frame. As well, she selected a few additional pieces that were more formal because of what Boris had told her about dressing for dinner. The choices she made were influenced by her circumstances, not by her past. After thanking her grandmother, Dee asked to be excused.

Constance was disappointed, for she expected Dee to model the clothes and ask her opinion like Phoebe did. It reinforced the fact that there was no relationship between them. She knew she had to give her granddaughter time to adjust to her surroundings. It reinforced the fact that both of them needed time to adjust to the situation. "There will be plenty of time to talk later. Why don't you go outside and look around." Dee could use some color on her pale skin. She had been through a traumatic experience that had mentally and physically exhausted her.

Dee felt as though she'd been given a reprieve. The look of relief was evident as she made a quick exit. Dee wandered around the gardens she had viewed from her bedroom window. Sunbeams filtered through the trees and Dee enjoyed the warmth on her skin. She strolled along intertwining walkways through the immaculately manicured gardens. She shaded her eyes from the sun as she stopped to watch a wren bathe in one of the fountains. It was busy flicking its short tail repeatedly to splash the water up. She listened to the birdsong around her and for the first time since her arrival she allowed herself to relax. Her smile was natural and real. It was reassuring knowing that she could draw on general knowledge from her past. Hopefully, in time, her personal memories would emerge as well.

Returning to the lobby of the hotel, Dee took the time to survey her surroundings. She hadn't paid any attention to the hotel when they had arrived. At that time she was so disoriented. She appreciated that the lovely Victorian hotel had maintained the rich heritage of the original building on the inside. The reception area was exquisite. The mahogany counter between the solid wide columns had been burnished to a high gleam. Beautiful antique furnishings sat on deep rich carpet. On a side wall was a Victorian table with a fresh bouquet of flowers. Above it hung an ornate mirror with side sconces representative of the era that the hotel was built. Standing next to it was a display unit containing pamphlets highlighting all that London and area had to offer. Similar columns encased a gas fireplace where traditional styled sofas welcomed guests to sit. For those guests who preferred a more private sitting area they could retire to the cozy alcove with its majestic windows. *I may not remember my past but I don't think I lived this kind of lifestyle.* Just as she was about to enter the lift Dee felt a hand on her shoulder. She turned and it was Rowan Le Baron.

"I would like a word with you in my office," he demanded abruptly.

Why did she feel like she had been summoned to the Bear's den? Dee knocked his hand away and met his eyes without wavering. No way would she allow this man the satisfaction of seeing how much he had unnerved her.

Rowan put his hand firmly under her elbow and pulled her along. She tried to pull away but Rowan wouldn't let go. The man's office was large and comfortably furnished. It was an extremely masculine room. A large mahogany desk faced the door, custom built shelving and filing unit filled the side wall. Across the room rich leather furniture accented the room in an informal setting by the gas fireplace. Dee's eyes were drawn to the formal self-portrait hanging above the fireplace. *Pompous ass.* He obviously held a position of importance.

Rowan got right to the point, "I know what you're going through is very painful and you're frightened but it doesn't excuse your sulky attitude and your ungrateful indifference towards your grandmother. Not to mention your dreadful lack of manners. One can only overlook a certain amount of rudeness for a short period of time."

Deliberately, in an act of self-defense, Dee lifted her chin to mask her vulnerability. "Are you Brits always this direct?"

Rowan was undeterred, "Only when the situation calls for it."

"So your controlling attitude is just habit? You think you can kidnap someone against their will and then manhandle them." Dee hesitated, as if she was going to say something more, but, reading Rowan's expression, thought better of it. *Arrogant, self-important jerk.*

Rude, bad-tempered brat. Ignoring her insolence, Rowan continued, "I escorted you here as requested and your grandmother went to a lot of trouble to bring you here. You don't appear to appreciate her efforts. You might try and show a little gratitude toward her."

Dee could see no change of expression on his rigid face. Her own mask slipped and her eyes projected a scary desperation. "I don't need anyone's pity." There was no way she was going to let him think it mattered to her.

"Oh, you've made it abundantly clear about what you don't want." Rowan caught himself just in time for he was about to say that Constance had lost family as well but this was something Dee still didn't know. Choosing his words carefully, he continued, "This is hard on your grandmother as well. You weren't the only one meeting a stranger. You were dropped into Connie's life and disrupted it and the first thing you do is hurt her. How do you think it makes your grandmother feel when you mope around? Connie didn't ask for this either." He stopped knowing he must guard his words and rein in his anger.

Inwardly Dee flinched. Her grandmother had expressed the same comments at breakfast. "I'm not responsible for a situation brought on by you. What do you expect from me? Because I don't know!"

Unaffected by the resentment in her voice, Rowan continued, "Your situation was brought on by fate. Now you're here. Deal with it and accept the situation and try to be pleasant. And you can make an effort to get to know your grandmother. When you do you'll find her to be a decent person who is unpretentious and down to earth. Be as bitter as you want around me. Just don't hurt Connie." The note of affection was evident in his voice when he added, "She's a great lady."

Dee's voice was clipped and resentful, "I didn't ask for any of this. You dragged me half way across the world to be here. Well, here I am with no past and no future."

Rowan was unable to hold his anger, "People died in that accident. You survived for a reason. You do have a future so stop feeling sorry for yourself."

"Well the future I face is bleak." Furious, Dee stalked across the room to the window pretending to look out although her vision was blurred. She refused to give him the satisfaction of seeing her tears. Dee opened her mouth to retaliate and then stopped. Instead she stuck out her tongue, a childish gesture of defiance.

Rowan watched her struggle with her emotions. The sadness in her voice made him forget his irritation. "You need to be aware of the time of day it is. The window catches your reflection perfectly. Don't you know it's rude to stick your tongue out at someone?"

The calmness of his voice only infuriated Dee more. When she whirled back around her eyes were wide and dark with anger. "I hate you. Leave me alone." Stomping her feet, she stormed out of the room, slamming the door behind her. She stuck out her tongue a second time. She heard Rowan laugh as if he knew exactly what she did. Dee was still fuming when she entered the flat. *Damn the man.*

Constance stopped Dee as she was going to her room. While Dee was out, Constance had decided that if Dee was going to fit in she couldn't be allowed to use her room as an escape. She knew that she was going to have to be patient while Dee adjusted and that it would take time before her granddaughter felt comfortable. But that wouldn't happen if she shut herself away. "You look upset; did something happen?"

Unable to recover her composure, Dee frowned at her grandmother. "I had the bad luck of being detained by Mr. Le Baron," she said sharply.

More sharply than she intended. "He's a very obnoxious man. He dragged me into his office where we had a rather unpleasant discussion. I thought you said he was a caring man," Dee said miserably. Dee squirmed when she saw a flash of hurt cross her grandmother's face. She could tell that she'd upset her grandmother but Dee was used to speaking her mind.

"Sarcasm doesn't become you, Dee."

Dee felt guilty at being scolded. "I'm sorry. He and I definitely got off to a bad start. *All that man does is confuse me or make me mad.* I may have overreacted." Dee refused to allow her anger at the Bear extend to her grandmother. In an attempt to make amends, she forced a smile and deliberately changed the subject, "The gardens are beautiful and so is the hotel."

Constance nodded in agreement. "If you're up to it let's go out and explore our neighbourhood and browse in the shops. We can purchase those necessities I'm sure I've missed." Knowing it would be rude to refuse, Dee agreed.

Together they strolled along the cobblestone streets and Dee was soon happily engrossed in the scenes around her. A street vendor chatted away with the Bobby on the corner. Dee enjoyed her grandmother's stories of the local street vendors they met. She found the people open and friendly as they welcomed her.

Constance led Dee into a quaint bookstore and introduced Dee to the owner. Mr. Vickers was a small man in his late fifties. Horn-rimmed glasses framed sharp blue eyes that twinkled and he greeted Dee with a warm smile. To Constance's delight the book she ordered was in. Dee quickly became distraught while listening to the exchange between the owner and her grandmother. She didn't understand the currency or the local jargon.

At Dee's request, they stopped at a chemist shop where Dee purchased a few additional toiletries and treated herself to some make-up. Dee felt uncomfortable asking, for she had no money to pay for her purchases.

Constance made a mental note to have Rowan set up an account for Dee downstairs.

Dee was more subdued by the time they returned to the hotel. "Are you feeling okay?" Constance was concerned that this may have been too much for her granddaughter.

Attempting to sound more cheerful that she felt, Dee replied, "I'm fine. But if you'll excuse me, I'd like some time to myself right now." She strolled out to the terrace while her grandmother went to find Boris. Dee curled up on one of the chaise lounges and rested her head against the back. Rowan's words earlier still had a sting. All afternoon the incident kept picking at her. His attitude toward her didn't make any sense and it confused her. He obviously didn't understand how terrifying this was. Nobody could. She hated him more and was determined to stay as far away from him as possible.

Dee was pulled back to the present rather abruptly when she heard Constance talking to someone. Immediately she recognized the familiar voice of the devil himself. *Doesn't this man ever work?* She leaned closer to hear what they were saying. To her surprise they were making plans for the evening which included her.

Her grandmother seemed to be making every attempt to make Dee feel at home and fit in. "Let's have dinner downstairs to celebrate Dee's arrival. It'll get her out of the flat and we can introduce her to a few of the live-in residents. You and Maeve can join us."

Dee's stomach filled with frantic butterflies. *More strangers.* And she had vowed to stay away from the Bear. Dee was less than thrilled when Rowan agreed. *Insufferable.* It was the only word to describe him and she dreaded their next encounter. Dee remained outside moping, dreading the evening ahead.

When it came time to change, Dee chose a simple black dress. The color was intentional. She felt it fit her mood for she was not looking forward to the evening. Thanks to her purchase of some make-up Dee was able to apply some artificial color to her drawn face. Though her features were still pale she was able to erase the dark circles under her eyes with concealer. *I can do this. I only need to sit and make polite conversation. I can be just as damned civilized as any Brit, even if it kills me.* Gathering her nerve, she joined her grandmother and they went downstairs. Together they entered an impressive dining room. The entire room preserved the original grandeur of the hotel.

"Good evening, Mrs. Malone. Your table is ready as requested." Constance Malone was greeted like royalty and escorted to a very private table. No one would have guessed Dee's underlying anxiety as she moved with unconscious grace across the room with Constance. The table was beautifully dressed with fine linens, elegant place settings and expensive crystal glasses. The centerpiece of fresh cut flowers was eye-catching in its simplicity.

Constance and Dee were seated at the table when Rowan walked over. "Maeve will be here shortly." He looked over as a tall, willowy blond waved at him. "Here she is now."

Dee's eyes drifted past Rowan to focus on the striking blonde as Maeve Spencer crossed the room smiling and confident. The woman knew how to make an entrance. She was exquisitely attired in a dress that stated its exclusiveness. *Sleek, professional and slick,* Dee thought at first glance. Dee immediately felt like a school girl in her simple frock. There was no denying that Maeve was beautiful and classy. But there was an air of aloofness, a hauteur surrounding her. *So this is Rowan's assistant. She looks like an Ice Maiden with that smile frozen on her face.* Dee assessed her as a cool, self-possessed woman who loved what she did and she loved what went with it; the recognition, the attention and the opportunities of being in the limelight.

A young man sauntered over to join Maeve and Dee eyed him skeptically. He had an athletic build and was more casually dressed. He had curly, sun bleached hair that was too long, bright blue eyes and an irresistible smile complimented by adorable dimples. *He's a charmer.*

Maeve glided over and hugged Constance. The woman's perfect features were set in an expression of disinterest and she looked through Dee as though she didn't exist.

Sudden tension rose in Dee. *Some people you dislike on sight. This is one of them. This woman is cold and calculating.*

Maeve tucked her arm through Cal's. "I hope you don't mind that I invited Cal. He just popped down from Manchester and will be staying for a few weeks."

Without waiting for a reply, Cal turned to Rowan, "Be a good chap and pull in another chair." He turned to his hostess as if his presence was long-standing and welcomed and Dee observed his flow of charm. "Good evening, Mrs. C. It's wonderful to see you again. You look lovelier every time I see you." His smile would captivate any female at any age. He turned to Dee, "And who is this beautiful young lady?"

Constance Malone laughed up at Cal. "Cheeky as usual, young man. I haven't seen you for awhile. It will be a pleasure to have you join us. Cal O'Brian, I would like you to meet my granddaughter, Dee Dare."

Dee looked at him and saw the glint of amusement in his bright eyes. She recognized Cal straight away for what he was, an outrageous flirt. But there was also a calm assurance about him that she liked.

Cal immediately moved into the chair next to Dee and grinned his infectious boyish grin. Instantly, Dee grinned back and felt at ease for the first time since she'd been thrown into this horrid prison.

Constance continued with introductions, "This is Maeve Spencer, Rowan's assistant."

Dee attempted a polite smile. "Hello, Miss Spencer."

Once Constance introduced Dee, Maeve's manner changed instantly. "Please call me Maeve," she insisted. Her smile was perfectly cordial as she welcomed Dee. Although Maeve kept her expression composed, the look in her eyes remained frigid.

Too bad your smile doesn't reach your eyes. They're as green as Chinese jade and just as cold.

Throughout the evening Maeve was courteous, but cool, to Dee. Cal, on the other hand, was totally attentive so Dee found herself enjoying dinner. He used his charm shamelessly as he engaged her in casual conversation. It was impossible not to be disarmed by his attention.

Occasionally, someone stopped to visit their table. Constance was impressed by the natural grace with which Dee presented herself to those she was introduced to. As for the Bear, Dee kept as much distance between herself and him as possible.

After coffee and dessert, Maeve put her hand on Rowan's arm, "Darling, why don't we move over to the lounge? I've booked a new singer and she's playing tonight."

Dee surmised that there was more to their relationship then just business.

Constance, who was tired, excused herself but insisted that Dee stay.

Maeve was not impressed, her smile became less polite. In a dismissive tone, she turned to Dee, "You must still be suffering from jet lag. We certainly understand if you decline."

Dee would have preferred an early evening but there was something about Maeve's haughty attitude that immediately rubbed Dee the wrong way. She was under no illusion that Maeve wanted her to leave with Constance. Some small defiant part of her surfaced and Dee was unwilling to allow this woman to intimidate her. She smiled sweetly and said, "I would love to join you. When you're young you recover much more quickly from change." The annoyed look on Maeve's face was rewarding.

Cal grinned, admiring not only Dee's spunk but the subtle shot she gave Maeve. His smile was so contagious that Dee grinned back at him.

On the way to the lounge Maeve captured Cal's arm and slowed their progress. "You've certainly been chatting up the waif all evening. You usually prefer sophisticated and elegant women who return your casual flirting without emotional involvement. Like you, they don't expect any lasting commitment, which you have avoided like the plague. Smitten, Cal?"

"I don't know what it is about her but she's definitely different. She's such a 'Deelicious' morsel for a change, so fresh."

The play on Dee's name didn't go unnoticed by Maeve. Through pursed lips she said, "Always the playboy, aren't you. Best be careful. One day you might get played instead."

Cal laughed and once again went and sat next to Dee. She was comforted by the easy warmth she felt between them. There was an enthusiasm about Cal that touched Dee. He was amusing and she was flattered by his attention.

Turning more to face Rowan, Maeve effectively excluded Dee from their conversation. Dee sat back unaffected by the intentional snub. When the lounge singer began to sing she was soon captivated by her lovely voice. Dee found it to be both dreamlike and soothing. She turned to Cal and smiled, "Music makes a person feel more alive." The rest of the evening passed pleasantly. Dee heard the singer say, "For my last song I'll be singing a new release from a young band from the States." To Dee, it was a familiar tune. Unexpectedly, an immense feeling of sadness engulfed her. Like a ghost from the past it haunted her as she returned to the flat.

The flat was still but Constance had left a light on. Dee appreciated the gesture and thought what a kind lady her grandmother was. Then she realized that this was the first time that she had thought of her as her grandmother instead of a new acquaintance. As happy as she was to have family, she wondered about those in her past. Because of their earlier conversation, Dee knew better than to ask her grandmother.

On her way to her room Dee was drawn into the parlour. She walked over to the piano and sat down, her heart pounding, her hands trembling. Finally, she leaned forward and placed her long slender fingers on the ivory keys. The trembling stopped as a familiar feeling flowed through her and she smiled. It felt natural to caress the keys of the piano. Then Dee began to do something she loved, something that never failed to comfort her. She played. That's when it began. Slowly, tentatively, hesitantly and unknowingly. A connection to the past. There was nothing that soothed her more than music. It was a beginning. When she stopped playing, Dee was filled with an overwhelming sadness, as though she had lost something precious. A memory was nagging at the corners of her mind but she failed to remember for the vision slipped away. But from that moment on the piano became her oasis.

When Dee retired and turned off the lights, her thoughts took over. It was, all things considered, a pleasant evening. Her mind went back to the song the lounge singer sang. *I know I've heard that song before tonight.* The familiar words brought her comfort. *It must be a memory. It was too real not to be.* For the first time since her accident she was filled with hope and had a dreamless sleep.

CHAPTER THREE

Constance leaned back in her chair and analyzed the last few days. Time together had become more comfortable between her and Dee but it was evident that it was going to be a slow process before they were completely at ease with each other. Right after breakfast Dee had once again made her escape.

Rowan entered with Maeve who looked around the room. "Where's the waif?" Constance frowned at Maeve's crisp, impersonal tone.

Rowan wasn't amused either. Unaware, his protective instincts kicked into gear. "Don't be insensitive. The poor girl has gone through a lot." Constance was surprised and touched at how quickly Rowan had come to Dee's defense. He went and sat next to her. "Dinner was pleasant the other evening. It was nice to see Dee relax. I believe she even enjoyed herself."

In hopes of redeeming herself, Maeve smiled at Constance. "Your granddaughter and Cal seemed to strike a chord."

"Dee is a very charming young lady." Constance ignored Rowan's raised eyebrow. She looked over as Boris entered the room. "Please go ask Dee to join us for tea. I believe she may be in the garden."

Dee sat alone on the bench. She wore her unhappiness like a heavy cape that smothered her natural exuberance. Staring into space, she could hear the wind crying through the trees as if it shared her sadness. Today she was filled with an incredible sense of emptiness and nothing helped to ease the pangs of loneliness. Everything seemed hopeless. Dee felt she had no control of her future or her destiny. She was thoroughly miserable.

Boris found Dee sitting in the vine-covered gazebo. She looked lost in thought and the thoughts did not appear to be happy ones. He could tell she'd been crying. "I'm sorry to disturb you, Miss Dee. Madam has guests and would like you to join them for tea. It's Mr. Le Baron and Miss Spencer."

Dee now knew his aloofness was not unfriendliness. It was an air of reserve that served him well. His job required him to be detached. Dee looked up, tears still clinging to her long lashes. She quickly wiped her eyes. Although she smiled at him she couldn't mask the look of despair. Dee knew the invitation was one of kindness. There was no way her grandmother knew how uncomfortable she felt in the presence of both of her guests.

Boris recognized her silent plea. The poor child was in such a bizarre situation. His heart went out to her but his face remained impassive.

Dee's shoulders sagged as her depression grew. She looked up at him, "I don't fit in here, Boris. Everything is strange. I'm not familiar with sayings and the way things are done. People greet each other in a different way. When my grandmother and I strolled through the village, she picked up a book she had ordered at the bookstore. Just that simple outing became overwhelming. I had no clue about the currency. There are so many different coins. And people talk funny here. You pronounce everything in your own way and use slang words."

Boris interrupted Dee as she stopped to catch her breath and he sat down beside her. "We may talk differently but you'll learn. However, you won't learn everything in a couple of days so let me help you get out of the gate with some basic information. 'How do you do' is a greeting, not a question. The correct response is to repeat it back to the person. You do this when shaking hands with them. 'Ta-ta' means good-by but 'ta' means thanks."

Dee remained frustrated as she wrestled with her confusion despite Boris's sincere efforts. Everything had been alien since she'd arrived. "There's so much to learn because it's all so odd. Including everyday living here at the hotel."

Boris nodded in understanding. "You'll learn, Miss Dee. Give it some time and give everyone a chance. Madam would love to help you if you would let her. As will I. Madam's life style is very social. She entertains a lot both in her flat and downstairs so I will teach you the proper etiquette when dining."

Dee felt a surge of optimism as Boris continued, "Brits may seem a little stiff and formal because we are reserved and private people. This may cause us to appear cool and indifferent or very formal." For a brief moment he lowered his guard and placed his hand on hers. "It takes effort in the beginning to build a relationship."

Dee knew he was referring to her grandmother.

"I'm sure you've realized that the Brits can be snobs and have an obsession with class."

Dee laughed at his candor. *That describes Maeve Spencer perfectly.* She knew Boris was trying to boost her spirits. "I'm sorry. It's not like I can't do it," she said, as if trying to convince herself. "I hate this feeling of loneliness. Right now, it's the only real thing I know. Isolation makes the days seem twice as long. I feel like I'm living in a fish bowl and everyone is watching me. It's a very expensive fish bowl, Boris. What if I never fit in?"

Recognizing that Dee was still upset, Boris said, "I'll tell Madam that you must have gone for a walk."

Dee's eyes filled with gratitude. "Thank you. You're being incredibly kind. I'm sorry if I've been difficult to have around. It was never my intention to hurt my grandmother."

Boris smiled in understanding. "Up you get and toddle off. I don't want you making a liar out of me." With that he gave her a quick wink and left.

There was an old-fashioned dignity about Boris that Dee now respected instead of being intimidated by. She hadn't failed to catch the brief glimpse of his wry humor. It helped her to feel more at ease with him.

It was a beautiful day, for the sun was bright overhead and sunbeams filtered through drifting clouds. With her composure somewhat restored, she gathered enough courage to venture away from the hotel. She took the opportunity to look around and mindlessly explored the surrounding neighbourhood. Time passed too quickly. Reluctantly, she knew it was time to return to the hotel where she'd once again have to face and conquer her fears.

On the way back to the hotel, Dee reflected on the varying emotions she'd experienced in the small amount of time that she'd been here. She tried to piece together her feelings. Fear, anger and resentment immediately came to mind along with the image of Rowan Le Baron. He was the spark that ignited these negative emotions. Her grandmother had immediately welcomed her but the Bear and his attitude overshadowed everything. The man irked her to no end.

Dee managed to escape to her room until dinner. It was with a lighter heart that she joined her grandmother. In an attempt to make an effort, Dee shared with her how she had passed the afternoon. "I enjoyed spending time in the neighbourhood. Afterwards, I sat for a while and listened to a jazz band in the park. When I have more time I intend to venture further," Dee declared triumphantly.

Constance was thrilled that Dee was making plans on her own for the future. She hoped that it was a sign of acceptance. With a note of encouragement she informed Dee, "There are many outdoor activities happening all over London. It seems that there's always an event taking place along the Thames River, most of which are free." They continued to chat comfortably with one another and the evening passed pleasantly.

Later that night, Dee felt stifled in her room. Moonbeams cast streams of light across the room but soon the darkness would close in around her. She sat alone asking herself questions she couldn't answer, tortured by the fear that she might never have the answers. Dee wanted answers. She was tired of wondering who she was and what she was afraid to remember. She had no one to ask, no one to turn to. Unable to bear the loneliness within the four walls any longer, she stole quietly downstairs to stroll through the garden. She paused to enjoy the quiet of the night. When a young couple passed by holding hands she wondered if there was someone in America missing her. *More questions, no answers.*

Rowan's familiar voice greeted the couple and they chatted for a while. *He can certainly be friendly to others.* Dee's first instinct was to run but there was nowhere for her to flee. Attempting to hide, she moved to the darkness of the shadows and stood perfectly still. She prayed he'd turn around and retreat back to the hotel.

Unfortunately, her bad luck hadn't changed and he slowly approached her. Dee tried ignoring him, hoping he'd pass by. "Good evening, Miss Dare. Looking for an escape route?" His unnerving gaze remained locked on her.

This is absurd. Why is he determined to torment me? "Go away, I want to be alone." Suddenly, it occurred to her, "Are you spying on me? Of all the intrusive gall. You're an extremely offensive man."

Rowan ignored the insult she hurled at him.

"Thank God you're leaving for a few days. I won't have to worry about being stalked." *I wish it was forever.*

Rowan placed his hands on her shoulders to prevent her from leaving. "You might as well get used to me." His voice, if not exactly threatening, had taken on a steely edge, "I intend to keep a close eye on you while you're here and you better behave yourself." He towered over her, giving her his best glare, but Dee didn't cower away. She didn't appear to be at all intimidated as she matched him glare for glare.

"Take your hands off of me or I'll scream," she cried, while pushing against his chest. She wouldn't give him the satisfaction of letting him see how much he had unnerved her. "You don't frighten me," she exclaimed, although her knees were shaking as she stood her ground.

Rowan released his hold. "I'm not trying to frighten you. I'm simply warning you and you better listen."

"Both your advice and your threats are meaningless."

"Be clear on this, Dee. If you do anything to hurt Connie I'll make your life more miserable than what you think it is now."

Dee didn't doubt this for a second. Her eyes now reflected her unhappiness rather than fury. "What can be worse than hell?" She turned and fled.

Rowan watched until her slender form disappeared into the night. He was frustrated with himself for once again this young slip of a girl had gotten under his skin. If nothing else, Dee Dare did not lack spirit.

Instead of returning to her room, Dee escaped to the parlour and began pounding the piano keys. It was a long time before softer notes filled the room.

Dee once again retired to her room. She flung herself on the bed and stared up at the ceiling. Unable to sleep, she went to the window and wrapped the throw around her shoulders. She sighed and laid her head against the cool window pane. She gazed out, her lovely eyes shadowed, and released a weary sigh. She felt her whole world was turned upside down. Immediately, the Bear returned to her thoughts. *Infuriating man.*

Pushing a hand through her hair in agitation, she found it hard to let go of her anger toward him. He was instrumental in the current upheaval in her life which was on a downhill spiral straight to hell. How she hated him.

Giving in to fatigue, she climbed into bed. Slowly she drifted into an uneasy sleep. Along with sleep came the ghost filled dreams. They were more confusing than usual and along with them came the familiar fear.

CHAPTER FOUR

C al and Dee became fast friends. A few days after they met Cal called on her. After a flirtatious hello to Constance, he turned to Dee and handed her a brochure with a tour bus on it.

"What's this?"

"Our next outing if you don't have plans for tomorrow," Cal offered with a grin.

"My circle of acquaintances is next to none so I have no plans," she said solemnly.

Constance looked over at her granddaughter hating to see her distress.

Cal, unaware of the underlying significance of Dee's comment, continued, "You and I are going to enjoy hopping on and off sight-seeing buses and explore the city in depth. We can see London's iconic landmarks and attractions from the comfort of a bus."

"And we can hop on and off wherever we want to?"

Cal nodded as he handed her more brochures, "It's the perfect way to see London's most famous places. You'll enjoy the striking display of British pomp and pageantry as we watch the changing of the guard outside Buckingham Palace."

Constance liked Cal and knew Dee would enjoy the day he had planned. But she wished that Dee felt as comfortable with her as she did with Cal. There was such a natural ease between the two of them, while there was still an invisible wall between her and Dee. It wasn't as tall but it was still there. So, she smiled warmly and said, "I'm sure you couldn't have a better guide."

As promised, the next day was everything that Cal had promised. Dee felt like a teenager on her first date. All day long they hopped on and they hopped off. They were as awed as other tourists and giggled like little kids. The more Cal made her laugh the more Dee relaxed. They had the time of their lives as their friendship grew.

That day with Cal was a turning point for Dee. Day by day, Dee relaxed her guard. Constance and Dee grew closer as they became more at ease with one another and accepted each day for what it was. After her talk with Boris, Dee knew she had to give her new life and those in it a chance. Dee was less reserved and her smiles and conversations became more spontaneous. She made more of an effort getting to know her grandmother. As a result, conversations were more comfortable. Dee's smiles came more readily and her eyes no longer had a wounded look.

This week both Rowan and Maeve were away on business. Cal was off to Wimbledon to join a group of friends who had made plans months ago. So, for now, it was just Dee and her grandmother. Their time together was carefree and unplanned.

Dee enjoyed their excursions. They went to the ballet one night, a concert at Albert Hall another night. One rainy day they just stayed in and talked. Thinking of all she had to be grateful for, Dee forgot to be angry. Sometimes Dee caught herself wanting to say something, share a thought, only to lose it. She refused to give in to the feeling of frustration. She hoped in time to grasp the memory and hold onto it.

This afternoon they were at the Globe Theatre, an Elizabethan playhouse associated with William Shakespeare. Constance picked up the summer show schedule. "How wonderful, 'A Midsummer Night's Dream' is playing in a couple of weeks."

Dee turned with excitement to her grandmother. "Mom loved this play. It was one of our favorites."

Constance forced herself not to react but this was the first time that Dee had unconsciously shared a memory. This gave her hope that in time Dee would recall all of them.

It was mid-afternoon when they returned to the hotel. Dee was jubilant. "I remembered that Mom loved live theatre. I love it, too."

"What else do you remember, Dee?" Constance urged. "Do you remember your mom?"

"Yes and no. I remember holding her hand and twirling around. I remember her laughter. She liked to sing. She always smelled nice, like lilacs. I'm trying to remember more but it's like I drift in and out of a fog."

Keeping her voice calm, Constance attempted to encourage Dee, "I'm sure more of your memories will come back to you. If you don't force your mind, maybe they'll continue to surface on their own like they did today."

For a moment both were silent. They knew today was monumental as well as reassuring. It gave Dee hope.

"Why don't we plan on attending a live production this Saturday? I have box seats at St. Martin's Theatre. It's one of the few remaining privately owned theatres in London. Over the years they've staged many famous plays. 'The Mousetrap' is currently playing. Are you familiar with the play, Dee?"

When Dee shook her head, Constance enlightened her, "This classic Agatha Christie murder mystery is the longest continuous show in the world."

Dee beamed with pleasure. "I'd love to go with you. Who knows, maybe it will trigger more memories."

"I'd say your subconscious is letting you know you're not ready to remember everything. For now, a little at a time will have to do."

Dee looked up at her wistfully, "I thought all my memories would have returned by now." Dee paused, a faraway look in her eyes. When she turned back to her grandmother, her voice was very serious, "May I ask you something?"

Constance smiled graciously, "Of course, Dee. What is it?"

Dee gave her grandmother a long searching look, "Will you tell me about my parents?"

Constance knew the day would come when Dee would ask specific questions. "I would like nothing more. I don't get to talk about those years very often. Come, it's a beautiful afternoon, I'll ring Boris to bring us tea and biscuits and we can enjoy them out on the terrace."

Dee's feelings toward Boris had mellowed from when she first met him, for she recognized his devotion to her grandmother. "Boris takes such good care of you."

"Boris is a dear man and a good friend. He's really the one that runs my home. He quietly and efficiently goes about his business taking care of the flat and makes all aspects of my life easier. I appreciate all of his years of loyal service."

"I now know better than to interfere with his duties. But I still feel uncomfortable about him doing everything for me. I doubt very much that I was catered to in my past."

Dee's reference to the past was with acceptance rather than bitterness and Constance felt that they were making progress.

When the tea arrived Dee looked over to her grandmother. Constance remained silent for a moment, knowing she had to choose her words. She began slowly, feeling her way carefully over a minefield of words. The wrong words could set off a bomb which could scar her granddaughter for life. There were definite signs that Dee had found her road to recovery but she was still unable to recognize all the signs.

Mentally, Constance took Dee by the hand and started down the road together. "Your parents went to school together. Johnny Dare was the most popular boy in school. He had an irresistible vitality, an aura that made every eye turn in his direction. Young girls threw themselves at him. But he only had eyes for your mother and Phoebe idolized him."

Dee smiled as Cal's image came to mind.

"Johnny always said that when he was eighteen he was going to the United States where he was going to become a star as a singer. He said this like it was a guaranteed fact. Johnny had no family of his own so it was an easy decision to make. His mom was a single parent who overdosed on drugs so he was raised by his grandmother. He never knew his dad. Johnny told us that he and Phoebe loved each other and they wanted to get married so she could go with him. Johnny promised us he would take good care of her. Of course we said no because they were both too young. They were barely more than kids themselves. Phoebe would argue with us and cry saying they belonged together and they would always love each other. There was nothing we could say to change her mind. I suggested that Johnny go on his own and Phoebe could join him once he was settled. To be honest, I was hoping they'd grow apart and move on with their own lives because I didn't want to lose my daughter." Constance's voice broke recalling her most recent loss. She had just lost a granddaughter and hadn't yet been able to grieve that loss.

"Your mother, Phoebe Olivia Malone, was our only child. I have to admit that she was spoiled by both of us but especially by her father. Phoebe was sweetness and charm and had the ability to wrap her dad around her little finger. From the day she was born, Oliver could never say no to his ray of sunshine. When he heard her call out in the morning, he would smile and say that the sun was up and he would smile again as he went to get her." The old lady's voice broke a little, "She was his life. He was her hero." For a brief moment Constance allowed herself to drift back in time. She smiled as she remembered how alive and vital Phoebe was as a little girl. She was a little spitfire who was full of life. Constance sighed sadly, for there was nothing that could bring those years back. Her eyes misted over knowing that Dee, too, would have to deal with that same loss.

Dee misread the tears and felt sorry for her grandmother who had lost her daughter so many years ago. She waited anxiously for her grandmother to continue.

"Phoebe was stubborn and strong-willed and absolutely sure of what she wanted. It became a contest of wills between Phoebe and her father. This was one time that Oliver wouldn't concede. Johnny was like a force of nature. Your grandfather was afraid Phoebe would be sucked up in his vortex and it would consume her. He didn't want that life for Phoebe, living in a crazy world with unstable people. I was also concerned that they would struggle with his chosen profession."

"Phoebe loved her father but she was in love with Johnny. Men don't realize that loving and being in love are two different things. Phoebe and Johnny believed in each other. They believed in the power of love. Being strong-willed and independent, she eloped with Johnny. When they told us they were married they'd already booked their flights. They were young and ready for an adventure with no fear of the unknown. We may think we know exactly what we need to make us happy. We believe we know what's good for us to have a happy ending. However, life has many unexpected twists and turns and reshapes our lives in unexpected ways."

Dee had the distinct feeling that her grandmother was no longer just talking about Phoebe. Suddenly she wondered if she'd be ready for the truth if her memories returned.

Constance sighed heavily, "Brits often have an inability to express their emotions. Oliver shut down when Phoebe left and seldom talked about her.

He pointed out that things were now different. Our daughter had made a rebellious move and Oliver believed that when you make decisions you must accept the consequences. Phoebe was very much like her father. She shared the same belief. We knew they struggled but she never asked us for money after she left. They severed themselves from their lives here."

Dee was wholly absorbed in her grandmother's narration and was hanging on every word. "What happened when they got to America?"

"When they arrived in California, they settled in a small dreary apartment where the rent was cheap. Johnny was unsuccessful as a solo artist so the early years were a challenge and at times their financial situation became acute. But your father was an intense young man who was eager and ambitious. So he formed a band and started touring and Phoebe travelled with him. I knew she was lost for awhile but she never complained. She loved Johnny too much to do that. Nothing had prepared her for life in the United States, but in time, she adapted to the American way. But she was lonely. She deserved a better life."

Constance leaned over and took one of Dee's hands in hers. "Your mother had a gentle spirit. They lived a nomadic life even after you were born." Constance had to catch herself, for she almost said you twins instead of you. Conversations like this seemed unfair because she couldn't be completely open with her granddaughter.

"Phoebe thought you were an angel and you gave her so much happiness. She considered her role as a mother to be important as well as rewarding. When Phoebe became terminally ill with cancer, she told Johnny that she wanted to be cremated and to let Oliver and I bring her ashes back to England. She died within the year. After the funeral we brought our daughter home. That was the last time I saw you." Her eyes glistening with unshed tears.

Emotion, and something else, rose within Dee but she pushed it aside.

"Oliver's life changed the day Phoebe died. His life became overshadowed by grief. I think Oliver lost his will to live that day, too. He died the same year. I'm sure it was from a broken heart. The sunshine had gone from his life. They're both buried in the family plot in a small rural cemetery outside of London." Constance lapsed into silence.

Dee waited a moment before quietly asking, "What happened to my dad?"

Constance hesitated before continuing, more sad news for this child to absorb. "A fatal heart attack took Johnny's life. Your dad did his best after your mom died. He wasn't a bad person. He just lived in a world different than ours."

Dee had to ask, "I have no other family?"

Constance couldn't bring herself to lie. She took a deep breath. "Not anymore," she said evasively. Her face revealed nothing.

Now Dee knew why there was no family for her in the States for her to go to. It answered a few of her questions but filled in none of her missing pieces. Dee was neither shocked nor upset by what she heard. She stated soberly, "You're all I've got for family now."

Constance clasped her granddaughter's hands in hers. "All we have is each other. You know you're everything to me."

They sat for a moment in silence before Dee asked, "What did my mother look like?"

Constance smiled reflectively, "She was the most beautiful girl in the world. You look exactly like your mother, Dee. I was a little shocked when I saw you standing there that first day. Let's go back into the house. In my bedroom I have photo albums stored in a chest. I'll share more stories as we look through them." Constance knew she would only share pictures up until Dee's parents left England. The rest of their story would have to wait for now.

Constance and Dee spent the next few hours in Constance's bedroom. There were so many things she wanted to tell her granddaughter. Sadly, she'd have to learn them for herself. "Both of your parents believed in a dream and their love for each other was real. It's interesting where life takes you if you are open to an adventure, if you dare to dream."

Dee recalled a voice saying the same words. They were both silent for a moment.

Constance saw the vulnerability in Dee's eyes and was dismayed. Her heart ached seeing how sad Dee looked.

"What's so awful that I can't remember?" Dee questioned, not for the first time.

It was a question left unanswered. Constance understood the poor girl's frustration, but for now, there was nothing she could say. That was something Dee would eventually remember. Constance reached over and gently touched her granddaughter's cheek as Dee looked at her with eyes full of hope. For now all she could offer Dee was silent supportive sympathy.

Constance got up and walked over to her dresser and opened one of the drawers. She pulled out a small velvet box and went and sat back down next to her granddaughter. A tear fell to her cheek as she opened it. Inside was an exquisite gold locket which Constance slowly opened. Inside was a picture of Phoebe. It could have been Dee. Constance could see that her granddaughter was so much like Phoebe in her loveliness, her energy and her stubborn nature. "I've been saving this, waiting to pass it down to my granddaughter." The old lady's voice broke. Wiping her eyes, she undid the clasp and placed the necklace around Dee's slender neck.

Dee's fingertips brushed the locket. "This will be something I will always treasure," she said softly, for this was part of her past as well as her future.

Constance smiled in delight. "You brought back memories I thought I'd forgotten. You've given me a greater gift than I can ever give you."

Dee thought about what her grandmother told her about her parents. She had told a story of loss and love. "Thank you, Gran."

This was the first time that Dee had called her Gran and Constance was genuinely touched. It endeared Dee to her as nothing else had.

In so many of the pictures Dee saw how much she looked like her mom. She touched the locket. It was weird to look so much like another person. Like twins. A shiver ran down her spine. As disturbing as the thought was, it was also comforting. Dee now felt an invisible tie to her mother and the past.

"I pray every day that you'll have your life back with your memories restored. I want you to be happy again."

"It's not that I'm not happy. Today you've helped restore my family to me. Thank you for telling me about my parents."

The new look of hope in her granddaughter's eyes was thanks enough. Constance was grateful for this extraordinary relationship that she treasured more every day.

The next day over breakfast Constance reminded Dee that she had appointments all day. "What are you going to do while I'm gone?"

"Nothing in particular. Cal's busy, too. Maybe I'll go out and explore on my own. Don't worry about me, I'll find something to fill my time."

Casual conversation confirmed that Rowan and Maeve were back. Dee always tried her best to avoid them but she didn't want to be imprisoned in the apartment. By mid-afternoon Dee was restless. Depression was quickly closing in so she decided to venture out.

As she strolled along Dee felt the gentle breeze caress her body as the hot sun broke through floating clouds. The streets were crowded and colorful; fruit and vegetable stands brightened the sidewalks. She'd forgotten that it was festival season. Dee laughed to herself for it was a normal forgetfulness. Her smile widened, for she was grateful that she could laugh at herself despite her situation.

Dee paused on occasion to glance at the latest displays in the windows. Unexpectedly, she caught a glimpse of her reflection. Goose bumps broke out on her flesh as a memory transported her back in time. The blood pounded in her ears as voices seemed to surge around her. Familiar voices that sounded like music to her ears. The maxi dress she was wearing had been bought at a flea market in Arizona and she'd been with someone. The reality around her blurred and vanished for a moment. A chill ran down her spine as the color drained from her face. The vision had been so real she knew her subconscious was coming to the forefront. Dee shivered in the bright sunlight and rubbed her bare arms to rid herself of her goose bumps. An elderly woman gently touched her arm. "Are you okay, luv?"

Dee attempted to smile, wanting to reassure the kind lady but she felt like she'd seen a ghost. "I'm fine, thanks," she lied, trying to sound calm when it felt like her whole life was turning upside down. "I probably should've worn a hat. The sun is awfully warm today."

Deciding a cold drink couldn't hurt, Dee went and sat at a patio table in the courtyard. It had only been a few weeks since her arrival but in some ways it seemed like an eternity. Dee tried to sort through the confusing images that seemed to slip away as quickly as they came. But this last memory stayed and she knew this one wouldn't fade away like so many others. As upsetting as it was at the moment, she took it as a positive sign that she'd be able to hold on to more of the memories that flitted randomly through her mind. Even though the sun was hot, she shivered again. Another memory continued to haunt her. It was so close but she couldn't capture it, and then it was gone. Suddenly another thought popped in. *Why was I in Arizona if they flew me here from California? And who was I with?*

Dee sat idly watching as friends and family talked and laughed with one another. The sudden yearning to be part of a loving, close-knit family overwhelmed her as a wave of homesickness make her ache inside. Were there friends who were missing her? Did she even have any friends? The huge blank screen that was her past continued to torment her. *God, I'm miserable.* She was so immensely lonesome that she started to cry. Dee knew it was childish to feel sorry for herself but she didn't care. She indulged herself with a bout of self-pity before wiping the tears from her eyes.

Dee pulled herself away from her deep thoughts and returned her gaze to those around her. She opened her eyes wide in disbelief as she caught sight of the familiar figure strolling her way. *Unbelievable, has this man been cloned?* Without hesitation she rose to leave.

"Dee, wait." Rowan grabbed her arm and turned her around to face him. He looked at her for a long while. He thought she looked pale and very sad. "Before you accuse me of stalking you believe me when I say that I'm not following you. I had an appointment in the neighbourhood and since it's such a beautiful day I decided to walk back to the hotel. Please sit back down and let me join you for a drink."

"Stop grabbing me." Eyes cold, Dee jerked her arm free. She immediately regretted the burst of anger and took a deep breath to calm herself. His being here could have been a coincidence but his sudden appearance had rattled her. She hated that he could make her react so quickly in displeasure. It wasn't fair if she kept snapping at him every time they spent five minutes together. But she would have bitten off her tongue before admitting it.

"Why won't you stay and have a cool drink with me?"

"Because," Dee declared, meeting his eyes directly, "I don't like you." She didn't bother to mask the disgust in her voice.

Her outrage made him want to laugh. She was so easily riled. "It's too fine a day to be upset. Sit down and finish your drink. It'll cool you off."

Dee didn't know how to take that remark and she didn't appreciate the fact that she could see amusement in his dark piercing eyes. Her lips tightened in annoyance, "Didn't you hear me? I said no."

Rowan frowned at her stubborn tone. "Come on, Dee. For some reason we seem to have gotten off on the wrong foot."

"Why? Because you've resented and mistrusted me since the day we met?"

"You're right."

Dee was bewildered by both his words and the gentleness in his tone. Her eyes narrowed as she shot him a suspicious glance, searching for signs of sarcasm, but his smile was perfectly sincere. Slowly, under his steady gaze, she felt her rage die down.

"So, will you please sit down and finish your drink with me?" he asked again, the tease of a smile on his lips. This time his smile reached his eyes, warming them a little.

"No," Dee said again.

Rowan seemed surprised at her answer. "Why not?"

Dee looked at him in disbelief. No one could make a clearer statement with an arch of an eyebrow. "I still don't like you." Without another word she started to walk away, her stride lengthening in a hurry for distance in case he came after her. Dee ignored his summons to come back and she heard him say, "My God, you're stubborn."

Despite himself, Rowan was still smiling to himself long after she had walked away. He had a hunch he had met his match in uncompromising strength of will and stubbornness. The girl had spunk and constantly pushed his buttons. And once she made up her mind, hell could freeze over before she changed it. Dee Dare exasperated him and captivated him. He headed back to the hotel deep in thought.

CHAPTER FIVE

London was experiencing a wonderful summer and Dee planned on spending part of her day outdoors. Dee had finally settled in at the hotel. She had come to terms with her circumstances and was adjusting. She wasn't the type to remain fixated on the negatives of her life. Although she hated the feeling of loneliness, she was grateful to be alive. There were times she had random flashes of memory, which she gratefully hung on to. Other times, there were glimpses of images that came and went too quickly for her to grasp. They were always just out of reach, never quite breaking the surface of her conscious mind. They came at unexpected moments, mere fragments that filled her with hope. There were odd times that she felt like she had done something or heard something before. They meant nothing but she knew they were pieces from her past. Hopefully, one day the pieces she gathered would start to fit together and she could put together the puzzle of her forgotten past.

Dee dressed in a pale blue summer frock and pulled her hair back in a single braid. She looked charming. Time in the sun had colored her bare skin with a warm golden tan. The dark shadows had disappeared from under her eyes that now sparkled with life.

Hunger pangs motivated her to leave her room, knowing a wonderful breakfast would be waiting. Dee smiled. Boris was the best. True to his word they'd spend a little time together when Madam was resting and he'd taught her new things about the Brits and their lifestyle. Dee was determined to learn and fit in. Today, she decided not to worry about the past or the future and just enjoy the gift of today.

Dee bound into the morning room smiling a greeting. She was surprised and very pleased to see Cal chatting with her grandmother. A little thrill of excitement ran through her for they had become fast friends. Dee enjoyed the fact that Cal was carefree and spontaneous and didn't ask a lot of questions, and as a result she remained at ease with him.

Cal turned to Dee and his dimples flashed when he grinned. "I dropped by hoping I could interest you in taking a ride in the country. Since you arrived you've spent all your time here in London. I thought you might like a change."

"That sounds wonderful." Dee looked at her grandmother with a questioning look. They didn't have any special plans and Dee had to admit she enjoyed spending time with Cal.

Constance nodded, "You spend enough time with this old lady. Go have some fun."

"Are you sure you don't mind me being gone all day?" Dee asked politely.

Constance insisted, "I'm fine. Don't take this the wrong way. I love having you here but I could use a little time to myself. I think I'll spend time in the garden reading. We've been so busy I haven't started the new book we picked up. I'll have Boris pack a picnic lunch and the two of you can spend the day touring around the countryside."

Breathless with excitement, Dee turned to Cal. "Well, Mr. O'Brian, you have a date."

Cal went over and kissed Constance on her cheek. "Mrs. C. I hope you have an enjoyable afternoon with a dashing gentleman of fiction."

Constance giggled like a school girl and slapped his arm. He was such a cheeky bloke but one couldn't resist his lighthearted charm. "You can join us for breakfast." Thanks to Dee her home was again filled with youth and energy. She hadn't realized how lonely she'd been until Dee arrived and filled that void.

Dee laughed when they arrived at Cal's car. Of course he would own a convertible. She wouldn't have expected him to drive anything ordinary.

Cal grinned back as he opened the car door. "Are you fine if we keep the top down? It truly is a grand day for a drive."

Dee nodded as she climbed in and settled back against the luxurious leather seat. She felt a thrill of exhilaration as they took off, along with pure joy in being open to the wind. It was amazing how liberated it felt to get away from the hotel, peering eyes and questioning remarks. She felt free for the moment from the tension around her.

As they drove through the lush countryside, Dee looked around with interest. The landscape was flooded with sunlight that streamed through wispy clouds that flitted across the sky. The view was breathtaking with the patchwork hills, dramatic dales and winding country roads. They rounded a bend and off to the left were beautiful lavender fields dotted here and there with stone houses in the distance. Fascinated, Dee gazed out the window. Cal turned down a side road and slowed down so they could enjoy the heady scent from the fragrant plants.

Cal enlightened Dee with a few relevant facts, "Farmers are looking for alternatives to growing wheat and barley so now parts of our countryside are turning an attractive shade of purple. Once the lavender is harvested the oil is distilled and left to mature. There is now a thriving business selling hand creams, soaps and lotions based on the essential oil."

Continuing along the country lane soon led them down to the river where they found a perfect spot for their picnic. The view was spectacular and the air was invigorating with the fragrance of lavender from the adjacent fields. It was a gem of a summer day. Cal grabbed the basket while Dee spread the blanket on the grassy embankment before being drawn to the babbling brook. The sparkling water was as clear as crystal as it rippled over the river rocks. Dee shaded her eyes as she took a deep breath and appreciated the beauty surrounding her.

Dee dropped down next to Cal, who had sprawled full length on the blanket. His long legs were stretched out before him, crossed at the ankles. Dee wrapped her arms around her knees and rested her chin on them. Both were relaxed in each other's company. "What a spectacular place. It's peaceful and still. I feel like I left all my worries back in the city."

Cal laughed as he looked over at her but was caught off-guard by her solemn expression. "Why would you have worries, young lady?" The tone in his voice changed and he quickly sat up, "I've been spending a lot of time with you but I hardly know anything about you."

"Well, Cal, truth be told, you probably know as much as I do."

Cal stared back with curious eyes. "What's that supposed to mean?"

Dee answered Cal's astonished stare with a sad reply, "I thought you knew I have amnesia. Everything about my personal past I've had to learn from Gran. I've even wondered if Dee is short for another name. I've tried to accept the name but it feels unfamiliar and doesn't mean anything. When I asked about it, Gran was evasive and I didn't push. I was told that I was coming to England to visit her and on the way to the airport I was in a car accident. I don't remember what happened but when I woke up in the hospital I had amnesia and no memory of my life before the accident." Unconsciously, she lifted her hand and ran it down her face. "When I saw my face in the mirror, it meant nothing to me. I was a stranger to myself. I was told I have no family left in the States. Gran is my legal guardian so she arranged for Rowan to bring me here when I was discharged."

"You don't remember anything?" he asked in disbelief.

"Nothing from before the accident as to what happened or who I am. There are things I know; things I'm sure of. I can draw on general information with ease. But my own face means nothing to me. I thought all my memories would come back in a day or two but it's been weeks. I do have occasional flashbacks but not everything stays. They float away like leaves in the wind. I treasure every memory I keep and I store it away. For now, all I have are tiny pieces that don't fit together. I hope in time I'll have enough to start piecing my life back together. I wish I could remember," Dee told him longingly.

Cal was dumbfounded.

"Gran is very protective and doesn't want to upset me. We're still guarded around each other but it's getting better. I feel both Gran and Rowan know more about me than what they're saying. They'll start to say something and then look at each other and stop. Because they were told by the doctor to let my memories return on their own I know they're holding back. I'm afraid to ask too many questions. Maybe I'm afraid of the answers," she confessed.

The wistfulness in her voice made Cal shake his head. "Gee, this is bloody awful. I can't imagine how you've been dealing with this. I'm not sure I could. What are you going to do if you never remember?"

Dee turned to look at Cal and the haunted look was back. "I have nightmares and I wake up thinking this is all a bad dream, but it isn't. I get scared when I think that I may not get my memory back and due to my present situation I sometimes feel imprisoned at the hotel. Those are the hard times, the times that I feel really alone. But I'm trying to adjust and accept that this is a possibility. This morning I realized that I'm tired of trying to figure out who I am. So, for now, I am just Dee Dare. I'm bravely venturing into a new world, discovering new people and experiencing new feelings."

Cal had been enthralled and totally fascinated by her tale. "If you're having sporadic flashbacks of memories I'm sure it's a sign that you'll soon get all of your memory back and everything will be back to normal," he said, wanting to give her hope.

Dee appreciated Cal's gesture and clung fiercely to the belief that it would happen. "I'm adjusting and learning to fit in. I feel like I've had time to heal on the inside, which has allowed me to think about things in a different way. More questions come into my head and I can't help but wonder what life I've left behind."

In an effort to put Dee back at ease, he changed the subject. "Your grandmother is an incredible lady. She's so genuine and kind. She enjoys it when I tease her."

"I'm very fortunate. Gran has been more than kind. She welcomed me and made her home mine."

"What do you think of her godson, Rowan?" Cal asked off-handedly.

Dee's joy faded as she looked absently at the flowing river. As always, thinking about Rowan caused her heart to race. "I can't stand the man but he is very loyal to my grandmother. I find it difficult to resent that loyalty. Has he always been insufferable?"

Cal's eyes were alight with amusement at her reaction. "Rowan's actually a decent bloke. Other than being too stern and rigid."

Dee was surprised by his comment and to her greater surprise she believed him. Her thoughts quickly switched to Maeve. "I try to avoid both the Bear and his Ice Maiden. I can tell that Maeve doesn't like me. I hear her call me 'Tweedle Dee' behind my back."

Cal nodded, for he understood Maeve completely. "Maeve and I are old friends. She dated my older brother, Graham. That is until she met Rowan, who was a much better catch. Graham wasn't really her type; nor was she his. Money is Maeve's major obsession along with social climbing. Her unwavering goal is to become Mrs. Rowan Le Baron. Even though

Rowan hasn't officially proposed, Maeve expects they'll marry next year. Nothing and no one is going to get in her way."

She can have him. They deserve each other.

Cal gave Dee a warning look, "Beware of Maeve, there's quite the temper under her icy exterior. I'm not saying this about her to be unkind. I'm stating a truth and telling you to watch yourself around her. Jealousy is a terrible thing and very dangerous. I get the feeling she doesn't like having you here. Maeve can be extremely charming to your face but watch your back."

Dee was unable to hold back a sharp retort, "So why are you friends with her?"

"Maeve tolerates me like she would a younger brother. Like a younger brother, it amuses me to annoy her at times. Our families have known each other for years. We still have mutual friends and I'm one of the few people that Maeve can be real with. She's always so perfect with her work and around Rowan. Speaking of Rowan, when is he back?"

Too soon. "I think the Bear is back today." Not wanting to spend any more of her time thinking of the horrible man, Dee teased Cal, "Maeve implies that you've got quite the reputation as a lady's man. She refers to you as one of the pretty boys."

Cal frowned in annoyance. His voice rose in his own defense, "I'm not just a pretty boy like Maeve portrays me. I graduated with Honors from Oxford. Top of the class," he declared proudly. "And come August I'll be back there taking my Masters in Economics. I like school, so I'm looking forward to the fall. The summer has been fun and I'm enjoying myself. Especially now while holidaying here in London and spending time with a beautiful young lady who enjoys my company. I'm not looking for more until I've finished school. I'm keeping it simple with good friends and good times."

Dee appreciated his openness and honesty. She was also relieved that Cal had no long term interest in her other than being friends. Her life was already complicated enough. She continued to tease, "Irresistible, well-mannered and intelligent; a powerful combination." Dee recognized that Cal had a strong personality but there was gentleness as well that he preferred to disguise with his cavalier attitude.

Cal resumed his relaxed position and continued to open up. He spoke of his life at Oxford and shared descriptive and amusing tales of escapades with his mates.

The two friends enjoyed the afternoon relaxing and chatting as the hours flew by. All too soon it was time to pack up and return to the city. They talked easily on the way back. With Cal she never felt that it was necessary to choose her words with care in case she was misunderstood or said the wrong thing. Dee looked at him and said, "Thanks."

"For what?"

"For being my friend. You're the only one I have so that makes you my bestie." A shadow crossed her eyes, for Dee was sure these were words spoken in her past and she wondered who her bestie was before. "I'm grateful for the time we spend together. You make me laugh. I didn't realize how depressed I was until I heard myself laugh."

Understanding her loneliness, it bothered Cal when he said, "I have to leave tomorrow."

Dee knew she would miss Cal for he had become a regular companion. He was totally attentive to her but never demanding. Dee failed to hide her disappointment. "Will you be back for another visit?"

"Yes, my little chickadee, I'll try to come back down the first weekend in September before my classes start."

It was late afternoon by the time they returned to the hotel. All in all, it had been a glorious day. It had been nice to spend time away from the city.

"We're back, Gran," Dee called from the front door.

"Did you kids have a good time?"

"It was a smashing day. I can't remember when I've had so much fun." Dee burst out laughing. "No surprise there, since I don't remember much."

Cal laughed with her. "No pressures from the past," he commented, with amused understanding. It was a comfortable banter between friends.

They were still laughing when Rowan walked in with Maeve draped on his arm. A sense of entitlement oozed from Maeve's pores and Dee found it amusing. *He's all yours, lady.* It struck Dee that they were a perfectly matched couple.

Dee's face glowed and Rowan realized this was the first time he heard her laugh. As well, there was a subtle change in her voice; it was much more musical when it was tension free.

Releasing her hold of ownership, Maeve went and sat beside Cal. "I've hardly seen you," Maeve pouted at him. "It's been boring with Rowan gone and you've spent all your free time with Dee."

Dee's eyes sparkled when she turned to Cal and smiled, "Cal has been very generous with his time. Without him, I wouldn't be able to live up to my obligation as a tourist. We've been hopping about all over London seeing the sights."

Cal laughed, knowing she was referring to the Hop-On, Hop-Off bus tour. "The pleasure has been all mine. I've seen things that, as a Brit, I've always taken for granted."

Rowan surprised everyone when he said, "We should do something special for Dee. Why don't we have a party? Dee's been here several weeks. She'd probably love to meet others since Cal will be back in school."

Dee was completely started by his suggestion.

Constance was immediately excited. "What a wonderful idea, Rowan. I should've thought of it myself. I want Dee to feel she fits in."

Dee stared at them in disbelief. This was not something she wanted. "You've already made me feel more than welcome."

Constance failed to hear the reluctance in Dee's response. "I'm glad, Dee. But I think you're ready to be introduced to my friends. I know I want them to meet you."

When Dee realized how pleased her grandmother was with the idea she knew it would be unfair to argue. Recovering quickly, she forced a smile and turned to Cal, "Can I put your name on the guest list? It wouldn't be any fun without my bestie."

Cal gave her a friendly hug, "Let me know when it is and I'll be there."

Dee accompanied Cal to the door and thanked him again for such a lovely day.

"Happy to oblige," Cal said easily, giving Dee a quick kiss on the cheek. She watched him go with regret. She knew she'd miss him.

Dee returned to the parlour to see Rowan turn to Maeve, "Would you mind helping Constance with making the arrangements?"

Maeve flushed in annoyance at being given the task of welcoming the despised twit. She didn't understand the need for all the fuss for a temporary visitor. Always the professional, Maeve resorted to trained manners as she turned to Constance and smiled. "Of course, we all want to do whatever we can to help make Dee feel at home."

Dee couldn't stand Maeve's condescending tone but had to admire the way she could coat her voice with warmth even while her eyes hardened.

After they left, Constance and Dee discussed the proposed party which opened up the topic of Dee's friendship with Cal. Constance smiled when she stated, "Cal is a very intelligent and definitely entertaining young man. He's as handsome as the devil and twice as charming and in time he'll find himself. When he does, he'll be a fine young man."

Dee smiled back, for she couldn't agree more. Cal had become a friend and she'd enjoyed spending time with him. He'd helped her to settle in despite her uncomfortable circumstances. She knew she'd miss him.

Dee hoped that Constance had forgotten about the party but a few days later she presented her with the guest list. "Please run this down to Maeve so she can order the invitations. We'll need to get them out at once since I've decided on the first Saturday in September."

Dee knew her eyes had widened in surprise and her response reflected her shock. "Invitations! I thought this would be a small dinner party. As generous as your offer is, I don't need a big party. I don't know anyone."

"Nonsense, silly child. This will be like a debutante party. I'll be introducing my granddaughter to my friends," Constance declared proudly.

Dee tried to be appreciative of all the effort her grandmother was doing to make her feel welcome. It was ungrateful of her not to be excited about the party. But, in truth, it was all overwhelming and this wasn't making her feel any better about herself or her circumstances.

With a heavy heart Dee went downstairs to Maeve's office. This was the first time the two had been alone together. Dee was immediately aware that the atmosphere was heavy with frost. "Is this a bad time? Gran asked if I would give you the guest list and she hoped you'd have time tomorrow morning to go over some details."

Maeve's expression remained frigid, "Tell Constance I'm available all morning. She can buzz me any time and I'll come up." Maeve returned to the correspondence on her desk.

Dee forced out a thank you that she didn't mean.

Maeve looked up and drummed her fingertips on her desk in agitation, "Was there something else? I am busy. I don't live the life of leisure like you."

Dee took a deep breath to control her anger. "I don't know what I've done to offend you. You barely know me."

"Everything you do offends me. Ever since you got here it's been all about poor Dee. Don't you think it time you drop the mystery girl routine, Tweedle Dee?"

Rising temper brought a flush to Dee's cheeks. "I see you've dropped the phony facade you present when you're around Mr. Le Baron and my grandmother. You really are cold and insensitive, the ultimate Ice Maiden."

A hostile look crossed Maeve's face making it clear that Dee had struck a nerve.

So the Ice Maiden reacts when her adversary fires back. Some primeval instinct warned Dee to be cautious. Apart from the fact that Dee disliked Maeve intensely, she didn't trust her. Cal's words of warning about Maeve returned. *Don't let your guard down around this woman.*

"Nice game you've got going. I'd go all memory loss too if I were in your shoes. But if you think this act will help you reel in a big fish like Rowan, you're fishing in the wrong pond."

He was the last man she'd consider romantically. "I couldn't be less interested in a cold fish like Rowan Le Baron. He's protective because of his obligation to my grandmother. But maybe you need to change your bait. Yours may be stale since it appears you haven't landed him in your net."

"Careful Dee, I can also be a bitch." She added a glare so Dee would back down.

It didn't work. Dee wouldn't be intimidated. In fact, she glared right back, ready to take on the Ice Maiden. "No secret there, Maeve," she flung back.

Maeve's eyes narrowed, "I can make things very uncomfortable for you."

Dee shrugged, "Save yourself the trouble. I've been uncomfortable since I got here." Just then Rowan appeared in the doorway and all conversation ceased.

Rowan's eyes locked on Dee. "Is there a problem?"

While Dee ignored him, Maeve rose and engaged him with her possessive smile. Dee was amazed at Maeve's ability to mask her feelings. *I wish I had that much self-control.*

"Dee and I were just getting to know each other better," Maeve responded with false sweetness. Like a chameleon, she changed her colors. She turned and smiled at Dee. Her tone was dismissive. "Thanks for bringing me the invitation list. I'm sure Constance and I will throw you a wonderful party. She's so delighted to have you staying with her for awhile. I'm sure you're thrilled as well, considering everything."

Containing her anger, Dee countered back, "My grandmother said you were exceptional at your job and she has every confidence that you will not let us down." *Take that!*

The smile died on Maeve's face.

Rowan regarded the two of them for a moment, than gestured for Dee to follow him. *Again to the office? Who does this man think he is?* Wishing she could stay and argue, Dee reluctantly followed Rowan. Squaring her shoulders, she prepared herself for another sermon. "I wish you'd stop pulling me around," she snapped as he grabbed her arm.

"Then keep up." Rowan led Dee into his office. "What was that all about?"

Dee chose to ignore his question. She knew if she answered he would just get mad.

Rowan's features were tight and unrelenting. "I asked you a question."

His demanding attitude got to her. "That woman infuriates me."

He grabbed hold of her chin and forced her to look at him. "Maeve is a strong woman to take on. I'm impressed to see you have a backbone and not just a sharp tongue. Even though it is cute."

Dee pushed his hand away. Rowan had touched a nerve. She was embarrassed by her previous behavior and it was just like him to remind her of her immature behavior. As if she didn't already have enough reasons to hate him.

Rowan's expression remained impassive but she saw the warning in his eyes. "I know Maeve can be very intimidating."

"If that's what you want to call it, go ahead. I think she's appalling, with a high and mighty attitude." *Just like you.*

"What you're thinking isn't very nice," Rowan pointed out.

"So, now you're a mind reader, too?" *I don't believe the arrogance of this man.*

Rowan laughed. "I don't need to be. Your face says it all."

Dee's cheeks turned pink with embarrassment. This man could infuriate her so quickly. "Good. Then you know how much I hate you."

Rowan was more amused than offended. "Oh, I haven't forgotten since the last time you told me."

This only made Dee angrier. "I don't have to put up with this." She turned and left, slamming the door behind her. She hated that she'd allowed him to upset her again.

When Dee returned to the flat, her grandmother informed her that the trunk had arrived from America. "I had Boris put it in your room." A second trunk had also arrived but it had been stored away. More secrets to keep.

Without hesitation, Dee ran to her room. Hopefully, there would be something inside that she would recognize. With nervous anticipation she opened the lid. The disappointment was crushing. Like everything else in her life, nothing was familiar. Then she saw the tambourine that lay at the bottom. Picking it up she felt a moment of recollection as a sweet memory washed over her. In a blink of an eye it was gone. Minutes later Dee got up, for she recognized that this was another exercise of futility. She went into the parlour, glad that it was empty, and began to play.

Constance followed the haunting notes of the piano. Dee looked up as she entered and her eyes once again had that hollow look. "I keep waiting and waiting for my memory to return." Dee was speaking slowly to keep her voice from trembling but she couldn't stop the tears that fell. "Questions. All I have are questions. Never answers. I was hoping that whatever was in the trunk would magically provide me with answers. I was hoping it would bring back my memory," she dared to whisper.

"This doesn't mean you should give up hope. Please don't be discouraged," Constance implored, reading the emotions that crossed Dee's face. "It takes time," she said, as much to herself as to her granddaughter. "It will come," she promised.

There was a yearning in Dee's fragile voice, "When? Obviously, not today." Her posture remained rigid.

Constance was sensitive and knew to leave Dee alone. However, it didn't stop her from saying, "When you build a wall around yourself, it may keep out the grief. But it keeps out everything else. Try to be patient and give it more time," Constance pleaded as she hugged her granddaughter tight before she turned and left the room.

Dee sat caught up in her own thoughts, her gaze far away. She felt the familiar sting of tears and shook her head, trying to throw off her self-pity. She began counting her blessings. The wall she'd built before she got to London had been slowly coming down. This was happening not just between herself and her grandmother but with others as well.

That night Dee was too sad to sleep, too lonely to let go. It had been another emotional day. Her life was a continuous roller coaster ride. She reflected on her day and began to ask herself more questions and she still had none of the answers. It was time to ask someone else. This time, her thoughts returned to Rowan Le Baron. Thinking over her conversation with Cal, she decided to confront Rowan about her documents in the morning. Her passport would have her full name on it. Dee couldn't believe how often Rowan infiltrated her thoughts. She closed her eyes tighter, attempting to shut him out of her mind. He wasn't worth another thought. Yet, she thought of little else. Finally, she fell into a restless sleep. The nightmares returned.

CHAPTER SIX

D ee woke and found herself breathing hard. Although her dreams were less frequent, they were more confusing and sometimes frightening. Last night Constance had reminded her that she had an afternoon meeting with Rowan and it was her weekly Bridge night with her friends. Constance had slowly returned to her regular routine. Even Boris was away. He left yesterday to visit friends in Scotland for a few days. Depression set in, as the day presented a rather desolate prospect and the dreaded sense of loneliness once again began to close in. Dee felt like she had been dealing with this hopeless situation forever. And she was missing Cal.

As if her day wasn't miserable enough, Maeve was in the morning room with Constance. They were deep in discussion going over decorating details. Dee hurried past, making her escape into the parlour. She sat still while eavesdropping on the conversation. It seemed Constance was determined to make the gala as extravagant as possible.

After Maeve left Constance joined her granddaughter, who was staring pensively out the window. "What are you fretting about?"

Dee's eyes widened. "Why do you think I'm fretting about something?"

Constance fixed her eyes on her with a knowing look, "You're twisting your hair like your mother did when something was bothering her."

Dee looked over at Constance with troubled eyes. "I overheard you and Maeve talking. I should be happy about my party but I'm not. I feel scared and confused. I'm socially inept so there's no way I can play the role of a well-bred young lady."

Constance understood Dee's anxiety. "Your lack of confidence is normal considering you have no experiences to draw from. Just be yourself and greet everyone with your warmest smile and people will like you for who you are."

Dee put on a happier face for her grandmother. But Constance could see behind the frayed façade. She quickly realized that Dee needed confidence in more ways than mere words and she knew exactly what was required. Dee deserved to look stunning for her coming out party. "Tomorrow you and I are going shopping for a new dress for your party."

"I have everything I need thanks to you. I don't feel right about you spending all of this money on me."

Constance smiled at Dee and her voice was filled with kindness, "What's money for if not to spend? Don't be concerned, Dee. I have a comfortable amount of money and I can do what I choose with it. I missed so many stages of Phoebe's life. I also missed out on you growing up. Please indulge an old lady."

Dee drew in a calming breath. "I'm glad we can make up for that now, Gran, but a new dress isn't going to make me more refined."

"Nonsense. You'll be surprised what the right dress can do for you. It can give you a world of confidence. You'll need a designer gown. Don't forget, you are the guest of honor and all eyes will be on you."

Dee's gaze wavered as anxiety resurfaced. "That worries me as well." She frowned as Maeve's image came to mind. "I hate to admit it but Maeve intimidates me. She's so poised and knows what to say at the right time."

"Maeve can be incredibly intimidating and she'll be dressed in a very chic outfit and looking to take center stage."

"I have to admit that Maeve has excellent taste." *Except in men.*

Constance firmly put Dee's comment aside, "Maeve's expensive to maintain. I'm sure Rowan pays her well and she gets a lot of perks with her job because of their personal relationship. Unfortunately, some people feel a sense of entitlement by association. They get confused about what their position is. Maeve works for Rowan though she doesn't always see it that way. She sometimes forgets that she only holds a position here like everyone else."

Dee was confused, "I thought you liked her."

"I tolerate her because of Rowan. I have no idea what he sees in that woman. She's shallow and a bit of a snob as well. And those aren't her only faults. She may be a pretty package but there's not much inside. Cool sophistication doesn't keep a man warm." Constance raised her eyebrows in a gesture of conspiratorial amusement. "So Dee, what do you say to my offer? Are you willing to upstage Maeve Spencer?"

Dee responded with an answering glimmer in her eyes. "You're quite the gal, Gran. You're full of surprises. You keep your devious side well hidden."

"I have to admit I also have a temper. Fortunately, time has helped teach me how to control it," Constance added pointedly.

Dee felt a surge of optimism as she smiled weakly, "So, there's hope for me?"

Constance nodded and smiled. "It's time to bring out the woman in you. Let's give Maeve a run for her money and I'm game to pay a dear price." They both laughed in conspiratorial glee.

Thankfully, her grandmother had helped Dee regain control of her fears. Dee felt her spirits lift. "Okay, I'm ready for anything."

Constance's smile widened, "This is going to be so much fun. I want this party to be perfect for you, Dee. I promise that you will have a marvelous time."

Dee looked at her grandmother with gratitude. Laughing joyfully, she replied, "Double dare, pinkie swear."

Constance gave her a strange look. "I don't know what that means."

"Never mind me. It must be an American saying." Dee knew she was having a flashback from her past. Even though they were more frequent, they were random and she still couldn't hang on to all of them.

The next day greeted the ladies with sunshine and high spirits. On their way out Constance handed the invitations to the receptionist for mailing. Dee swallowed hard knowing she was now committed.

It was a full morning. They looked through many of the big name stores. There were hundreds of dresses to choose from but they were unsuccessful in finding the perfect gown. Remembering a conversation she had overheard at the beauty shop, Constance got directions to Simone's Salon, a small shop by a new designer.

As soon as they entered the boutique they were welcomed by the designer herself. Simone Vanier was elegance personified. Constance informed the designer what the occasion was and that they required a special gown.

Meanwhile, Dee looked around with a feeling of awe. A person would have to be blind to miss seeing the exquisiteness of the fashionable garments displayed throughout the boutique. She turned and whispered to her grandmother, "Gran, they're all so beautiful but this appears to be a very exclusive boutique."

Ignoring Dee's protest, Constance was determined to spare no expense.

Within minutes Constance and Dee were introduced to a young assistant named Jillian, who proved to be excellent. Diligently, Jillian kept bringing Dee a range of styles and colors, from floral to metallic, body hugging to flowing. Dee modeled each one of the gowns while Constance sat back and smiled as she enjoyed every moment. She recalled the first day that Dee had arrived and how Dee had shared nothing as she selected a limited range of clothes. They had both come a long way from that tense day.

Dee came out and modeled a pale lavender halter dress in flowing chiffon that both she and Constance loved. When she was returning to the dressing room the sales clerk stopped her, "Don't get dressed yet, there's one more that Madam Simone would like you to try on." The assistant turned and left.

Within minutes Jillian returned with a gown that seemed to shimmer with every movement. "This isn't out on the floor but I've been given permission to show it to you. Madam Simone says that without a doubt it is the most superb dress she has created."

Dee was in complete agreement. She gazed at the dress entranced by its beauty. The ball gown was exquisite. Dee caressed the delicate fabric and the sparkles in the dress were no brighter than the sparkles in her eyes.

Constance was thoroughly enjoying herself as she watched Dee go through a wide range of emotions. "Go try it on, dear." Speechless, Dee did as she was told.

When Dee walked out, Constance stared at her in amazement. She reflected again how much this granddaughter was like Phoebe. She had seen it in many ways. The old woman's eyes teared up from the memories.

Dee used the same hand gestures when she spoke, the lift of an eyebrow when in doubt, the twirling of hair when she was deep in thought. And the beautiful smile that lit up her face when she smiled freely. Constance would do anything to see that natural happiness more often.

Dee glanced at herself in the corner mirror. Her breath caught in her throat as she gazed at herself with astonishment. She sighed in appreciation of the gown. It was perfect. She slowly turned and faced her grandmother.

Constance smiled, "It's breath-taking. You are your mother twenty years ago." In that moment she realized how much she still missed Phoebe.

Dee attempted to keep her voice non-committal but the joy on her face was undeniable. "Which one do you like better?" Dee knew which one she preferred but the price difference between the two gowns was substantial.

Constance only had to take one look at Dee's glowing face. "You look stunning in both but this silver ball gown is breathtaking. You look like a star from the heavens." Constance turned to Jillian. "We'll take both. Please have them delivered to the Conlyn Grand Hotel once the alterations have been completed."

Many would have been happy to take advantage of a grandmother's generosity or even take it for granted. Dee did neither. "Gran, I can't let you do that. I only need one dress and the silver gown is very dear. You can't keep buying me all these expensive things."

"Nonsense. At my age I can do whatever I like. My primary duty as a grandmother is to spoil," she added with obvious delight.

Dee smiled at her grandmother with unrestrained joy and was touched by how kind she was. "You've already spoiled me with so much."

Constance Malone beamed with pleasure. "Go change. We have more shopping to do. Now that we have the dresses, you need accessories to go with them."

The morning was long gone by the time they finished shopping. Constance tucked her hand into the crook of her granddaughter's arm. "Well, I haven't had this much fun for a long time. It's been a hectic day for an old woman. Now, my dear, we're going to share a very endearing custom. We are going to celebrate and have 'High Tea' at the Savoy in the renowned Thames Foyer. It's a very posh experience that is one of the must do's when one is in London." Together they climbed into the waiting limousine and proceeded to the Savoy.

Constance was welcomed by name and the ladies were escorted to a favorably located table. Once they were seated, Dee looked around in awe. Gorgeous chandeliers hung above stylishly set tables. In the center of the elaborately decorated room beneath a glass cupola was the hotel's resident pianist who quietly serenaded the guests. The stunning glass dome flooded the tea room with wonderful natural light.

Dee was overwhelmed. She turned to Constance with a look of awe on her face. "Gran, are you rich?"

The old lady nodded. "Filthy rich," she admitted sheepishly. "Despite my social position I prefer living a quite life."

Dee recalled Rowan having said basically the same thing to her the day she had arrived. She had always been impressed that her Gran never put on airs. Dee hung her head. Her voice was solemn when she spoke, "I've been so self-absorbed in my own misery that I haven't taken the time to learn about you. I would be honored if you would share who you are with me."

Constance was impressed. Dee didn't ask about her wealth. Instead she asked about her as a person. It said a lot about her granddaughter's character. "I've told you about your parents. Now I will tell you about your grandfather, Oliver Malone."

"Tell me about you first, Gran," Dee said respectfully.

Constance grinned, "Like Phoebe, I was an only child. And like Phoebe, I had the most wonderful parents."

Dee giggled, enjoying her grandmother's humor.

"Our family, an old established family, came from London, among a Society more elevated and wealthier than your grandfather's. The British are very proud of their long and rich history. My father was a stoic Englishman who was honest and well-respected. My mother was the perfect lady, kind and well-mannered, unless you riled her up. Then she was formidable. She was also independent, direct and strong." Constance looked at Dee. "It appears to be a family trait with the women in our family."

Dee was honored; she knew she had been included as part of the family tree.

"As I told you before, all of my family has passed away. You are all I have left. There are always times when I miss my mother and even more when I miss Phoebe."

Dee felt a wave of deep sadness and her own feeling of loss was intense.

"Your grandfather wasn't born into a rich family. His parents couldn't afford to pay for a college education so right out of school he took an entry-level job in a real estate office. He started as a mere office boy but he listened and he learned. One of the seniors took notice and became his mentor. He quickly recognized that Oliver was very clever. Oliver applied what he learned and saved his money. At the earliest opportunity he purchased a piece of real estate and from that moment on his life changed. He wasn't afraid to take chances. It was like he had the Midas touch and his wealth grew. He succeeded far beyond anyone's expectations. It took time and hard work but he was able to go well beyond the lifestyle provided by his parents."

"Everyone has hardships they encounter in their lives, but your grandfather was able to look past his as well as make a difference in the lives of others. Oliver was a logical and practical man with deep convictions and beliefs. Because he had faced life's harsh realities he never forgot about his roots. He had a wide range of friends and he was greatly respected and well-liked. Your grandfather was an incredible man. Oliver was direct, honest and intelligent." Constance smiled to herself, for she recognized similar traits in her granddaughter. Dee just didn't own them yet but in time she would. But first she needed to put aside her anger and stubbornness.

Dee was captivated by her grandmother's story. Wanting to know more she asked, "You said you were from different backgrounds as well as social status so how did you meet?"

Constance grinned like a schoolgirl. "Devine intervention. His family was visiting friends who had a son the same age. Even though Oliver wasn't rich he never felt that he wasn't worthy of everything life had to offer. On a dare they crashed a Society ball. It was evident that your grandfather was a stranger to his environment but that wasn't the reason I was drawn to him. Your grandfather was a dashing, handsome, fatally charming man who drew attention despite his obvious social ineptness. I admit I was quite smitten. Again, on a dare he asked me to dance. And as they say, the rest is history. Despite our different backgrounds we fell in love." Constance smiled reflectively, "I think that when people really love each other that is enough."

"Maybe my mom felt the same way with my dad," Dee said thoughtfully.

Constance nodded. "Maybe she did. A few years after we were married we settled outside of London. Most of Oliver's work was in London and that's where he met Preston Le Baron, Rowan's grandfather. Preston was a property developer, who like Oliver, had a passion for real estate. Preston's knowledge about land development and Oliver's ambitious beliefs worked well for them. They formed Malone Le Baron Management and started with small projects. Both men possessed sound business judgment. Their combination of innovation and hard work allowed them to make major acquisitions. The golden touch continued and their empire grew. Their acquisitions expanded to other cities as well. Due to a willingness to take occasional risks along with clever investments, they achieved great financial success."

The older lady's eyes teared for a moment. "I miss your grandfather. He was one of the most honorable men I've had the pleasure to know. Rowan is a lot like him. After Oliver died I relied more and more on Preston and now on Rowan. He is an excellent business partner whom I respect and trust. Even though I'm self-sufficient, independent and capable, it's always nice to have someone to lean on."

Constance didn't miss the look of disregard at the mention of Rowan's name. "For some reason you took an immediate dislike to my godson." Constance's expression wasn't one of anger, which might have been easier to bear, but rather one of disappointment. "You've judged Rowan unfairly. He's a very fair man but there always appears to be underlying tension between the two of you."

Dee couldn't deny it, so she chose to remain silent. She was aware that her grandmother and Rowan had a solid relationship. With a quick stab of resentment, it suddenly struck Dee that Rowan was more like family than she was. She felt a twinge of jealousy.

Her thoughts were confirmed when Constance declared, "I consider Rowan to be family so I'll share his legend with you as well. He possesses the old and highly respected title of Baron; he has wealth and an esteemed family name. The Le Baron family descended from hereditary privileges along with the rank of nobility and a title of honor. They were members of the upper class referred to as the Gentry and their social position was taken for granted. But they are and always have been business-minded."

"The Le Baron family manor, which the Le Barons have owned for generations, is in Kent along the coast. It's one of the unique moorland gems that date back to the fourteenth century that the Le Barons have owned for generations. It was considered one of the finest country homes in England. The main house sits high, offering breathtaking views of both the countryside and the coastline. No one has resided in the manor since the passing of Rowan's grandfather. Needless to say, it's been neglected but time has not detracted from its beauty. Rowan's roots are firmly planted there and he's been spending time restoring his home. Emmitt Barnes and his wife Winnie are his caretakers who reside in a detached cottage on the estate and take care of things in his absence."

"Rowan's grandparents reveled in the social life of London, especially Lynette. Their names were always on Society guest lists. Both Preston and Lynette came from affluent families. Nettie, as she was so fondly called, was a beautiful woman who was elegant and romantic. Nettie Le Baron was my dear friend. When she became ill, the Le Baron's withdrew from Society. In truth, they withdrew from life."

"Rowan was born into this rich, affluent life but was raised by nannies and spent most of his boyhood in boarding schools. I told you his parents died when he was young and that's when his grandfather, Preston, stepped into his life. But by then Nettie had also passed and Preston had moved into the city. Rowan didn't have a difficult childhood, just a lonely one. Preston's energy and time focused on the business and the manor was left neglected. Rowan and his grandfather were very close and Rowan misses him. Rowan was too serious at too young an age. Perhaps it came from knowing that the family responsibilities would fall on him. Sadly, he forgets to have fun."

Dee had to admit to herself that the word fun was not one that she would have associated with Rowan Le Baron. She wisely kept this thought to herself.

"This year Rowan has taken on the renovation of the manor to restore it to the grandeur of the past. So whenever Rowan has free time he goes there. He loves the old house and, like you, he is searching for parts of his past. His roots are there. It is and always will be his home."

A bewildered look came over Dee's face. Her grandmother had somehow helped to humanize the Bear. Dee quickly closed her mind, because the truth was that she was finding him interesting. She was suddenly thinking of Rowan Le Baron in a very different light.

Constance shared many amusing stories from the past over tea and Dee enjoyed getting to know more about her family. In time the topic returned to the reason for their outing and they discussed the upcoming party.

"Gran, I'm nervous about my party. I don't want to disgrace you because I'm not very sophisticated."

Constance knew that Dee was again comparing herself to Maeve. "You could never disgrace me. Sophistication comes from a great deal of worldly experiences and knowledge of art and culture. It comes from an in-depth learning about the world and people. It allows you to be comfortable anywhere you go and in whatever situation you may be in. Unfortunately, a person can get caught up with the material things with too much value placed on the high life. They begin to put on airs and become pretentious."

Dee knew her grandmother was once again referring to Maeve. She also recalled Rowan saying that her grandmother never put on airs, which Dee herself had found to be true.

Constance smiled with encouragement. "Elegance is graciousness and possessing a certain confident simplicity. You, young lady, are what one would call an elegant woman. You have proven to be self-assured even in uncomfortable situations. You may not be aware of it but you own a complicated confidence. You've changed in the last few weeks."

"I'm glad," Dee said, and she was. "A lot of it's because of your understanding and infinite patience. I owe you a lot."

"You don't owe me anything. You're my family," Constance said proudly.

It had been a spectacular day. And not because of the shopping. Dee felt closer to her grandmother now that she knew more about her background. Dee knew she had to process what her grandmother had shared about Rowan. She tucked those thoughts away for later.

Rowan stepped out of his office just as the shoppers walked in. Both ladies were surprised to see him. He wasn't due back for a couple more days. Constance glanced at him with surprise. "I thought you were supposed to be taking a few days off." It didn't go unnoticed by Constance that Rowan looked tired and drawn.

"Things went better than I thought. I even made a quick stop at the Manor. I plan to go back there later in the fall." He turned his attention to Dee to avoid further questioning. "How was the shopping spree?"

Dee's spirits were absolutely buoyant. She couldn't contain her excitement. "Incredible," she said, holding out both hands that were filled with packages.

Constance smiled at Rowan with pure joy on her face. "There's more in the boot. Lend a hand and bring the rest upstairs."

Rowan shook his head in disbelief but did as he was told. Both ladies laughed as they entered the lift.

CHAPTER SEVEN

D ee slowly woke from a deep sleep. With casual familiarity she rolled onto her back and looked up at the ceiling. A smile came as she recalled how out of place she felt at first. Thanks to her grandmother and Boris, she now felt comfortable and considered the hotel as her home. As Dee lay there, she acknowledged that she was no longer living in a world of strangers but she did feel that she was simply existing in a time warp. She didn't want to live an empty life. She was tired of simply biding her time with waiting. The realization remained that she may not regain her past but she knew she wanted to be present in the future. Dee knew she had spent too many days taking refuge in her anger and her self-indulgence. *I need to start living my life looking forward. I can't move forward if I keep turning around to see what's behind me.* It was time to conquer her fears and face her uncertain future, knowing life went on. Dee felt that she'd always been independent and she didn't want to live off the means of others. Although Dee was grateful, she wasn't content with doing nothing. Suddenly, it came to her. She needed a job. She'd spent too much time sitting around moping. It was time to take control of her life.

With that thought forefront in her mind, Dee went looking for her grandmother. She came across Boris first. "Do you know where Gran is?"

"Madam went downstairs to talk to Mr. Le Baron. She should be back soon. Is there something I can do for you, Miss Dee?"

She smiled at Boris affectionately. "No thanks. If you see Gran before I do, will you tell her I'd like to speak with her?"

Boris nodded on his way back to the kitchen.

Dee went to wait for her grandmother on the terrace. She realized summer was coming to an end as a cool wind blew her hair around her face. Dee sat staring into space wondering what she might have done in America. A small frown creased her brow as she shook her head sadly. Wondering didn't provide any answers.

Meanwhile, downstairs in Rowan's office Dee was the topic of conversation. Rowan looked at his godmother with a serious expression. He wondered how Dee was managing in the face of her current situation. "Is Dee doing better? Does she remember anything from her past?"

Constance let out a sigh before she shared the progress Dee had made. "There are moments when something unreadable flashes across her eyes but her face remains expressionless and I realize that she has mentally drifted away. Sadly, she can't hang on to those thoughts long enough to keep them. So she gets angry and frustrated and I can't blame her. Then there are times that I know she remembers something and her eyes light up. Her eyes, her face, her gestures are all so expressive. That's happening more and more for her. Maybe when Dee realizes that she fits in and accepts this as her home she'll feel safe. Unconsciously, until then the fear of the future may still be blocking her memories."

"Your granddaughter has a quick temper and expresses her anger very well."

"Especially toward you. You have to remember that in her mind you're the reason she's here. We're in what one would call a transition period. She's had such a difficult time."

Rowan failed to hang on to his tolerance, "Unfortunately, that's become an easy excuse."

Constance was stunned by the sharpness in his tone. "Rowan, you could try being nice to her. I think the poor girl is terrified of you."

"I'm always nice and I have tried." When Constance raised her eyebrow in an expression of doubt, he agreed to try harder.

"Dee opens up once she learns to trust you. Her spirits are improving. She was so hostile in the beginning and tries hard to hide her vulnerability. Dee doesn't run away from difficult situations. She just needs to learn how to handle them better."

Rowan's voice was impatient. "She needs to work on her quick temper. There's a sharp tongue under her soft demure. I find her to be constantly rude. She should appreciate your protection of her welfare."

"I must apologize for Dee. She does have a quick temper but a wonderful spirit. Even with her life in shambles Dee's thoughtful and kind and courageous."

Rowan was skeptical. "I'll have to take your word on that."

Constance was miffed by his comment. "Dee is appreciative and never assuming. You're only seeing one side of her. You should get to know her better. You'd be surprised."

Rowan spoke the truth when he said, "Oh, I have no doubt the girl is full of surprises."

"I'm pleased to say that Dee and I are getting closer and we're slowly building a relationship. I'm beginning to learn how she thinks, what she likes, what she dislikes. She's definitely her own person, authentic and non-pretentious. She isn't nice just to be liked. But I have to be honest. I know she can be spirited at times."

Constance laughed when Rowan nodded in agreement. "I find Dee to be genuine and sincere. She is gracious to everyone and takes the time to say hello to our guests as well as our staff. They all say she's friendly and sincere. She has a way of dealing with people that disarms them and converts them quickly into friends and admirers. She remembers the little details that are important to them. Dee now laughs when she's happy, cries when she's sad which is a more normal behavior than her guarded silence was. For now, she seems content."

"She sounds charming. But then, you know her better than I do."

Constance chose to ignore his sarcasm. "It seems that music is a trigger for her. Dee spends a lot of time in the parlour, that's where she feels safe and seems to connect to the past. Nights seem to be especially trying for her. I hear her playing the piano after I've retired. She often plays the same haunting tune over and over."

Rowan listened intently as Constance spoke of Dee. He was rather intrigued by some of the comments Constance shared and began to see Dee in a new light. Perhaps he was being a little insensitive. He could see how much Dee was starting to mean to his godmother and hoped that Constance wouldn't get hurt in the end.

Constance let out a sigh before continuing, "Dee has an inquiring mind so she asks a lot of questions. I answer what I can and circumvent the others. She hasn't sorted out the facts but I'm expecting some tough questions when she does. We've talked about her parents, up to a point. I make no mention of her twin sister. Rowan, I want to tell her that everything is going to be okay but I don't want to continue lying to the poor girl."

"We knew this wasn't going to be easy. We talked about this before."

Constance's tone changed to one of concern. "I guess doing what's best isn't always doing what's right. Can you imagine the damage a few careless words could do? But I truly believe she's going to get her memory back. Perhaps then the nightmares will cease."

Rowan's expression was chilling. So was his tone when he said, "Then there will be many more things to deal with. I share your concerns, Connie. It won't be easy for her without her sister." He felt sorry for his godmother. He also felt sorry for Dee.

"I know. We'll get through that, too."

Rowan took her hand and squeezed it. He knew Constance included him in the we and he would never let her down. He'd always been there for her in the past; he'd be there for her now. So he'd make an effort to get to know the spitfire child better.

Constance let out a heavy sigh. "We got sidetracked with Dee. I also came down to see how your business trip went. Did everything go okay in Manchester?"

"Not really, but I'm on it." Rowan declined to go into details. Constance had enough to deal with right now and there really was nothing she could do at this time.

"Well, if that's all you're willing to share, I best go upstairs and see what our young lady is up to."

As soon as Dee saw her grandmother she grabbed her attention. "Gran, I don't want to bother you but can we talk?" There was a definite note of eagerness in her voice.

Constance smiled at Dee affectionately, "You're never a bother, dear."

In typical Dee manner, she got right to the point. "I need something to do so I want to get a job. I can't continue living day to day without purpose. I'm tired of sitting around waiting for my past to find me. I'm ready to accept things as they are and move forward."

Constance smiled inwardly. Just when you think things are running smoothly everything changes. So much for Dee being content. Not that Constance was surprised. She was aware that Dee had adjusted to and accepted her circumstances. So it was natural for Dee to want to move forward.

Dee was quick to add, "I'm settled and happy." More, she realized, than she would have believed possible. "I just want a normal life. Gran, I appreciate everything you've given me and I don't mean the material things. You unconditionally accepted me into your home and into your life. The only constant in my world right now is you and you've supported me in every way. I know how lucky I am to have you. But that's not what this is about. I know my presence has intruded on your life and your time with your friends. You've given me so much of your time and I'm sure I've completely disrupted your routine. I don't want to be a burden."

"You haven't been a burden. I've enjoyed every minute of our time together."

"So have I, Gran. This isn't about money. It's about acceptance and commitment to starting a life here." Dee may have lost her memory but she had found her sense of self.

Despite Dee's emotional dependency on her, Constance admired the courage her granddaughter had shown in the past few weeks. She reached out to Dee with empathy, "Why don't you speak to Rowan. He might have a job here that may interest you." Constance knew that if she asked Rowan he would find something for Dee but she also knew her granddaughter had to start taking control of her own life.

Dee's initial reaction was panic. *How can I avoid this man if I have to work with him?* "I can't ask him for a job. He treats me like a child. I'll have you know I'm twenty-four." *Another memory.* Dee grabbed it and held onto it.

Constance knew it was time for some motherly advice. "If you want to be treated like an adult, you must act like one. You really must learn to behave like a young lady with him."

Dee cared about what her grandmother said. And she hadn't missed the hint of disapproval, which put Dee on the defensive. In an attempt to justify her behavior, she complained, "He brings out the worst in me. He dislikes me and doesn't trust me." Trying to keep the tone of annoyance out of her voice, she asked, "I know that he carries a significant position here but what can he do?"

Constance Malone felt that now was the time to expand on a few more facts in regards to not just herself, but also her godson. "Do you remember when we stopped for tea at the Savoy and I told you I was rich?"

Dee nodded her head. "After you told me, I admit that I've wondered about different things. You definitely live here in luxury. The staff treats you with the utmost respect; it's almost like you own the place."

"I do," Constance replied simply. "Along with Rowan."

Dee was stunned by this information. For once she was speechless.

Constance watched Dee as she absorbed the shock. "Close your mouth, dear. The name Conlyn was chosen by my husband and Rowan's grandfather. They combined my name and Rowan's grandmother's name, Lynette, and renamed the hotel when they bought it. At their passing, both men were wealthy beyond account. Rowan doesn't like to use his title but he truly is a Baron. His ancestry has rich association with English nobility and he holds a title of honor. Rowan has little interest in the pursuits of London Society. Maeve on the other hand can hardly wait to be a Baroness."

Constance laid a hand on Dee's, hopefully to reassure. "I trust you and I have every confidence in your capabilities. Go and speak to Rowan. I'm sure he'll be willing to help you."

Dee wasn't so sure but she didn't argue. She was frustrated at being placed in such a position. "Fine," agreed Dee, without conviction. "It's not like I have a whole lot of options." *Back to the Bear's den.*

Constance smiled to herself as Dee left. Her granddaughter didn't give in easily. Like mother, like daughter. It's too bad the child inherited the Malone stubbornness in spades.

Dee slowly made her way towards Rowan's office determined to remain cool and in control. Realizing she was stalling for time she picked up her step. Maeve had just closed the door to Rowan's office when Dee got there. Dee couldn't believe her bad luck. It seemed to follow her everywhere like her shadow. "Is Mr. Le Baron in his office?"

Maeve positioned herself between Dee and the door. "He is. What do you want?"

"If it was any of your business, I'd tell you," Dee replied as she slipped past her. Dee was sure Maeve would've stopped her but one of the guests had called her over. Dee sighed with relief but she stood at the door undecided. Her stomach was in knots and she had to swallow hard. Ignoring the fear running through her veins, Dee knocked lightly.

"Come in."

It took every ounce of courage Dee could muster to walk through the door.

Rowan looked preoccupied and distant. His eyebrow rose when he saw who it was.

Dee was relieved to see he wasn't scowling but he did look surprised. "Mr. Le Baron, do you have a few minutes or are you busy?" Dee remained at the doorway waiting for him to invite her in. As usual, he had a disturbing effect on her.

Rowan nodded and motioned for her to enter and sit as he continued to shuffle papers.

Obviously this man wasn't going to say anything to make her feel comfortable. He was just going to sit there like God Almighty. Dee remained standing in front of his desk.

Her unconscious act of defiance didn't go unnoticed. Rowan didn't say a word for a long time. Finally he spoke and his tone was cool, "What brings you to the Bear's den, Miss Dare?"

Dee had the decency to blush. Swallowing her pride, she answered, "Normally, I wouldn't presume to impose on your time, Mr. Le Baron. However, I would like to get a job and Gran thought you may be able to help me."

Rowan, caught completely unaware, stroked his chin while studying her candidly. He could see she was nervous and the combination of fear and hope in her voice bothered him. He placed his elbows on his desk and laced his fingers together. "That's a complicated situation under the circumstances. Based on your current situation I don't believe you can be officially employed." Rowan's eyes suddenly filled with compassion, for Dee hadn't been able to prevent her disappointment from surfacing.

Dee couldn't believe what the man was saying. She'd put no thought to the legal aspect of not having an identity. This was one of those complicated circumstances that still had not been addressed. Her frustration was evident as her mind filled with unexpected panic. To hide her disappointment she became defensive. "I would like to see my passport," she demanded.

Rowan searched for a way to change the topic. Realizing that she wouldn't let it go, Rowan decided to be as direct as Dee. "Your documents have been turned over to the government until you regain your memory. All you have for identification is a visitor's visa with the name, Dee Dare. It's locked in the hotel safe for safe-keeping while we wait to see what the future brings." Rowan hated to see the tears in her eyes that this news brought, especially since he knew he was the cause of her distress.

Even though she had to accept his explanation, there was no way Dee could hide her frustration. "So what am I supposed to do now?" She felt the same anxiety she felt when she had woken up in the hospital. "This is my future we're discussing." Dee looked at him in desperation as she tried to hold back her tears. In that moment, Rowan saw beneath her guise of bravery which Dee usually wore while facing her world that was both strange and challenging. Suddenly Rowan felt the need to remove the distraught look from her face. His heart softened. Ignoring the protest he knew Maeve would make he stated, "I'm sure we can work something out here at the hotel."

Dee hated having to be beholding to a man she detested. Before she could respond Maeve walked in. Dee almost groaned out loud.

Rowan immediately explained Dee's situation to Maeve.

Maeve had been curious to see why Dee wanted to see Rowan but she certainly hadn't expected this. "That seems a bit extreme considering her stay here is only temporary until she regains her memory."

"We're dealing with Dee's current state of affairs. If, and when, that status changes we can always reassess."

"What can she possibly do, Rowan? The girl has amnesia."

Rowan attempted to reassure Maeve, "I doubt that she's incompetent. I'm sure Dee won't have any problems learning what she needs to know."

Irritated by his patronizing voice, Dee snapped back, "I have no doubt as I do have a working brain."

Maeve's voice remained impersonal. "What kind of skills do you have?"

"As you so callously pointed out I do have amnesia. So do you really think I know that?"

"What an interesting question, Dee. None of us know what you know. It doesn't matter. You won't need to draw on your past. As Rowan said, we can train you. You look smart."

Dee's reaction was immediate, "Looks can be deceiving." She quickly bit her lip from adding, *"You look smart too."* Dee caught the spark of humor in Rowan's eyes. She knew he had read her mind. Dee now had her back up. "I'm sure I'm a very capable person. What I don't know I can learn. I learn quickly." *It didn't take me long to figure you out.*

Continuing to scrutinize her closely, Rowan sat back and watched the exchange. Rowan realized that the atmosphere in his office had never been so tense.

If he doesn't quit staring at me, I'm going to get up and leave the room. Job, be damned.

Maeve's tone was indulgent, "Well, what would you say your strengths are?"

"I'm good with people in general." Dee caught the flash of Rowan's grin. Thinking he was laughing at her, it took every ounce of effort not to react. She humbly stated, "I'm willing to do anything." Dee braced herself, expecting the worst since neither of them were receptive to hiring her.

Totally unemotional, Maeve turned to Rowan, "I think we're wasting our time but it's up to you." She merely gave Dee a curt nod and left.

Rowan had been observing both women the whole time. He stated simply, "Actually, Dee, it's up to you. Are you willing to work with Maeve?"

Dee's response was defensive, "You know I have no choice." Dee wasn't about to concede easily, "I'm sure we'll get along as long as I follow Maeve's rules and meet your expectations."

"See there, I knew you were a quick learner. For now you work for me, not the hotel. Meet me here at my office Monday morning at nine o'clock sharp. That'll give you a few more days to enjoy the life of leisure."

Dee frowned at his cool dismissal. She hated the fact that she had no other options. So it was with a feeling of apprehension that she accepted. Not trusting her voice, she simply nodded her agreement. *My life is going to become more complicated because that woman hates me and I hate the Bear. And I thought my life couldn't get any worse.*

Dee turned and left. She barely resisted the urge to slam the door on her way out. She knew she should have thanked him but somehow the words had stuck in her throat.

Rowan sat back and smiled. *We're making progress. That's the first time she didn't slam the door on the way out.* He wasn't concerned about hiring Dee. Constance spoke highly of her and he trusted his godmother's judgment even if it might be a little biased. His apprehension was with having Maeve and Dee working together. Then, he smiled again. This could be interesting and it sure as hell wasn't going to be boring.

CHAPTER EIGHT

Dee was excited. Tonight she and Constance were going to the highly anticipated performance of 'The Mousetrap' at St. Martin's Theatre. She was humming as she entered the kitchen to join her grandmother for breakfast. "Morning, Boris. It's another beautiful day, isn't it? Where's Gran?" Dee's warm smile lit up the room like morning sunshine.

Boris was setting a breakfast tray and looked up. "Madam isn't feeling well today, Miss Dee. She's asked to have breakfast in her room."

Dee's reactive disappointment was quickly overtaken by concern. "Let me take the tray to her." She was anxious to see for herself what was ailing her grandmother. Dee was relieved to see Constance sitting in her chair with a warm throw over her legs. A knit shawl was draped over her shoulders.

Dee loved her grandmother's bedroom with its delicately carved furniture. Painted lamps cast a soft light around the room. It was the charming dressing table with the oval mirror above it that always caught her eye. Dee could visualize her grandmother sitting and getting ready for an exciting night at the theatre or opera. But not tonight. "Morning, Gran. Boris tells me you're not well."

Constance grimaced. "He fusses too much. I'm fine but my arthritis has flared up. I'll feel better once my medication kicks in. It's a nuisance growing old."

Dee could see that the poor lady's ankles were swollen and she'd been rubbing her stiff knuckles when Dee had entered the room. "I hope you'll feel better soon."

"There'll be a change of weather blowing through. Don't be surprised if we have an early fall. I'm sorry that our plans for tonight will have to change."

"Oh, Gran, don't give it a second thought. We can go another time when you're feeling better," Dee replied, trying not to sound disappointed.

Constance smiled happily. "You're still going dear. Rowan was here earlier. He offered to take my place."

Dee smiled back at her grandmother with great effort. Constance had just thrown Dee into a total state of inner conflict. Despite her ongoing resolution to avoid the man, here he was again intruding in her life. This was the last thing she wanted to happen. Dee would have loved to give an excuse not to go but she couldn't think of a gracious way to decline. Besides, she wouldn't disappoint Constance after all she'd done.

Dee gave her grandmother a reassuring smile that did not reflect her true feelings. She forced a lightness into her voice, "That sounds perfect." *Perfectly awful.* She hoped her disappointment didn't show.

Constance beamed with pleasure, "Rowan is an excellent escort. I'm sure you'll have an enchanting evening."

Only if I'm hypnotized, Dee thought in misery. They chatted a while longer before Dee went to join Boris for breakfast.

Both ladies spent most of the day in their rooms. Constance resting, Dee sulking. In the safety of her bedroom, Dee went and sat on the familiar window seat. It had become her personal place of refuge. She sat in stillness, frowning and lost in thought. Despite her resolution to avoid Rowan Le Baron, she was now doomed to spend the entire evening with the man. Desperation clutched at her throat every time she thought about the evening ahead. Her nerves began to fray as the time grew closer.

Dee had no problem deciding what to wear. She removed the pale lavender chiffon gown from the closet. As soon as she put the dress on Dee felt the excitement. She dressed carefully, attending to the details of her appearance as she hadn't done for months. She took extra care with her make-up and pulled her hair up except for soft tendrils at her ears. The only jewelry she wore was her mother's locket and fine gold hoops in her ears. She gave one final look at the woman in the mirror and the nervous tremors in her stomach eased. Dee saw what she needed to see. Over the last few weeks she had moved from girlhood to womanhood. *I may not want to go but I'm at least going to look sophisticated.* With her chin up, she left the safety of her bedroom determined not to let her proxy date spoil the thrill of the evening.

As Dee walked into the parlour she was the epitome of elegance and grace. Rowan was positioned by the fireplace, his arm resting on the mantle. He was chatting away with Constance. *They have such a comfortable relationship.* Dee was conscious of a stab of envy. Dee had to admit she'd never seen the man look so fine. Rowan was the personification of power and wealth. He, too, was dressed in formal attire. Black suited him. Rowan presented himself with all the natural authority of a gentleman of his social stature. The man did everything well; it showed in every line of his assured manner.

Rowan's reaction was immediate and involuntary. He knew the dress was expensive and it looked incredible on her. The pastel purple highlighted her soft creamy skin and flowed softly from her slender frame. Her face seemed more delicately sculptured with her hair drawn back. His sweeping gaze appreciated her efforts. She was beautiful in a natural fresh way. He also knew he was staring but he couldn't help himself.

As Rowan looked at Dee a genuine smile curled the corners of his mouth, momentarily softening his features. It made Dee catch her breath. Noting Rowan's astonished stare, his gaze was everything she'd hoped it would be. Dee felt triumphant. His look of approval was reward enough for the effort it took to commit to the evening. She smiled with satisfaction. When his expression altered she saw something in his dark eyes she couldn't identify. It made her heart beat faster. She thought it was due to fear and found herself at a loss for words. Dee stared back at him and swallowed nervously.

The tension of the moment was broken by Constance as she clapped her hands in glee. "I was hoping you'd choose that dress. You remind me so much of your mother. Phoebe would be as proud as I am."

Dee smiled warmly at her grandmother.

"Doesn't she look stunning, Rowan?"

Rowan drew a deep breath and regained control. This was a side of Dee he hadn't seen. She had completely mystified him. "Your granddaughter is a vision of beauty, Connie." A shudder went through Dee when Rowan stepped toward her. "Well, Miss Dare, shall we go?"

Dee prayed that she would get through the evening. The last thing she wanted to do was spend time with this man. Rowan smirked at her as if he knew.

Unaware of the undercurrent of tension, Constance gave them a joyful smile. "Enjoy your evening."

Dee gave Rowan a doubtful glance as she went over and kissed her grandmother on the cheek. The evening might be an ordeal but at least she had made her grandmother happy.

Rowan opened the door and assisted Dee out with a hand under her elbow. With proper etiquette, she allowed it. "Thank you, Mr. Le Baron," she responded with perfect composure. There was a quick twinkle of amusement in his dark shrewd eyes.

The shiny black limousine was parked at the curb. It took Dee back to the day she arrived in England. The chauffeur behind the wheel was the same driver who had picked them up at the airport. So much had changed, yet nothing had changed.

During the drive, Rowan spoke casually about the London West End district they were driving through and provided history of the privately-owned theatre itself. Dee began to relax once she swallowed her resentment and disappointment. Rowan recognized that behind the cool exterior still lay a defenseless young woman. Recalling his reaction to her earlier, he could hardly continue to think of her as a child.

Dee's excitement grew once they arrived at the theatre. It was exactly as Rowan had described. The exterior had been preserved since the doors were first opened in 1916. The interior woodwork was paneled in dark mahogany and burgundy curtains draped over the boxes and cloaked the stage. Dee appreciated that even with extensive refurbishing the atmosphere remained perfect for period pieces. Rowan led them to their seats. He sat down next to her and handed her the program. His size was intimidating and so was his nearness. The seats were so close she could feel the warmth of his body. She also felt his overpowering magnetism. It frightened her and her tension returned. This was going to be a long evening to endure.

Dee waited breathlessly for the show to start. She exhaled audibly when the lights dimmed and the music started. Her face came alive as she sat back in her seat and visibly relaxed and smiled in the darkness. From that moment on she forgot everything as her eyes remained transfixed with fascination through every scene. She never once turned her attention from the stage.

Rowan's own gaze was fixated on Dee, watching the joy on her face, which was flushed with excitement. Her expression was tension free as she sat lost in the performance. He'd never seen her so relaxed and so peaceful. Rowan wondered if she had any idea of her effect on him. With her defensive wall down she was mesmerizing.

Dee watched engrossed until the final curtain lowered and the house lights came on. The applause was deafening through several encores and then the curtains closed. Dee's eyes danced when she turned to Rowan. Her voice flowed like soft music, "It must be wonderful to perform like that." And then she smiled one of her breathtaking genuine smiles that had captivated him on the rare occasion she had shared it with someone else.

Rowan sat there with an odd look on his face. He looked away and Dee had the disturbing feeling she sometimes had that this man knew more about her than he should.

Rowan had been a charming and attentive escort, a side to him she hadn't seen. Upon their return to the hotel, he politely invited her to join him in the lounge for a nightcap. Smiling politely, Dee declined using the opportune excuse that she wanted to check on her grandmother.

Rowan escorted her upstairs. "Your grandmother cares a great deal for you." His genuine smile softened the lines of his handsome face and made him seem so much less arrogant.

Dee smiled back and could no longer deny how she felt. "I love Gran," she said easily.

"I've always loved Connie. She's always been a part of my life." Rowan realized that this was the one thing that they were in agreement with and had in common. Tenderness came into his eyes when he smiled at Dee, "I'm glad that you enjoyed the performance."

Dee replied with genuine pleasure, "I loved it. Thank you for a wonderful evening." She really meant it. It came to her that she had been at ease in his company for the first time. For one brief moment she felt something different, a warm glow. Dee didn't pause to appraise the pleasure she took in having shared this experience with him.

"Good night, Dee." Rowan enjoyed seeing her lips curve in one of her hesitant smiles as she lowered her eyes.

"Good night." The automatic response was no more than a whisper.

Rowan took a polite leave and walked back to the lift. He shook his head. Dee was an enchanting creature as well as a mystery.

CHAPTER NINE

Monday morning Dee woke early. She went and sat on the window seat and stared out at the coming dawn. The morning glow was incredible as the sun began to peak over the London rooftops. *A new day dawns on a new beginning. A good omen.* Dee looked forward to a day filled with hope and promise. Not sure of what her role of employment would entail, Dee donned a basic navy linen dress and pulled her hair back in a low ponytail. Filled with nervous excitement, Dee made her way to the morning room.

Constance turned and smiled as Dee entered the room. "You look lovely this morning. You look like you're ready for anything. I'm very proud of you, Dee. This is such a positive step for you. I know this will work out."

So why did Dee have this nagging doubt? Still feeling nervous, she only nibbled at her toast as she continually glanced at the clock. She dare not be late.

Constance understood that Dee was nervous so she kept the conversation light and refrained from mentioning Rowan or Maeve. All too soon it was time to go downstairs. Constance gave Dee an affectionate squeeze and wished her good luck.

"Gran, you realize this is a huge step for me in creating a permanent life here. I appreciate the opportunity Mr. Le Baron is giving me. I'm excited, but a little scared too." Seeing the concerned look on her grandmother's face, Dee promised, "I'll be on my best behavior. I'll listen intently and say and do all the right things including holding my temper."

Constance was impressed and knew she wouldn't have to worry about her granddaughter. Dee may be feisty at times because that was her defense mechanism when she was feeling insecure. But behind her tough exterior was a very intelligent young lady who was witty and bright, vibrant and full of energy. Dee was also strong-willed and had a mind of her own. Constance knew her granddaughter wouldn't be a pushover. Neither Rowan nor Maeve knew what was in store for them. Constance smiled to herself, thinking how much things had changed around here since the arrival of one Dee Dare. And it had just begun.

Promptly at nine o'clock, Dee knocked on Rowan's door. She was filled with anxiety, though mixed with that anxiousness was excitement. Rowan opened the door and to Dee's chagrin Maeve was seated in one of the chairs, her long legs crossed and looking indifferent.

Rowan motioned for Dee to take a seat. "Maeve and I will go over a few things before we take you for a tour of the hotel. Even though you've been here for a while, we want to introduce you to everything that our hotel has to offer."

Maeve turned to Dee as she sat down. "Rowan and I discussed your unusual situation last night over dinner."

Again the claim my man game, thought Dee.

Maeve threw another superior glare at Dee. "Due to your circumstance, both being a foreigner and handicapped by your memory loss, we intend to move slowly to see what you're capable of."

The hairs on Dee's neck started to rise as she clasped her hands together tightly. "I'm not an idiot. I lost my memory, not my mind. I can learn fast with the right teacher."

The intentional dig was wasted on Maeve but it didn't escape Rowan. He quickly interjected, "I understand that Connie shared the history with you as to the early business relationships between our two families."

"Do you remember?" Maeve asked with a mocking look.

The claws are out early. Stealing herself to sound calm when she was livid inside, Dee replied, "Fortunately, I have no problem with my memory since my unfortunate accident, Maeve. Please don't continue to be concerned in that regard. As well, I believe that moving forward I will prove myself capable of being trained in whatever role you've chosen."

Without saying a word, Rowan walked over to the window. He was fully aware that these two women didn't like each other so he wasn't surprised by the exchange between them. He realized that Dee would be able to hold her own with Maeve. Not that he ever doubted it. Dee looked up and his reflection in the window winked at her.

Rowan turned and his dignified voice was filled with pride, "A hotel is much more than the handsomely constructed shell. The Conlyn Grand Hotel holds a certain mystique that welcomes guests from around the world. We provide a high level of luxury that we feel is exclusive to the Conlyn. We have thirty seconds to impress so it is the front-end staff that is our most important asset. They are encouraged to listen and build relationships with our guests. The Conlyn strives to go above and beyond in offering exceptional guest services at every level throughout our guests stay. Together, Maeve and I will be doing hands on training rather than enrolling you in our basic training program. Again, due to the circumstances, this will be more advantageous for all concerned."

Dee had been observing Maeve while Rowan spoke and the lady's lips had been pursed most of the time. "I'm here to learn," Dee said earnestly. Knowing she lacked neither intelligence nor ability, she was ready.

Throughout the detailed tour, Dee listened with every ounce of concentration. New information was coming fast and furious so there was plenty to absorb. Rowan took the time to introduce her to staff members. He was impressed at how many Dee already knew by name. During the tour, he watched Dee. Her eyes were alive with curiosity as she continued to observe at every opportunity.

Rowan surprised Dee with his patience as he answered her dozens of questions, as one question led to another. She surprised him with her eagerness and general knowledge. Maeve, on the other hand, was completely bored.

Dee had to admit that Maeve was the perfect assistant. Not once did the smile leave her face in front of others. But there were several times that Dee felt the daggers from her when Rowan wasn't looking.

After they returned to the lobby and were standing outside of Maeve's office Rowan excused Maeve. "I know you have things to do to prepare for the arrival of the Duke and Duchess of Devonshire this weekend. Don't forget to compliment them with ballet tickets for Saturday evening and see that her favorite chocolates are included in the gift basket."

Maeve knew she'd been dismissed but disliked the fact that Dee would now have Rowan's undivided attention. She was quickly overtaken by a surge of jealousy.

Rowan turned back to Dee, "I'll show you where you'll be working." When they arrived at Rowan's office, he led her across the room and opened a side door that Dee had never noticed before. It opened to a small adjoining office. "You'll be working here, right next to me."

Dee couldn't resist, "Afraid I'll steal the family coffers?"

Rowan continued as though she hadn't spoken. "This way I can keep a close eye on you as well as help you to avoid making any big mistakes."

Dee felt even more intimidated knowing he'd be so close and constantly observing her every move so she resorted to her go to defense of sarcasm. "I believe I already have but at the moment I have no other choice."

Rowan chose to ignore the barb. "This will be your office so feel free to make it your own. If there is anything you need, let me or Maeve know. This morning I'd like you to shadow Maeve. She's expecting you in her office. If all goes well, I'll have time with you after lunch. You'll be working Monday through Friday until four o'clock. Do you have any questions?"

"What about work attire? Will I be required to wear a uniform?"

"You're not enrolled in our training program, so you may wear your own clothes. Trousers are not acceptable. You may want to take your cue from Maeve. She always dresses professionally."

Dee had to agree. Maeve draped her frame with exquisite perfection. She also had to acknowledge that Rowan was also always impeccably dressed. Today he wore a pin-striped gray suit that fit his hard toned body flawlessly.

"Anything else?"

With a gesture of resignation, Dee shook her head. She was feeling a little overwhelmed at the moment. And she was dreading having to spend the morning alone with Maeve.

"Aren't you curious about your salary or are you confident that your allowance will continue?" Rowan braced for a strong reaction.

Instead Dee said solemnly, "I expect you'll be fair but I'm sure I'll have to prove myself for you to determine my worth. I have no credentials with which to impress you so I'll have to let my work speak for itself." Dee was a person with ethics. Her moral principles were more important than money.

Rowan was impressed by her response. Certainly not what he had expected. He began to doubt that he'd ever understand her. "Dee, now that we'll be working side by side every day I think it's time to drop the formalities and call me Rowan. It would also please your grandmother. She thinks you don't like me."

Deliberately, Dee tilted her head and looked him in the eye. Mindful of their new relationship, she smiled politely before responding, "Grandmothers can be so intuitive, Rowan."

Rowan's reaction surprised Dee. He let loose a hearty laugh. This was the first time that Dee had heard him laugh. It had a deep rich sound. She didn't think he laughed often. "Well, off you go, brat. Maeve is expecting you."

Oh, joy. I can hardly wait. By the time Dee arrived at Maeve's office, her hands were clammy and her nerves were stretched tight.

Maeve looked up in annoyance. "This idea of Rowan's is definitely going to be an inconvenience. I don't like the interruption your arrival has created in the routine around here. You rely on your relationship with Constance, and, therefore, misuse that power over Rowan."

"Gran's and my relationship is totally irrelevant."

"You only got this so called position because of who your grandmother is. This was only an act of kindness. If you were anyone else, Rowan wouldn't give you the time of day."

Dee was unable to dispute the truth of Maeve's words. It was because of her relationship to Constance and not her own abilities that she was given a job. Dee knew she'd have to prove herself even more to show Rowan that he made a good decision.

Maeve's attitude verged on abrasive. "Needless to say your job description is undefined. Rowan just created a job because he wants to make Constance happy. My job is very involved as I'm Rowan's right-hand assistant. I also act as hostess and I'm the front person in his absence." There was no doubt that Maeve felt herself to be superior to the rest of the staff.

This woman is nothing but an egomaniac who suffers from illusions of grandeur. "Just tell me what to do and what you expect. I can be very adaptable and useful."

The look Maeve gave Dee could freeze water. "I want to make it clear that I don't like you. I don't like your attitude. In fact, I don't like anything about you."

Dee wasn't intimidated by this woman. "Well Maeve, we certainly cleared that up. I hope you can curb our own personal feelings and keep them separate from work."

Maeve was not used to anyone countering back, "You might want to keep your personal life separate from work as well. You need to pay more attention to your duties than to Rowan. I heard that you and Rowan attended the theatre Saturday night. You work fast, don't you?"

"What I do outside of work is none of your business. Besides that, I answer to Rowan."

"You answer to both of us. Don't forget it. Now, let's get started." Throughout the morning Maeve remained businesslike. Dee unwillingly had to respect Maeve's work ethics and she quickly recognized Maeve's skills. She was a capable woman who was very efficient and extremely professional. Her occupational smile never left her face around her guests and she always gave them her undivided attention.

Dee listened carefully to all of Maeve's instructions. Dee felt Maeve intentionally talked down to her even before she asked, "Clear so far?"

"Perfectly," Dee said coolly.

Dee was more than relieved when Maeve said, "I have several calls I need to make. I'll give you a few things I feel you can do on your own. If Rowan isn't back after lunch, come back to my office."

"Wonderful," Dee mumbled under her breath as she turned and walked back to her own office. She proceeded to work on the menial tasks that Maeve gave her, which included a huge stack of mail. While sorting the mail for the hotel as well as the hotel residents, Dee was surprised at how many replies there were for her party. She put them off to the side and would take them up to her grandmother at the end of the day. Dee was less anxious about the upcoming party but this was evidence that it was very real and much bigger that she had imagined. Having completed her assigned duties Dee wasn't sure what to do. Not one to remain idle, she began rearranging the office and making it her own.

After lunch, Dee returned to Maeve's office. "This afternoon we'll move on to the computer program we use here at the hotel. The program itself is really quite simple."

Dee didn't miss the degrading tone but chose to bite her lip to refrain from responding.

There was no polite small talk as Maeve got right into the training. Dee was quick to realize that the computer program would take practice but she wasn't overwhelmed. She took to the computer just like she had to the piano, for the keyboard keys felt familiar. Within minutes her slender fingers were tapping away entering data and updating guest files in the computer. Dee was quick to realize that the information on each guest could be more detailed and even more so on the live-in residents. She was smart enough to refrain from saying anything today but she would store it away for later.

By mid-afternoon Rowan had not returned and the tension between the two women had intensified. Maeve was obviously annoyed. Her professional manner slipped and her approach became more personal. "We can dispense with polite small talk when we're alone and it would be wise to stay out of my way."

"It will be my pleasure to stay out of your way as much as possible," Dee flung back.

Maeve smiled coldly, "I'm glad we're on the same page."

Maeve's attitude infuriated Dee. "We're not even in the same book."

"I can make your job here miserable so let me give you some free advice."

"Don't bother, I'm sure I'd pay for it one way or another." Dee looked over her shoulder on her way out, "Beware Maeve. I've never avoided a challenge."

Rowan overhead the last part of the heated exchange that was taking place and he decided to keep on walking. He no sooner sat down at his desk and the spitfire entered.

Cheeks flushed with temper, Dee marched past Rowan, muttering under her breath. "She doesn't like this, she doesn't like that. She doesn't like one damn thing as far as I can tell."

Rowan got up and entered Dee's office. Dee was startled by the interruption. He wasn't about to mince words, "I don't care if the two of you don't like each other but you will learn to be civil and get along. Which means you will do what's necessary to work together. This is business, pure and simple."

"You're the boss."

Her sarcasm didn't go unnoticed by Rowan. This time he didn't let it go. "That's an order I just gave you. Do not mistake it for a request. Understood?"

"Is that all? Or do you have more orders to give me?" Rowan studied her closely as she glared up at him. Dee wasn't done. "How come I'm always the one in trouble and not Maeve?" Wanting to further defend herself, Dee was frustrated when Rowan interrupted her.

"Yes, how come?" Rowan shot back. "Maybe if you'd adjust your attitude and hold your tongue along with your temper you might make life a little easier for yourself. When are you going to stop being angry at everyone?" Rowan turned and left, for Dee had failed to hide the hurt in her expressive eyes. Why did this little slip of a thing always have to confront him? She was proving to be more of a challenge than he imagined and it was only the first day.

Dee slumped back in her chair in defeat as she struggled with her wounded pride. What happened had shaken her confidence and self-esteem. Rowan's words had stung. Letting out a long-suffering sigh, she pressed her fingers to her temples, trying to massage away the tension that made her head feel as if it was going to explode. She hated that she once again had lost control. Her promise to her grandmother hadn't lasted long. Both Rowan and Maeve left her alone for the remainder of the afternoon. Dee was relieved to finally see four o'clock. It had been the longest day of her life. After gathering her grandmother's mail, she got up to leave.

Rowan stood in the doorway, leaning comfortably against the door jam. Dee looked up and glared at him. Rowan felt bad about coming down on Dee, especially on her first day. "Sorry I couldn't spend time with you today."

Dee was calm again. "I'll get over it. And I'll try harder to tolerate Maeve. But I'm not going to apologize because I meant what I said."

It took all of his effort not to smile. *Baby steps but it's a start.* He attempted to make amends. Rowan looked around, "I like what you've done with your office. It looks good with the desk angled like that. It opens up that corner of the room. Would you like a table and extra chair for the other corner?"

Dee nodded, surprised that he took an interest in what she'd done. She'd been hesitant to make the changes as she didn't know how long she'd have her job. But then she decided to think positive and believe in herself and make it hers. Dee was relieved by his comments. The lines on her face relaxed a little and she actually smiled. The tension between them eased.

Dee dared to ask, "Would it be possible to have a coffee maker in here?"

"No problem. It will all be set up for tomorrow. Off you go. Tomorrow is another day."

Dee returned to the flat frustrated and tired.

After dinner, the ladies retired to the parlour. As expected, the conversation turned to her new job. Constance thought Dee looked exhausted and discouraged. "How was your first day?"

Dee didn't want to tell her grandmother that she had another round with Rowan. She didn't want to share her burdens, but, more important, she didn't want to disappoint her. Dee knew she'd have to make more of an effort to curb her tongue and hold a reign on her temper. She knew this would be easier if she took the time to process her thoughts instead of just reacting. Dee promised herself she'd work on it. Her reply was non-committal, "It was fine. I did menial tasks all day. I know I have to start somewhere but it's demoralizing being scrutinized every minute."

It took all of Constance's effort not to smile. "Might you be exaggerating? Is it possible you're being a little over-sensitive? All new employees are watched over in the beginning."

Dee knew she shouldn't feel discouraged so quickly. "I suppose that's true."

"Your situation is unique and so is theirs. They don't know what you're capable of any more than you do."

Dee sat back and thought about what her grandmother just said. Rowan's comments filtered in as well. She knew she was overreacting. Maybe an attitude adjustment on her part was called for to be fair to everyone. She turned to her grandmother. "I hate it that you're right." She hated it even more that Rowan was right.

"I can appreciate that everything is difficult for you without being able to fall back on memories of your life and experiences. You're a brave girl facing your challenges every day."

Dee realized that she'd sounded ungrateful but she was tired. It had been a long and stressful day. "I'm sure that I've dealt with women like Maeve in my past. She likes to intimidate but I don't intimidate easily."

Constance smiled to herself, for there was no doubt in her mind.

"I guess there's no sense worrying about all of the mistakes I could and probably will make. That's part of any new job." She looked at her grandmother with determination. "I'll move forward with an open mind." Fighting another yawn, Dee realized how tired she was. "If you'll excuse me, I think I'll retire for the night. Tomorrow will be another long day." She hugged her grandmother good night and retired to her room.

As soon as Dee lay in bed the day became a jumble of thoughts in her mind. But not for long. A few minutes later she was sound asleep.

Dee stepped into her new role with ease. Her life now had purpose. The next few days were full and that kept her mind off her problems. Daily routines were established fairly quickly. She enjoyed the challenge of learning new systems and skills. She listened and learned. But by the end of the week she was exhausted.

All week Rowan had been patient and understanding and very professional. Dee was grateful and found she was very comfortable with both her job and her boss. Their relationship had altered. The changes were subtle and had been so natural she hadn't even been aware of it.

Dee was exactly what Rowan expected. He had to admit that Dee was conscientious, diligent and disciplined. Old skills had come back unaware. As a result, Dee was constantly revealing new facets of herself. She was a natural organizer, continuously observing and her questions were endless. Dee was eager to learn and under Rowan's watchful eye she blossomed. "You're really good with computers. You must have done this before."

The mischievous gleam was evident in her eyes. "Your guess is as good as mine." But she knew he was right. Some things came naturally and she didn't have to think about them. Like playing the piano. It all felt so natural using skills she obviously had. The work she was doing began to fill her with a sense of fulfillment, as well as stretching her mental ability.

Despite her early misgivings, Rowan proved to be a fair employer. The benefit of his sharp mind combined with his physical presence guided her daily but he didn't hover over her watching her every move. Instead, he'd come in periodically to check on her and see if she needed any help or had any questions. He proved to be both reasonable and patient.

It was the end of her second week and Constance and Dee were having a late dinner. "Are you still enjoying your job?"

Dee loved the work. It felt good to be busy and she was proud of how well she was doing. Her eyes lit up. "To be honest, I find it all fascinating. And the staff is amazing. I'm impressed at how well trained they are so I watch them and I listen so I can learn. They're always friendly in such a polite manner. They've helped me more than once through a situation that could have proven embarrassing."

"That's because you not only take an interest in things around you but you always take time to acknowledge them by name. Your interest in them is genuine."

"I learned that from you, Gran," Dee said sincerely.

Constance could tell that her granddaughter was adjusting not only to her job but to her situation. She was impressed with Dee. "You haven't complained about Maeve for awhile."

"I realize I shouldn't complain about her. It won't change who she is. I hate the fact that I have to tolerate her and I don't like having her always in my face. Maeve still loves to give me menial tasks but I'm learning something from everything I do. We seem to have called a truce as we strive to maneuver through the rough spots in our working relationship. I have to admit she's a hard worker and I've learned a lot from her. She's extremely professional. I know she wants what's best for the hotel." A little of the old Dee surfaced as she declared, "Right after she does what's best for Maeve."

Constance dared to ask, "How is it working with Rowan?"

Dee hesitated, trying to gather her thoughts. "He's a fair boss," was all that Dee would admit to. Silently, Dee recognized she was no longer immune to the man. His image drifted into her mind with such ease that Dee shook her head in an effort to dismiss him. He lectured, he guided and he teased her. Dee was honest enough to admit that there was a part of her, a very small part, that found the man intriguing. Despite her best efforts, she no longer hated him. As a result, her feelings for him were more confusing.

"You've had to adapt through so many difficult times. "I know it hasn't been easy but you're learning to cope very well. Have I told you how proud I am of you?"

Dee's face lit up as her grandmother's words warmed her heart. "Maybe once or twice. But I never mind hearing it. I want you to be proud but more important than that I want to be proud of myself. So I'm working on it."

It was the beginning of another work week and Dee and Constance were chatting over breakfast. Constance reminded Dee that her party was next weekend.

"Already? The days go much faster when you're busy. Do you remember how anxious I was when you first mentioned it? Actually, I was terrified. I'm sure it's going to be a fabulous evening. You and Maeve have put a lot of time and effort into the plans." Dee's voice waivered, "You've helped me fit in and accepted me as family. It will be an honor to be introduced to others as your granddaughter. I'll do my best to make you proud."

Constance took Dee's hand. "I count my blessings every day that you're here with me. It makes me happy to see that you've settled in and are moving forward."

Dee glanced at her watch. "Gotta run. Punctuality eliminates persecution from the warden." Both women knew Dee meant Maeve and not Rowan. Truth be told, Dee had to admit that she worked well with Rowan. He had earned her respect.

The work day had no sooner started and Maeve and Dee were at it again. "Why haven't you done this? I've shown you this before and it's really quite simple."

"As usual Maeve, you're right. It's simple and I do know how to do this. I just don't understand why we have to do it this way."

Like every other day, Maeve wore her superior attitude. "I don't like change."

Instead of losing control Dee kept her voice calm, "Even if it helps someone be more informed in their job? If you want my opinion?"

Maeve abruptly cut her off, "Which of course I don't."

Rowan, who was within ear shot, came over. "I'm curious to hear what Dee has to say."

Dee turned to Rowan, "I've been waiting for the right time to talk to you about this. The first day when we were touring the hotel you stated that the most important advantage is how we treat our guests. Registration does provide exemplary service. However, I believe we can add more personal information in our return guest's profiles and definitely more in those of our permanent residents."

Dee had a point so Rowan asked her to continue. Maeve knew better than to interrupt.

"It would be beneficial if there was a link to a page marked Notes or Remarks for quick reference to this information. For example, it might be advantageous to document the file that the Duke and Duchess of Devonshire have a dog named Beasley. I understand that they're always anxious about leaving their baby behind. It would mean so much to them if we would mention him. They don't have any children so it's like asking them about one of their kids. It may appear trivial to us but not to them."

Rowan was impressed and let Dee continue.

During her time at the hotel, Dee had made it her business to get to know the live-in residents by name and she was finding out something personal about each of them. "As well, the information on our permanent residents is very limited. These residents are our extended family. Actually, to some, we are their family. I see that birthdays and anniversaries are flagged in your system. It's Frieda Unger's birthday next week. What does the hotel do for special occasions?"

Maeve was quick to jump on this. "We hand-deliver a birthday card and if they come down for dinner it's complimentary."

"Frieda is turning eighty on Thursday. This is a special birthday. Can't we do more?"

"You can't come in here and start making changes and demanding things." Maeve turned to Rowan with a look of total disgust on her face.

Choosing to ignore the outburst, Rowan immediately instructed Maeve, "Please order two dozen red roses to be delivered the day of her birthday. I will invite Frieda to join Connie and myself to dinner and we'll have a birthday cake for her." Rowan was curious as he turned back to Dee, "How do you know this?"

"I've reviewed the files on each resident. Since they are our extended family, I feel we could expand their profiles with additional information and flag details like special dates."

Rowan agreed with Dee. "I think that's a splendid idea. We'll see about implementing some of your ideas right away. This is something that can be incorporated in all of our hotels." Rowan was curious, "How do you know so much about Frieda if it's not in her file?"

"Frieda invited me to join her for a cup of tea in her flat Sunday afternoon. She's a very interesting lady who has travelled extensively. She can't anymore due to her health but her albums are full of pictures and her stories are endless. Frieda's grandson is coming from Germany to visit her at Christmas and will be staying for the holidays. I created a Remarks link in her file and entered this information. There will be a pop-up on her file the week before as a reminder. We can see if there is anything special we can do for them during his visit."

The casual use of we angered Maeve. Who did Dee think she was trying to change everything? "We here at The Conlyn will do whatever we can to improve. As you so wisely pointed out we are all family."

Dee thought Maeve's teeth should rot with all the sugar coating on her words. "Exactly." Feeling there was nothing further to discuss, she turned to go to her office.

Rowan, who had followed right behind her, placed a hand on her shoulder. "Sit down, Dee. I'd like to talk to you."

Dee recognized his serious tone and tensed. Without a word she obeyed, dropping her hands into her lap and clasping them together. She blinked her long lashes and waited.

"I'll be away for the rest of the week, probably until Sunday night. I have a constant round of appointments up north and if time allows I may stop at the manor on the way back. Maeve is also out of the office on Friday so you'll be on your own. I've scheduled a meeting with the three of us for first thing Monday morning to discuss the Benefit Ball which will fall on October thirty-first. The upcoming Charity Fundraiser is an annual black tie affair. We donate the venue and host the Event in the main ballroom. The money raised this year is going to Evelina Children's Hospital."

"It sounds like a special Event for a worthwhile cause." The excitement in Dee's voice was evident as she said, "My Dad always said it's important to give back whenever you can."

Rowan, like Constance, recognized that another memory had just escaped. It was happening more frequently. When Rowan continued, his tone was more businesslike, "Keep in mind that the Benefit is two-fold. It's about raising money and public awareness. While I'm away I'd like you to review the file on last year's Event. It will give you an idea of what we do and how we will proceed with this year's Benefit. I want someone with fresh ideas and a good head to review the file. A new perspective might offer new insights. I'd value your input."

Dee stole a quick look at Rowan, confused by the trust in his voice. "May I have the file for the weekend?"

"I'll leave it on your desk."

Dee ended up shadowing Maeve for the rest of the day. When she returned to her own office, the file was on her desk as promised. Immediately after dinner, she excused herself and closed herself in her room. After reviewing the file, Dee had a good understanding of the Event. Then her brain shifted gears to the Charity. In hopes of getting a better understanding of this year's recipient she decided to spend Saturday at Evelina Children's Hospital. The rest of the night was spent doing research. Dee was impressed. The hospital's positive reputation was built on high quality, compassionate and innovative care.

Right after breakfast Saturday morning, Dee informed her grandmother, "I'm going out for the day. It's work related but I can't tell you about it yet."

Constance could hear the excitement in Dee's voice. This job was a good thing for her. It had brought purpose for Dee and helped to take her away from her forgotten past. Constance didn't question her but she couldn't help but wonder what the child was up to. And would Rowan approve?

Dee grabbed her jacket, as the days had gotten cooler. It was only the end of August but fall was hovering around the corner. "Gotta run. I'll be back before dinner."

At the hospital Dee met with Rebecca Grieves from administration. Together they spent the morning touring the hospital and over lunch she answered a lot of Dee's questions. Returning to her office, Rebecca handed Dee a package along with her business card. "Inside are some brochures and pamphlets about Evelina's. It has wonderful information about the hospital as well as what we offer to both our parents and their families. You'll find it enlightening."

Dee had been given a lot to think about. "Thank you for seeing me without an appointment and giving up your valuable time to show me around. Your hospital is a worthy Charity and we will do everything to represent you well. I'm also glad that you mentioned your Volunteer Program. I'll stop by Human Resources on my way out and provide them with whatever they require to see if I can meet their criteria."

It had been an inspirational day and Dee was more than impressed with the hospital. But it also brought back the feelings she had before she came to England. Loneliness took over for a moment but Dee refused to succumb to it. After seeing so many young patients, many of them terminally ill, she would have been ashamed not to count her blessings.

On her way out there was a young girl sitting in a wheelchair off by herself staring out the window. Dee guessed her to be maybe six years of age. The patient wore a scarf so Dee couldn't help but wonder is she was here because of cancer. For some reason, Dee was drawn to her. Without hesitation, Dee went over and sat down beside her. She looked so cute with her heart shaped face and turned up nose dotted with freckles. "Hi there, I'm Dee."

The child possessed a quiet charm and introduced herself as Elizabeth. "But everyone calls me Beth, except for my mom. She calls me Bethie." She kept her penetrating gaze on Dee, "You talk different."

Dee gave her a warm smile. "That's because I came here from the United States of America. I'm staying with my grandmother for awhile. Starting on Wednesday I'm going to be volunteering here at the hospital. Do you like music?"

Beth nodded. "You're really pretty. You have beautiful hair," she said, her tone a little wistful. "Your hair is as black as midnight."

Dee studied Beth carefully. "Thank you. That's a very pretty scarf you're wearing."

In a voice that was very direct, Beth declared, "Usually I don't wear a scarf. I'm completely bald."

Without even realizing this could be an awkward moment, Dee asked Beth what color her hair was.

The little girl answered quickly, "It was fire engine red and very unruly."

Dee smiled at that knowing Beth had heard this more than once from her mother. "Well, now you don't have to worry about tangles in your unruly hair, do you?" They both giggled.

"What are you two laughing at?" The nurse, who just arrived, smiled at Dee. She was pleased to see Beth open up with someone. She usually kept to herself. The nurse turned to Beth, "It's time to go back to your room."

Beth looked disappointed. Without pause, Dee stopped the nurse, "I'm Dee Dare and I'll be volunteering here in the Music Program on Wednesday nights. Can Beth come to our music session and I'll take her back to her room afterwards?"

"Please, can I?" Beth pleaded and the nurse nodded.

Dee leaned down and gave Beth an impulsive hug. "See you Wednesday," Dee called after them as Beth was wheeled away.

Beth was an odd little girl but Dee found she liked her. At first Dee thought Beth was shy but she soon realized that she was probably reserved with new people. Dee could relate and realized she was looking forward to Wednesday night.

The time spent at the hospital was more than Dee had hoped for. While she was able to obtain valuable information, Dee found it much more moving than she expected. As she made her way back to the hotel her mind was in a whirl. She could hardly wait to get started. Along with the information she gathered about the hospital, Dee began to formulate a plan. Dee's mind had kicked into high gear when she heard the date and she needed the weekend to prepare her proposal. She couldn't let go of the fact that the date fell on Halloween night so she decided she had to incorporate a Halloween theme into the Event.

Dee bounced into the flat with a burst of excitement. Her grandmother was there to greet her with a questioning look. "I still can't tell you what I've been doing, not yet." Dee's intent wasn't to be evasive, she simply wanted time to process her ideas and formulate her plan. Blessed with an overactive imagination, her head was full of ideas. One idea initiated another and she was anxious to get her thoughts on paper.

As curious as Constance was, she respected Dee and left her on her own. She knew Dee would reveal everything when she was ready. Dee again closed herself away in her room. For a brief moment, Dee doubted herself. Was her idea too bizarre? She recovered quickly and laughed to herself. What was the worst that could happen? Deciding she had nothing to lose, Dee proceeded. She worked on her proposal long into the night.

The next morning Dee dressed in shorts and a sleeveless tank top. She bundled her hair up on top of her head, wanting it out of her way. After breakfast she grabbed the Benefit folder and went out to the terrace. Once she had wiggled into a comfortable position at the table, she again poured over the file. Based on her theme, her mind was working furiously. Dee was overflowing with purpose, her formulated ideas now being transferred to paper. Her notepad was soon filled with detailed ideas and simple sketches. Throughout the morning she kept jotting down more notes. There were papers in various piles with sticky notes attached everywhere. Her creative mind went into over-drive when she started working on the menu. There were moments when she laughed out loud. The specialty drink names were unique.

A sudden memory made her pause and sit back in her chair. She realized that she had a knack for creating and wondered where it came from. With a shake of her head, she refocused her attention and began working on the outline for her presentation. Dee let out an impatient breath for she was struggling with the words. Deeply absorbed in what she was doing, she was unaware that Rowan was silently observing her from the doorway.

He watched as the gentle breeze caressed her skin and teased her hair. She lifted her hand to tuck a loose strand behind her ear. Her legs were long and thin and time in the summer sun had warmed her skin to beautiful honey gold. He recalled how pale she was when she had arrived. Today she looked wholesome. As he strolled over, Rowan's movements were easy. "Enjoying the summer sun?" A smile briefly touched Rowan's face. "You were lost in thought. What were you thinking about? You looked so serious."

Dee smiled up at him, her face eager and excited when she heard his voice. Until that moment, she hadn't realized how dull everything had been without him. She couldn't believe that her feelings for him had changed. "I was lost in my own thoughts. I had one of those déjà vu moments again. I have them more often and I remember more but I still can't put everything together. It's rather frustrating at times but I'm refusing to get discouraged. I can't make it happen. It will happen or it won't."

As much as Rowan wanted this for Dee, he felt bad knowing that her life would be forever changed when she did.

Misreading Rowan's concerned look, Dee said quietly, "I realize I can't change anything and I'm grateful to those who helped to make my unwilling transition easier."

Rowan smiled and with accustomed ease he went over and dropped into the chair next to her at the table. "Reviewing the file?" he asked as he poured himself a glass of lemonade. He leaned back and took a long, cool drink. "Trying to get in good with the boss?"

"No, I hear he's a real tyrant," she bantered back. Dee was pleased when he laughed with her instead of at her. It almost made the Bear human. "I've studied it earnestly," Dee said, as she closed the folder. She had a million ideas but wasn't willing to share them. He would have to wait until Monday.

"Do you have any questions?" he asked with a curious expression.

"Not yet," she replied simply, choosing not to discuss the subject with him.

Dee appeared to be nonchalant but he knew she wasn't. A few minutes later Constance joined them and the three of them spent the rest of the morning in comfortable conversation.

After Rowan left, Dee was more determined than ever as she went back to her notes. She knew she needed to be prepared right down to the last detail. Time slipped away from her and it was only when the sun slipped behind the rooftops that Dee closed the folder and allowed herself to smile with satisfaction. Dee was tired but exhilarated.

CHAPTER TEN

Dee sat at her desk with a sense of anticipation waiting for Rowan. Just after nine o'clock Rowan walked into her office. "Did you have time to finish reviewing the Benefit file?"

Dee looked up and smiled wide. "I spent the whole weekend thinking about nothing else. I propose we do something totally different this year that will fit in perfectly with both the date and the selected Charity."

"What do you have in mind? Better yet, do up a proposal for me to look at."

Dee opened her desk drawer and pulled out an impressive file. "I already did," she informed him as she beamed with pleasure. "I hope you'll hear me out without interrupting because I'm sure it isn't what you have in mind."

Rowan looked at her questioningly. *What in heaven's name was she up to now?* "Bring it to my office and we'll take a look."

Dee's heart was pounding as she followed him. For better or worse, she was committed.

Rowan went and sat behind his desk and opened her folder. Just then Maeve entered the room. "Have a seat, Maeve, and join us. Dee wants to share her ideas for the Benefit."

Maeve's smile faded immediately. "Great," she said without a trace of interest.

Sudden panic set in with the realization that Maeve would definitely veto her presentation. Both turned to Dee, waiting for her to proceed. Dee remained standing, unconsciously taking control.

Rowan motioned for her to start. With customary ease, he leaned back and watched her.

Dee experienced a sudden panic similar to stage fright. A feeling she realized she was familiar with. As in the past, she took a deep breath. Although she was nervous and excited at the same time, she had no doubt about her proposal. "I think we should host a masquerade party focusing on a Halloween theme. The date itself opens the door to such an Event."

Maeve was so astonished she laughed out loud.

Recognizing the spark of annoyance on Dee's expressive face, Rowan turned to Maeve. "Please be respectful and give Dee the opportunity to continue." He turned back to Dee as a slight smile touched the corner of his mouth.

Undaunted by Maeve's negative reaction Dee continued, her enthusiasm increasing from detail to detail. When Dee was done she sat down, relieved but anxious.

Maeve hadn't been the least bit interested in her proposal.

Rowan, on the other hand, had occasionally jotted down notes. He found Dee to be amazing. She was bold and courageous in her plans and he couldn't help but admire her confidence. She had obviously unconsciously drawn on experiences from her past. Her proposal was brilliant, even addressing the finest details. She seemed to know what would be required. There were many sides to Dee. Strange how he was affected by every one of them.

Rowan had yet to comment and Dee was unaware that she was holding her breath. His expression was non-committal. Rowan couldn't find anything wrong with the presentation, including the theme. He was impressed with what Dee had come up with and he was positive she'd continue to come up with more ideas. The way she had presented even the small details he could see how they would all fit together into an impressive whole. It would be an experience in itself to see the process through to the finish line.

Dee gave Rowan a long searching look. Her gaze remained on him but his expression didn't tell her anything.

The prolonged silence continued until he finally said, "Interesting. You have a vivid imagination and a brilliant mind to go with it. I may have a few more questions but I can see you've done your homework and have provided a very thorough presentation."

Dee drew a deep breath of relief.

Rowan remained reserved and guarded. Dee had a concept that was worth considering but he wouldn't give her the satisfaction of having him agree right away. "I'll let you know."

Maeve, on the other hand, looked at Rowan in disbelief. "You can't be serious," she said in a tone that suggested he was out of his mind. "We've always held a formal black and white affair."

Rowan did his best to remain serious. "This is still a black and white affair, Maeve. Dee's just adding in a lot of orange. Maeve's style is typically expensive and ornate," he informed Dee.

Maeve was not amused. "Why change what works and has proven to be successful?"

Dee was not intimidated. She interjected before Rowan could respond. "That's a good question, Maeve. A question I asked myself. But then I thought, why not? This may be even better. Sometimes people enjoy the unexpected and take pleasure in a change."

Maeve's next question to Dee was a total blow, "Who helped you with this?"

Dee was insulted. "Use your head, Maeve. Who do I even know to ask? I simply thought maybe people would enjoy a change, especially since it will be on Halloween night."

"This is hardly a change. It's a ridiculous idea. There is absolutely no way that what you're presenting would ever suit our venue and clientele." Maeve couldn't hide the astonished expression on her face when she turned to Rowan. "The girl can't be serious, Rowan. The cream of Society is going to be in attendance deciding how wide to open up their purse strings."

Ignoring Maeve's rant, Rowan informed Dee, "I'll review my notes and your presentation. I'll get back to you." There were things that he wanted to discuss with Maeve.

"Thank you, that sounds reasonable to me," Dee uttered.

"Reasonable! This is ridiculous," Maeve snapped.

Dee snapped back, "Please don't hold your opinion back for my sake."

Rowan took the folder and placed it on the corner of his desk.

Taking this as a dismissal, Dee took her leave and went back to her own office and closed her door. She sat back in her chair and closed her eyes. It was going to be unbearable waiting for his decision. She could hear Rowan and Maeve deep in conversation but their words were too muffled to decipher. She wished she'd left her door open. Her surge of confidence began to fade as time ticked away. She got up and paced back and forth. To calm down, she grabbed a coffee and carried it to her desk, where it sat untouched as she waited some more.

Meanwhile, in Rowan's office the atmosphere became volatile as soon as Rowan asked Maeve what she thought about Dee's presentation.

The ensuing explosion was entirely predictable. "You can't be considering this. It's the stupidest thing I've ever heard of. Tweedle Dee may have lost her memory but it's no excuse for you to lose your mind, Rowan. Have you even thought about this?"

Rowan turned to Maeve in anger. "The fun is over, Maeve. Dee deserves respect. Moreover, she has earned it. Do not let me hear you call her that again."

Their heated discussion continued, neither of them willing to concede.

It was late morning when Rowan and his minion entered Dee's office. She held her breath as she waited for his answer. Maeve was just as anxious.

Rowan's look was directed at Dee. "I like your proposal. It was thorough and well thought out. There's a ghost of a chance this will work," he said quietly.

When Dee saw the laughter in his eyes, she let out a long pent-up breath.

"Great," Maeve responded without an ounce of enthusiasm. She gave Dee her best disgusted look to which Dee paid no attention.

Dee, quick to pick up his meaning, responded. "I promise you this will be a howling success and everyone will have a wicked good time." Dee's comment made Rowan laugh. The change was astonishing. It made him look years younger.

Maeve was hardly amused, "You're both batty."

Dee suppressed a giggle and kept her face serious with tremendous effort, "See, even Maeve is getting into the spirit."

Rowan saw the glimmer of mischief that lingered in Dee's bright eyes. Her humor was contagious. "Oh, oh, there's mischief brewing now."

This was a side of Rowan that she'd never seen before. Who would have believed he had a sense of humor? His usual formidable disposition had masked this particular attribute.

Rowan winked at Dee, "You must have cast a spell on her." He wasn't sure if he'd ever engaged in such a ridiculous conversation.

"This isn't amusing," Maeve snapped. Their laughter echoed as Maeve left the room.

"I think Maeve's warming up to my idea," Dee said straight-faced.

Rowan laughed harder. "You have an odd sense of humor, very unique and somewhat warped." He felt that he was beginning to discover the real Dee that was slowly emerging from behind her veil of mystery.

Dee was the first to regain her composure. She pulled out another folder from her top drawer. "I have more sketches and notes I'd like to show you."

Rowan couldn't believe how easily Dee took control. "I do have a question. We've always had a live band for the dance. Why do you want to use a DJ instead of a band?"

Dee quickly responded, "We can't ignore the fact, as Maeve so adamantly pointed out, that this is obviously a less formal event. A DJ can be more selective of the music selection. The crowd will love to dance to theme songs like: Monster Mash, Transylvania Twist, Spirit in the Sky. You'd be surprised at how many theme-related songs there are. I've already spoken to a local DJ and he has agreed to dress up as Wolfman Jack."

My, God, this girl has been busy. "You were very thorough, not knowing if I'd agree to your proposal."

"You have to come in with your best anytime you want something, especially if you want others to believe in you. *Where did that come from? I'm hardly done yet.* I was thinking we could have a special menu for the bar and they'll serve signature cocktails."

"I'm nervous to encourage this. Do you have specific drinks in mind?" Rowan knew she did and could hardly wait for her reply.

Without blinking an eye she rolled off her list, "Morgue-a–Rita, Pina-Goulada, Bloody Mary, an obvious, and Vampire Kiss Martini which will have fangs hanging on the rim." Rowan couldn't get a word in even if he wanted to, as she continued, "The main course can be traditional but I think we need to have themed side tables. The appetizer table will feature items like deviled eggs, lady fingers which look like fingers with almond slivers for finger nails, as well as mummy wraps, small carved out pumpkins filled with dips."

Rowan felt he should take a deep breath on her behalf.

"The dessert bar will have a display stand featuring cupcakes that look like spiders and others will be adorned with witch hats. There will be trays with mummy pops, bat truffles, spider web cakes, monster strawberries dipped in chocolate."

"Besides being sure of yourself, you're very efficient aren't you?"

Dee nodded. "If you're going to do something, why not go for the gold?"

"I like your spirit, no pun intended this time, as well as your eagerness." Rowan was a smart man. He knew he'd struck gold with Dee. In spite of her inexperience she'd proven to be efficient, capable and an enormous help. She was a definite asset, youthful, energetic and enthusiastic. Besides everything else, he recognized that Dee paid attention to detail. He recalled the drawings she presented laying out the ballroom. She had captured all the details of decor with candelabras, cobwebs draping the doorways, black chair covers and tablecloths. He also remembered seeing a list of several costume rental shops with contact numbers and addresses. Dee had thought of everything.

Rowan was impressed with her presentation and with what she'd come up with just over the weekend. But he was somewhat concerned that all of her efforts had been focused on the party and not the Charity. Rowan decided to address this right away. "We've only discussed the banquet. You should take some time and educate yourself with Evelina Children's Hospital."

Dee took his comment at face value. She knew her proposal was only on her concept of the party segment. Now that he asked, she was ready with additional revelations. Because she had hit the floor running, she was already one step ahead of him. In a voice tinged with pride she began, "I researched the history of the hospital. I know it was founded in 1869 by Baron Ferdinand de Rothschild whose wife, Evelina and their child died in premature labor. In 1999 it was decided to re-establish Evelina Children's Hospital as a specialist hospital for children's services. The new hospital was completed five years later."

Rowan was pleased to see that Dee had done her homework in regards to the Charity and their facility.

With her enthusiasm mounting, Dee continued, "I spent Saturday morning at the hospital. It's a beautiful facility that doesn't have the feel of a hospital which I was pleased about. But I also had to appreciate the fact that it provided a comprehensive range of hospital services and care for patients from before birth, through childhood and right on up to adult services." Her enthusiasm continued to spill over. "I spoke with several of the administration staff as well as nurses and therapists. Besides the health centre, they provide services in schools, community buildings, even in patients' homes. They offer a wide range of support and counseling. I brought their pamphlets back with me so I can review them in depth and get an even better understanding of this wonderful facility."

Rowan was overwhelmed, not just with her knowledge of the Charity but her compassion for it. "Dee, I need an organizer, someone creative and not afraid to work hard. You've shown incredible initiative and I feel you'll thrive with this project. I would like you to be my co-chair for this Event." Rowan was confident that Dee would work with creativity and style and she was obviously very resourceful.

The unexpected request surprised Dee. "Your confidence in me is overwhelming."

"As well, you're very personable and mostly pleasant," Rowan teased.

"Is that a compliment?"

He smiled but refused to concede. "An observation."

"Have you discussed this with Maeve? I doubt she'll be very happy about this. You may have noticed that Maeve and I don't see eye to eye."

Rowan's brow lifted at the regret in her voice. "In the end, I can overrule her objections if I feel it's required. In time, she'll come around. She'll want what's best for the hotel."

The conviction in his voice eased Dee's concern. "What about my other duties?"

Rowan brushed this off as inconsequential. "This is a big project and very important to the hotel. So for now, you'll devote all of your time to this Event."

Dee was drawn to the idea and her mood lightened at the thought of not having to work with Maeve looking over her shoulder every day. She thought she witnessed a light smile from Rowan as if he knew what she was thinking.

Rowan wanted to reassure Dee, "Maeve will be here if you need her. She knows a lot but right now she isn't on board."

"You can say that again."

"Give Maeve a little time and she'll come around to your vision." Rowan had all the confidence in the world in Dee. "You haven't answered me yet."

Dee knew she was competent. "If I agree to your proposal I'd like you to provide me with a budget as soon as possible. And I want the freedom to come and go without question. We'll meet every Monday morning so we can share ideas and updates, but more important, we can discuss foreseeable problems. I'd like Maeve to let me talk to the staff and see who would be interested in some overtime. I'll pick my own team who will work directly with me. Besides a menu committee, I'll need a committee to help with decorating the hall."

"You're very direct."

"It saves time."

"I don't foresee any of your requests being a problem."

Rowan was being so agreeable that Dee shot him a suspicious look. "Let me ask you this. Are you willing to leave me on my own and allow me to come and go without reporting everything I do each day? I'm not willing to be cross-examined about everything I do. You either trust me or you don't."

"If I didn't trust you, I wouldn't have asked," Rowan said simply.

Dee let out a long breath while organizing her thoughts. Uplifted by such a vote of confidence, she agreed. "I'm your girl. Trust me, I've done it before." Dee laughed at the look on Rowan's face. "Just kidding. But I know I can manage this." To Dee's relief, he laughed.

Rowan was aware that Dee was filled with strength of mind along with her vibrant spirit. He was amazed that she could joke about her memory loss. Here again was another layer to this woman. "I know you're more than competent. You have tremendous instincts, you've got tenacity and you have the ability. And you'll have a challenge with Maeve if we go with this. But as you stated previously, you're always up to a challenge."

Dee knew Maeve didn't always understand her actions, let alone her humor. Unfortunately, Maeve had never made any effort to get to know her. Just knowing that Rowan believed in her made her feel more confident and less anxious. Dee knew she'd be busy and challenged every minute of the day until the Event was over.

Rowan called Maeve back into the office. "Dee and I have been talking and she has presented more points to consider for the Benefit."

Maeve looked irritably at Rowan while dismissing Dee with a shrug, "I have better things to do than run in here every time she has another bright idea."

"I agree, Maeve. So, Dee will be my co-chair as your time is better spent elsewhere." Maeve actually seemed at a loss for words. In an obvious huff, she excused herself. Rowan turned back to Dee, "For the next few days you and I can brainstorm and consider your inspirations." He paused before asking, "No sarcastic comment on Maeve's reaction?"

Dee thought about her answer. This was the time to rethink her attitude and take the high road. "Only on the inside. I'm learning to hold my tongue."

Rowan's eyebrow shot up in disbelief. "Since when?"

There was laughter in her eyes. "Since today. One has to start sometime."

"I wonder how long this will last."

Dee saw a glimmer of warm amusement in his eyes. Her own amusement faded and her tone became serious, "I will work really hard. But believe this, Rowan, I intend to make this Event a wonderful evening."

Rowan was impressed with her new maturity. He had no doubt she'd do just fine with both the Charity Event and with Maeve.

Dee was nervous about her volunteer shift at the hospital. Since Wednesday was Constance's Bridge night, it was the perfect night. It would break up her week and give her something to look forward to. Dee felt liberated in doing something independent of the hotel and her grandmother. She was surprised that she was nervous when it came time to meet the kids. She saw Beth in the corner and waved. The kids all laughed at Dee's accent but music was a universal language with the power to connect with everyone. It didn't take long to feel accepted.

The time flew by and all too soon it was time to take Beth back to her room. Beth was bubbling with joy. "That was so much fun. I can hardly wait until next week." They looked up when the nurse entered the room. It was time to get Beth settled so Dee took her leave.

As she was leaving, Dee noticed a young man cleaning up the art room and wondered if he was a volunteer. Dee stopped and smiled as she surveyed the disorder. There was stuff all over the floor. "Hi, I'm Dee. Would you like an extra hand?"

He stood up and rubbed his hand down his jeans before shaking her hand. He was casually dressed in worn jeans and long-sleeved shirt open over a cotton T-shirt. "Thanks, Dee. That would be great. The kids out-did themselves tonight. My friends call me Woody." He was of medium height with a slim build so he didn't loom over her slender frame as so many men did. Dee couldn't say that Woody was stylishly handsome but he had an interesting face and warm hazel-colored eyes. Humor was evident in the tilt of his brows and curl of his mouth. She noticed that he had a slight accent that was hard to place. Dee looked around the room and shook her head. Pieces of cut tissue paper in every fall color were all over the floor. "Whatever you were working on with the kids made a big mess."

"We finished making fall trees. Just wait until next month when we carve pumpkins. I try to schedule a project relating to an upcoming occasion like Halloween. It gives them something to look forward to. We'll dry the pumpkin seeds and use them when we do mosaics for Thanksgiving. Are you visiting someone?"

"I'm a volunteer and I just started tonight. Funny you should mention Halloween, that's what first brought me here to Evelina's. I'm co-chairing a Benefit that's raising money for this hospital. Because I'm not from here I wanted to see what the hospital was like and how and where we could help. This facility is amazing."

Woody studied her, appreciating her beauty. "You're American, aren't you?"

"I am. What about you? I haven't been able to place your accent."

"My mother is French and I studied art in Paris."

"The artwork displayed throughout the hospital is impressive," Dee expressed with genuine sincerity.

"The Virtual Artisan British Arts Organization had some of their artists collaborate to make the interior as fun and colorful as a hospital can be. They brightened up the rooms and hallways with murals and artwork. It helps make it seem like you're not in a hospital."

"It definitely helps to make the building feel more friendly. For some reason, I keep being drawn to the art pieces by Ashton Underwood."

Instantly Woody's curiosity was intensified. "What is it about his art that you like?"

Dee thought a moment before answering, "There's a free flow in his strokes with a subtle hint of light in his presentation. Even though there's an underlying sadness in some of his pieces, one is still left with a feeling of hope. His pieces remind me that hope is eternal." Dee was embarrassed when her eyes teared. She had no idea what brought it on.

Woody smiled in understanding. "Have you studied art? You're very knowledgeable."

"I don't think so. I know my Mom loved art in every form so I'm sure her passion was passed on to me."

Dee was unaware of her vague response. Her comment intrigued Woody even more. He knew he wanted to know more about this mystifying young lady. "You've made me curious. Can we grab a coffee after we're done?"

Dee's reply was hesitant, "I don't know you."

Woody's eyes danced. "You will if you agree to have coffee with me. I can't be too bad if I volunteer with kids, which I've been doing for over two years."

"I can't tonight. How about next week?" Woody seemed to be a very intriguing young man and she had liked him immediately. And he really had wonderful eyes. Intent and serious, and just a little shy.

"I'll look forward to it. See you next week," Woody said with a happy grin.

CHAPTER ELEVEN

Constance popped into Rowan's office with the hope of having a chat. She wanted to get Rowan's version on how things were proceeding with Dee and her new job.

Rowan rose from his desk. Constance seldom came to his office. They usually discussed business upstairs in her suite. He had a good idea as to why she was here.

"Am I interrupting anything?" Constance asked lightly.

"Of course not. Come, let's sit by the fireplace where it's more comfortable."

After a few minutes of idle talk, Constance casually asked, "How is Dee working out?"

Rowan smiled slowly, "Nobody has strangled her yet, but it's early. That's a positive start for now." They both laughed. He quickly came to Dee's defense. "I didn't really expect to be impressed with her but I am. From the first day she's proven her worth. Not only is she a quick learner, but she's also competent and responsible. Dee is making a conscious effort to control both her temper and her mouth. It doesn't always work. But she is trying."

"I have to admit that Dee's a lot like her mother. Phoebe was always feisty. How is it going between Maeve and Dee?"

"Interesting to say the least. Dee's fearless, so she can give as good as she gets and she doesn't back down. I can feel the tension brewing. Dee's like a volcano. I keep watching her because one day she's going to spew. And other times she's as cool as an iceberg and just as dangerous. The girl is definitely a contradiction. Under that cool veneer lays a fiery temper and she can go from frost to fire so quickly I just stand back and stare in amazement. Fire and ice."

Constance understood Rowan's comment and laughed.

"The Benefit is coming together beautifully. This is a good project for Dee. I like a lot of her ideas and I'm glad I gave her a chance. Dee is competent and extremely creative. Besides being highly organized, Dee likes to be in control. She's taken charge and is the boss of everyone. Dee definitely knows what she wants and when she wants it and in the end she usually gets her own way."

"Just like her mother did."

"Despite everything, I do like her, Connie. You were right, she does grow on you. She's young and full of passion. She can be amusing, adolescent and annoying. Occasionally, all at the same time. And then, unexpectedly she's mature and witty. I enjoy her energy and her enthusiasm. And yes, she can also be charming, bright and entertaining but always challenging."

"Sometimes they surprise you."

"You're right. There's no telling about people until you get to know them. Every time I figure some part of Dee out she surprises me with something else." Rowan had to admit that he was intrigued by Dee.

Constance felt better when she left Rowan's office knowing he was seeing her granddaughter in a better light.

Rowan called out to Dee as she was passing through to her office. Dee changed direction and went and sat down in front of him and asked, "What have I done wrong now?"

Rowan had difficulty controlling his smile as he handed Dee an envelope. In answer to her questioning look, he informed her, "It's month-end. Here's your first paycheck and well earned I must say. I don't know what you did before but I do know that you've proven yourself. I didn't expect you to be so capable." He rewarded her with an appreciative smile.

To her surprise Dee realized that she cared about his opinion

Rowan enjoyed the glow on her face as she brightened at his praise. "As you can see, it's my personal cheque. Due to the circumstances you can only deal at my bank. I've set an appointment with my bank manager who is making an exception so that we can get an account set up for you. I realize that independence is important to you so I knew you'd appreciate having your own account. We're meeting with him this morning at ten."

Dee was beginning to ask more questions now that she had adjusted to her circumstances. "I don't know why this has to be so complicated."

For a moment Rowan didn't know how to answer her questions. Rowan had to surrender the passports and the birth certificates for both Delaney and Desiree Dare to the authorities. Those authorities had put restrictions in place that would be removed once Dee regained her memory and positive identity could be confirmed. It was becoming more and more difficult to avoid revealing her past. Rowan shared what he could. "As previously discussed, the British authorities are holding your legal documents until you regain your memory." He couldn't share all of the details so he now understood better how Constance was struggling with the situation.

Dee frowned. Another obscure response but she let it go.

At the bank, Mr. Edwards, the bank manager, helped Dee through the process as though it were perfectly normal. With Rowan Le Baron as her guarantor it was all effortless.

They walked out of the bank with Dee feeling elated. She was no longer totally financially dependent on her grandmother. "Thank you. I really am grateful for my job and for your help today." This job was important to Dee and had become very personal. Dee believed she was drawing from her past and it was helping to restore confidence in herself and regain her sense of self. As a result, more and more flashbacks were occurring and puzzle pieces were beginning to piece together. Nothing significant, but it was a start. The weeks had gone by so quickly that she hadn't realized that August had slipped into September. It was also a reminder that her party was on Saturday.

CHAPTER TWELVE

Dee was trembling with excitement for the day of her party had finally arrived. She couldn't believe how it got here so fast. When her grandmother had first decided on the party, Dee was terrified with the thought of meeting more strangers. She could now accept that in time strangers become friends. Cal's image immediately came to mind. She was missing his perpetual smile and contagious laugh. Dee hadn't given up hope that she'd see him this weekend as promised.

Earlier in the day her grandmother had taken Dee to her bedroom. Constance pulled out a velvet box from the dresser drawer and lifted the lid. Inside laid an exquisite diamond chocker and earring set. "I had Rowan take these out of the vault this morning. This seemed the perfect occasion for the Malone diamonds. Please do me the honor of wearing them."

Dee could only gaze in wonder as Constance presented them to Dee. They were dazzling. Speechless, Dee nodded. She knew they'd be the perfect accessory for her dress.

Once Dee had finished dressing, she blinked in disbelief at her image in the mirror. Then she smiled, recognizing herself for who she was; a beautiful and well-dressed young lady. Taking a deep breath Dee took a final look in the mirror and pushed her fears aside.

When she joined her grandmother in the parlour, Constance beamed with pleasure. Her granddaughter looked elegant and poised.

Dee smiled at her grandmother in gratitude. She knew she looked fabulous. "You were right. A dress can definitely make a difference. I feel like I'm ready for anything."

"This is a very special night, my dear. You look stunning. Are you nervous?"

"Not really. My stomach is full of butterflies but it's because I'm excited, not because I'm worried. Thanks to you and our talks I think I can hold my own and do you proud."

"I have the utmost confidence in you. You're going to do fine so enjoy yourself. This is a very special night for both of us. I'm so excited to be introducing my granddaughter to everyone. It's going to be a wonderful party." Constance kissed Dee gently on her cheek.

Dee hugged her grandmother tight and whispered, "Thank you." And then it was time to go. Despite her grandmother's reassuring words, Dee couldn't suppress a tiny tremor of anxiety.

When they stopped at the entrance to the hall Dee believed she'd never attended such an extravagant affair before. She stood in awe. Her grandmother and Maeve had done a wonderful job of selecting the decorations. The primary colors were silver and black with a touch of purple for contrast. There were flowers everywhere and their heavenly fragrance filled the room.

Dee felt like she was about to step into a fairy tale and suddenly realized that everyone was looking at her. She pretended to be unaware of their stares and remained composed. Gratefully, not everyone was a stranger. There were a few familiar faces and her eyes were immediately drawn to Rowan.

Rowan and Maeve had arrived at the reception hall just before Dee entered. His face lit up in appreciation. It was as if a star had fallen from heaven and blessed everyone with its presence. Rowan's eyes remained on Dee without him being aware of it and he surveyed her from head to toe, missing nothing. Dee was breathtakingly beautiful. The silver evening gown was spectacular and fit her to perfection. Her black hair was pulled back in a chignon at the nape of her slender neck. Other than the flicker of apprehension in her awestruck eyes, her features were flawless. He continued to stare at her for a long moment. A tightness in his chest made him realize he'd quit breathing.

It had not gone unnoticed by Maeve. Perhaps Rowan's interest in Dee Dare wasn't as impersonal as she thought. Maeve's fierce ambition was to become Mrs. Rowan Le Baron and no one was going to get in her way. Maeve had to admit that the waif had morphed into an unexpected lady overnight. She was a glittering vision and her gown was a marvel. Maeve hadn't expected Dee to have such an amazing dress. She recognized the diamond chocker and earrings and had to admit that they were the perfect accessory. Maeve, who always draped her own frame with exquisite perfection, felt upstaged and jealousy quickly surfaced.

With a look of pure joy on her face, Dee turned toward the doorway, recognizing the infectious laughter of Cal O'Brian. She observed him as he came toward her. This was the first time she'd seen him in formal wear and he wore it well. He was so stylish and had so much swagger. "Cal, I'm so glad you made it. I must say you're looking very dapper." Dee smiled as Cal wrapped his arms around her. His timing couldn't have been more perfect.

"You look smashing my little chickadee. You're a vision and you will certainly be the star of the evening." With exaggerated gallantry, Cal put out both arms and said, "May I have the privilege of escorting the two most beautiful women here?"

Both women smiled in agreement. Constance because she enjoyed the flirtatious cad for who he was. And Dee for exactly the same reason.

The stream of guests seemed endless. Through it all Dee smiled warmly. Rowan introduced her to the Duke and Duchess of Devonshire. Dee liked them immediately. The Duchess was very impressed when Dee asked about their dog Beasley.

Maeve, unable to release the role she lived by, also made introduction to invited quests. "Let me introduce you to Leroy Jackson. He's one of our regular guests from the States. Leroy, this is Dee Dare, Constance's granddaughter."

Mr. Jackson, a portly man, extended his hand, "How do you do, Miss Dare."

Dee extended her hand and replied, "How do you do."

Constance smiled. Her granddaughter had been quick to apply the etiquette lessons that Boris had taught her. Boris always kept Constance informed of the times they spent together, including the first afternoon in the garden.

"Thank you for the invitation, Constance. I didn't realize you had family in the States." Leroy regarded Dee with interest. "Have we met before, Miss Dare?"

It was times like this that frustrated Dee. She stood staring at him unable to answer.

To her surprise it was Rowan who came to her rescue, "Nice try, Leroy."

Throwing Rowan a glance of gratitude, Dee smiled and answered pleasantly, "I'm new to London, Mr. Jackson. I'm staying with my grandmother for the time being."

Maeve recognized the protective move. She chose not to let it go and interjected, "Dee is originally from the States. Is it possible you met Leroy there?"

The composed tone of Maeve's voice made Dee look at her closely. Her phony smile annoyed Dee. She knew Maeve was baiting her because, of course, she knew that Dee wouldn't remember. With a calm maturity, Dee responded by purposely turning a question back to Mr. Jackson, "Where are you from?"

"I live in California but my business takes me all over the country. I'm in sales so you know how that goes. Do you like London?"

Dee realized that she really did. "I love London. It has so much history that I find very interesting and the city tastefully mixes the old with the new. Nor is there a shortage of things to do. I especially enjoy the theatre district." Rowan smiled at her in his knowing way and Dee colored slightly.

"Are you here on vacation?" Leroy inquired politely.

Dee was learning how to redirect and answer uncomfortable questions. "I have no definite plans at this time." If Dee's composure was ruffled, she never showed it.

Rowan, who had stepped away to request another setting be added at the head table for Cal, patted Leroy on the back. "If you'll excuse us our table is ready."

Maeve was annoyed that Rowan retained the seat next to Dee and placed Cal next to her.

Cal leaned over to Maeve, "Nose out of joint?"

Maeve let her cool mask slip for a moment. "Shut up, Cal."

The head table was elegantly set, the crystal glasses filled with carefully chosen champagne. Once everyone was seated Rowan helped Constance to her feet.

Constance raised her glass of champagne and turned to Dee. "Life can take us on very interesting, and at times, very complex journeys. The road is not always easy. There was a void in my life when my daughter, Phoebe, moved to America. Today, I'm happy that her daughter is now living here with me. Please join me in welcoming my granddaughter, Dee Dare."

Now that the initial introductions were over Dee forgot to worry and started to enjoy herself. Rowan engaged her in conversation on carefully chosen topics and shared stories about a few of the guests. His efforts to relax her were appreciated.

The band struck up as soon as the meal was over. Cal immediately rose and appeared at Dee's side. "May I have the pleasure of the first dance, Miss Dare?"

Dee accepted gracefully.

Cal took her hand and led her onto the dance floor. "I thought I better grab you while I can. I swear every man in the room is staring at you. Do you want the line-up of men who want to dance with you to form a line to the left or the right?"

Dee giggled. She loved his light-hearted teasing and realized how much she'd missed her dear friend. The music ended and Cal escorted her back to her seat where a young man was waiting. Dee took a quick sip of champagne and then accepted his hand and returned to the dance floor. She was enjoying herself tremendously and when she smiled her eyes sparkled with excitement.

The guest of honor was unaware that she had a presence about her that was magical. In no time Dee was surrounded by laughing young people, mostly men who were trying to capture her attention. They were drawn to her like a moth to a flame. Dee chatted politely throughout the evening as she was introduced to an unlimited blur of faces, and names could no longer be remembered. She floated with the mood of the crowd as the music and laughter surrounded her.

When the band struck up a new tune that was light and lively, Cal and Dee were back on the dance floor. They both moved with wild abandonment. When the dance ended, Dee's eyes were drawn to Rowan as he crossed the floor with the firm step of one who was intent on a particular goal. He moved toward her with an amused smile on his face. Instinctively, Dee took a step back to increase the distance between them.

When Rowan tapped Cal on the shoulder, Cal politely stepped aside. "Would you do me the honor of a dance, Miss Dare?" He smiled down at her and his mood seemed easy. Dee's heart beat frantically when she found his face only inches from hers.

The glint in his eyes made her heart pound a little quicker. Blinking quickly, she managed to struggle free of the momentary spell. The band began to play a slow dance. Rowan smiled as he took her in his arms. She had never noticed how broad his shoulders were. His warm breath sent a shiver of pleasure down her neck, making it difficult for her to concentrate.

"Without a doubt, you are the belle of the ball and a beauty to behold." She blushed, he smiled. Dee was transfixed by the look in his eyes. Rowan held her in the firm grip of his hands as he twirled her around the dance floor. She felt like she was floating in a dream, light-hearted and worry free. As soon as the dance was over Dee backed away and swayed unsteadily. Rowan took her arm and escorted her to her table.

Dee took a much needed gulp of champagne as she sat down next to her grandmother.

"Just a few sips, dear. A little champagne can settle your nerves but too much can be disastrous."

Dee giggled and took another sip. It was helping her to relax. Her eyes were automatically drawn to Maeve and Rowan on the crowded dance floor. She watched the power couple as they moved around the floor with such ease. They were so comfortable in each other's arms that Dee felt a twinge of longing. She didn't know why.

The night passed quickly. Cal was off in a corner chatting up a young lady who was obviously captivated by the dashing young man. Dee smiled. Cal really was a charmer with the ladies. Dee again filled her glass, now unaware of how much she'd been drinking. She let out a soft sigh. It had been a wonderful evening. She'd been surrounded by her grandmother's guests and their immediate acceptance of her was pleasing. The night had been both exhilarating and a little overwhelming.

Dee smiled contentedly and swayed to the music as she watched the dancers. All of a sudden the room became unbearably hot and it began closing in on her. Fanning her flushed face with one hand, Dee looked around for a means of escape.

"It looks like you could use some air."

Dee looked up in surprise at Rowan, "I thought you left."

"I escorted Constance up to her flat. Did you miss me?"

Dee looked deep into Rowan's dark teasing eyes. "Like a bad toothache," she countered.

"I told Constance I'd take care of you and make sure you got back to the flat safely. Come with me, Dee. The night air will cool you off."

"I am a bit warm," Dee confessed.

Rowan pulled her gently from her seat and arm in arm he escorted her out to the garden.

It was a clear night but the air was cool. Dee was grateful for the light evening breeze that helped cool her warm cheeks. She paused and took a deep breath. The fresh air seemed to help and after a minute or two her head quit spinning. Eyes dreamy, she stared up at the stars.

Rowan removed his jacket and placed it over Dee's shoulders. "Feeling better?"

Dee nodded, pulling the jacket tight. "You're so good to Gran and I know she's grateful to you for always keeping an eye on me. I don't like it, but I'm getting used to it." The champagne had loosened the young lady's tongue. It had been so long since she'd thought of Rowan as arrogant and unkind. A new and unfamiliar emotion seemed to have replaced it. His expression had changed as well and she saw something in his dark eyes she couldn't identify.

Dee turned to Rowan, eyes large and dejected. "This was an enchanting evening that I'll remember forever. Tonight was a fantasy. It was perfect. But my real life is very lonely. I feel like I'm alone on an island surrounded by a sea of strange faces. The waves of despair rise higher and higher. The rescue ship with all of my memories won't come and save me."

Rowan had never seen her look so vulnerable. Her words revealed the loneliness and the fear in a way that he had only sensed before. "It's on its way, Dee. Be patient a little longer."

Suddenly the color drained from Dee's face. "I don't feel very good."

"You're going to feel worse in the morning," Rowan said sympathetically. With a gentleness she hadn't expected, he lifted her in his arms. "It's time to call it a night, Cinderella."

Unaware of what she was doing Dee dropped her head to his chest. She looked up, her eyes meeting his, "Are you my Prince Charming?"

Rowan's voice was warm and sincere, "For tonight." He placed a light kiss on her cheek.

Dee felt the gentleness of his kiss. It sent a strange tingle though her. Dee touched her cheek and informed him, "Sleeping Beauty gets the kiss, not Cinderella."

Rowan smiled. She was such an unpredictable mix of worldly knowledge and naive innocence and he never knew which one would surface.

Dee felt awful when she woke up. Her first conscious thought was that her head ached. It more than ached, it throbbed. Unwilling to leave the comfort of her bed, she rolled onto her back and lay quietly as memories of the party flooded in. Her party had been wonderful and more that she expected. Finally, her eyes remained open. With a lethargic sigh, she forced herself to get up and face the day.

Dee looked a little heavy-eyed but she greeted Boris with her usual smile as she entered the kitchen.

"Good morning, Miss Dee. Madam is having coffee on the terrace. She said to let you sleep in. She's been talking about your party all morning. Did you enjoy yourself?"

"I think I had too much fun and too much champagne." Dee glanced over at the sideboard laden with hot plates of scrambled eggs and sausage. "Thanks for keeping breakfast but I think I'll just have coffee. I don't think I can eat anything."

Boris handed Dee a much needed strong cup of coffee as his eyes twinkled with understanding. "Let me know if you change your mind."

Dee passed through the French doors and joined her grandmother. The morning air was crisp and it felt refreshing. "Forgive me, I'm sorry it's so late."

Dee expected a well-deserved look of disapproval. All she saw was sympathetic understanding. "There was no reason to get up early. I knew you'd be tired after your big night. How are you feeling?"

"Not so great," Dee answered truthfully. She was filled with humiliation. "It's no excuse but I don't think I drink as a rule. I didn't think I had that much champagne because I was just sipping and I thought my heady feeling was due to the excitement of the evening. I hope I didn't do anything to embarrass you."

Constance smiled at her granddaughter with empathy. "Rowan informed me that you were a perfect lady. He discreetly brought you upstairs using the private lift."

Dee's eyes widened. "You've already spoken with him this morning?"

"No, I was still awake when he brought you up last night. Did you enjoy your evening?"

A contented sigh escaped. "Gran, it was a spectacular evening. It was like a dream and I floated through the evening on a cloud of happiness. Thank you."

Constance's heart filled with joy. "I heard the most glowing remarks about you all evening. Not only were you beautiful but you were graceful and poised. Sophistication at its finest. I think you out shined all of the other ladies." They laughed and both knew who in particular they were talking about.

"I'm glad you persuaded me to get my lovely gown." Dee smiled again remembering how beautiful it was. Together, they relived the wonderful evening but Dee kept the encounter in the garden with Rowan to herself. She was determined to put it out of her mind.

"What are you going to do today?"

There was no hesitation in Dee's response. "Not much. I'm going to go out to the garden for awhile. The fresh air feels good and I'd like some alone time after last night."

"Off you go. Grab a jumper; it's getting cooler."

Sitting in the garden, shaded by low hanging tree branches, Dee realized that her grandmother was right. Autumn had come early. Many of the leaves had turned color and had already begun to fall. The days were getting shorter and today there was a definite nip in the air. The sun hid behind a cloud, contributing to the growing chill that cut through her sweater. Shivering, Dee pulled it tighter before putting her hands in her pockets.

The refreshing breeze helped to clear her head. The entire evening was released from her memory so she sat quietly replaying the night over and over in her mind. She remembered how it felt to be in Rowans' arms when they were dancing and how it had made her feel. The knowledge of his power over her, and her own reaction, caused her to tremble. She tried to piece together her feelings.

Dee touched her cheek where he had kissed her. She closed her eyes knowing nothing had ever been sweeter than his soft lips on her skin. Dee smiled ironically. *As often as I've prayed to remember my past, I'd like to forget last night's kiss.* She refused to believe she could be so deeply affected by one small kiss. Especially from the arrogant man she had disliked from the moment they'd met. Reflecting back, she recalled her reaction to him the first day in the hospital as he stood in her room looking so formidable and unapproachable. Over the last couple of weeks, she'd seen a different side of Rowan. He was such a magnificent man in so many ways and she didn't want anything to spoil the new relationship she'd established with him. She remained lost in thought, unable to understand her unfamiliar feelings.

The man in her thoughts had been watching her. Rowan walked over and stood in front of her. His voice was tender, "I came by to see how you were feeling. May I join you?"

Dee quickly lowered her eyes. For some reason, her heart was beating very fast. Managing to regain her composure, Dee slid over to make room for him to sit. "Probably better than I should. Not good, just better. How did you know where to find me?"

"Isn't this where you usually go to escape?"

Dee nodded, wishing desperately for her heartbeat to slow. "I came here to think." Dee felt she had to clarify a few things between her and Rowan. She had put no thought to what she was about to say; she was merely reacting on an emotional level. She brushed her hair back over her shoulders and looked directly at Rowan. Her tone was serious when she spoke. "I have two things to say to you."

Rowan wondered what he was in for now.

With sober words, she started, "First, I want to thank you for taking care of me last night and seeing me safely back to the flat. For one reason or another, you always seem to be there for me." Dee hated the fact that she'd made a fool of herself and of course it would have to be Rowan that came to her rescue.

Rowan sensed that whatever Dee wanted to say next was very important because she seemed to be taking an unusual amount of time thinking about it.

Dee finally exhaled a deep sigh and said, "Second, I owe you an apology. When I first got here, I was very angry inside and it was so easy to take my anger out on you. I resented you for forcing me to come here. I felt so powerless because I couldn't control the situation and it continued to fuel my anger and I felt justified. I was feeling sorry for myself. Unfortunately, I was too angry to think clearly." She now realized that anger had helped to mask her fear. "I'm tired of being angry. It's such a negative emotion and I really hate the poor-me-attitude."

Rowan let her continue, shaking his head in bewilderment. She was innocent and open, and despite a strong will and a sharp tongue, she was still incredibly susceptible.

"Sometimes I regret that I can't keep my mouth shut so I'm sorry about the awful things I've said. I would like to say I didn't mean them. But at the time, I did. I would like to say it won't happen again but we both know that would just be a lie. However, I am working on it." Dee had spoken candidly and it had been a difficult conversation for her.

Rowan sat still, silently studying her, aware of her inner turmoil. Something in her had changed and he appreciated her honesty.

Dee hung her head in shame, for the man next to her had tolerated her angry tirades. She was grateful to him for being patient with her, for his gentleness and many other admirable qualities. She looked up at him as she bravely continued, "But sometimes one has to be honest with oneself. I was wrong. I judge people by the way they treat me and by the way they treat others. I feel I have judged you harshly. I may have thought of you as arrogant and rude. But you were never unkind. I didn't expect you to be so fair and reasonable. I will not make excuses for my behavior but I do apologize for it."

Rowan was impressed. She had endured so much, this fiery girl with her amazing courage. She had gone through such hardships and rose above them with her spirit intact. He tipped her chin looking deep into her eyes. "You are the most extraordinary creature, Dee. You're a constant surprise to me. One moment you're expressive and volatile. The next you're serious and strong-willed. You can be generous and kind. You continuously present a duality of opposites and interchangeable personalities."

Dee saw his expression alter. For an instant, she thought she saw a flash of tenderness.

"I've never dealt with a woman like you. Sometimes I don't understand you." Now that Rowan had begun to get a better sense of who she was he was curious to know more. "Who are you, Dee Dare?"

"I ask myself that every day." Her voice was barely a whisper.

Once again he saw the haunted look in her eyes. Neither of them said a word. Dee sighed and rose. Rowan stood up at the same time. They walked back into the hotel in silence but it was not an uncomfortable silence.

Late in the afternoon, Cal called on her. "I wanted to see you again before I left. Can we go for a walk?"

Arm in arm, they walked along the streets. Agreeing they were both hungry, they stopped at a pub in the neighborhood and ordered fish and chips on newspaper. They took a corner booth that offered a little privacy.

Dee studied him, thinking what a sweet person he was. Suddenly, Rowan's image came to mind. There was no comparison. To the outside world, Cal appeared to be a man without a care in the world. He always wore a devil-may-care attitude. He was a charmer, yes, but Cal was also very intelligent and caring. Today, Cal appeared to be troubled. She searched his face, noting the uncharacteristically grave eyes and set mouth. "Is something the matter, Cal?"

Cal tried to keep his tone casual, hoping to conceal his feelings for this incredible young woman. She had captivated him from the moment they met. Now that he had seen her again, he realized he cared for her more than he realized. Besides being beautiful, smart and funny he knew she was also sensitive and compassionate. "Did you miss me, Dee?" Cal knew he had missed her. He had thought of her often.

"I missed you so much at first and my loneliness returned. My heart filled with joy when I heard your voice last night. My bestie was back." Dee's generous smile lit up her face.

Cal's eyes never left hers. His voice was low without its casual lightness as he confessed, "You've stolen my heart, Miss Dee."

"I doubt that your heart is that easily taken. You'll leave tomorrow and return to Oxford and continue to charm all the girls."

The unintentional rejection hurt Cal more than he could imagine. He didn't bother to confess that it was different with her.

Dee looked at him more closely. Seeing the hurt in his eyes she suddenly realized he was serious. Cal's charm had captivated her and, to make everything more complicated, she genuinely liked every single thing about him. So why didn't she have the same feelings for him? She knew it wouldn't be fair to allow a relationship to blossom between them. She valued their friendship too much to do that. When Cal took her hand, she realized she had mentally drifted. And then it hit her and her heart skipped a beat and a flicker of new emotion crossed her face. Dee was completely unprepared to deal with the earthshaking thought. Was she falling in love with the Bear? Dee immediately shook her head in denial.

Some of the brightness had gone out of his day when Cal realized his feelings weren't reciprocated. He was quick to recover and the momentary sadness in his eyes was gone as he smiled one of his charming smiles, "It was good to see you again. I'm heading back early in the morning. Mail me an invitation and, if I can, I'll come back down for the Charity Benefit."

Dee was sad that Cal was leaving again. She kissed his cheek gratefully. "Cal O'Brian, you truly are my best friend. You were my first friend I had here. However, we should go before they think I've forgotten my way back."

This was one of the many things Cal enjoyed about her. She wasn't afraid to make fun of herself and her unique situation.

They chatted good-naturedly on the way back to the hotel. A troubled wind had sprung up and large thunder clouds had gathered overhead. It was only a matter of time before the bulging clouds would burst. They stayed close to each other as the wind whipped through the open spaces between the buildings and thunder cracked in the distance.

Hand in hand, they walked into the lobby. Both Rowan and Maeve were standing at the reception desk. Maeve scowled as they passed by while Rowan gave them a brief nod.

Dee retired early but couldn't sleep. Now that her party was over, it was time to dedicate her energy to the Charity Benefit. She grabbed her folder and crawled back into bed where she began making a list of things she wanted to accomplish the next day. The project made her feel alive and it gave her a reason for getting up every morning. Dee knew that the invitations were priority so she needed Rowan to approve them right away so they could be ordered. Once her list started, it continued to grow quickly as new ideas came to mind. When she started to yawn she glanced at the clock. It was late. She turned off her light, reminding herself that she'd put in a better days work with a good night's sleep. She smiled to herself as she rolled over. She was content because she loved working and enjoyed what she was doing.

Dee slipped into the private lift, pressing the lobby button while mentally going over the morning work. As soon as she was in her office, she pulled out her list from her Benefit file. All of her information was entered in the computer but she still made a hard copy folder for quick reference. She could take it along with her and jot down notes. After drawing up her timeline she started making detailed notes of what needed to be done first. She had gone down early but promptly at nine o'clock Dee joined Rowan in his office.

They were chatting away when Maeve joined them. She was miffed. It was evident that Rowan and Dee were getting along all too well now that they were working together every day.

Respectful of everyone's time, Rowan quickly passed the meeting over to Dee.

Dee glanced down at the list on her clipboard and got right to the point. "The priority items on my list are the invitations and the guest list." When Dee looked up she took immediate exception to Rowan's look. Thinking he was mocking her, she gave him a look. "Yes, I make lists. It helps me to organize my thoughts and formulate a plan. If you're not organized, you end up worrying about every detail. Lists are the key to true organization."

"Well, it appears to work for you. You're very efficient and you certainly know what you're doing," he admitted as he looked over his own notes.

Dee continued to run through her list. At the end of the meeting, she asked, "Any questions?" Both shook their heads so Dee rose and motioned to Rowan, "Good, then come with me and you and I can get down to business." Rowan obediently followed Dee.

Dee opened another folder on her desk. "These are the invitations and thank you cards that I'd like to order. If you'd check them for possible errors or changes and give your final approval, I'll order them today. As you can see, I'm adding an insert with names of several costume rental stores. This will help those who would prefer to rent instead of coming up with their own costumes."

Roman placed his hand on Dee's shoulder as he leaned forward to take a look. "I love the theme 'Spooktacular Masquerade Ball' and your layout is great." He saw her file folder. "I see you've named your file Project Orange. Are you trying to push Maeve's buttons?"

"Maybe a little," Dee confessed with a wide smile.

Rowan enjoyed seeing Dee's sense of humor and he was seeing it more often. He also realized she wasn't a pushover and fought back in subtle ways.

"If we order the invitations today, they'll do a rush order and will courier them to the hotel by the end of the week. Would you be able to check over the invitation list from last year and amend as necessary?"

Dee just continued to impress Rowan. "How do you manage to get these favors done?" When Dee smiled he laughed. "It never hurts to ask, right?"

"Right. That and my irresistible charm. Once I reminded them that we are long time customers, they agreed to expedite our order at no extra cost. As soon as the invitations arrive I'll get them labelled and mailed out." Once again, Dee had to wonder what she did in her old life. Dee got up and headed over to the coffee machine. "Would you like a coffee?"

"Sounds good."

Dee poured a cup and handed it to him before she poured her own.

"Thanks. Any suggestions for my costume, Dee?"

Dee started to giggle. "You dare to ask? You're on your own with that. I haven't even taken a minute to decide on my own. Rowan, this week I'll talk to staff members in an informal interview and see who would be interested in some overtime. I have a couple in mind, and as I said, I would like to pick my own team."

"Check with Maeve." Rowan stopped mid-sentence as soon as he saw Dee's expression.

The offhand comment stung. Dee was grateful to Rowan for giving her the Charity Benefit project. But his casual remark immediately got her back up and she decided it was time to make things clear. "I'm the co-chair of this Event," Dee announced with a determined look.

Before she could say anything else, Rowan stopped her. "I owe you an apology. You're right. I put my trust in you for a reason." It had impressed him that Dee had refrained from blurting out a comeback and actually exercised self-restraint. "Aren't you going to tell me how offended you are?"

"I thought you could read minds." Dee waited a minute. Once again in control of her emotions, she continued, "I was about to add that I will, of course, run it by Maeve so there will be no conflict with scheduling." She turned and left.

Rowan felt he had been put in his place and had to admit that he deserved it.

Dee noticed the boxes on her desk when she arrived at work in the morning. She called out to Rowan in excitement, "They're here; the invitations are here!"

Rowan entered and sat on the corner of her desk. "Open a box so we can take a look."

Like a child on Christmas morning, Dee tore into the box and pulled one out and handed it to Rowan and then took one for herself. She looked up and giggled in delight, "This is real."

Rowan smiled at the excitement in her voice and nodded his approval of the invitations. "Let's get them addressed and in the mail. It's time to see how Society will respond."

At the end of a hectic week Dee was sitting at her desk having a full blown panic attack. *What if no one decides to come because they don't like the theme? Should I have hired a band instead of going with a DJ? Will guests take offense to the menu items and novelty drinks? What if Maeve is right and no one likes the photo booth? God forbid if Maeve is right.*

Rowan popped in for a quick chat. Right away he could sense that something wasn't right. "What's wrong? Did Maeve upset you?"

Dee's brow was creased in a frown and her head was throbbing with a tension headache. Her usual confidence had vanished and her eyes were clouded with worry. "What if we made a big mistake going with a theme night? What if I was wrong? I don't want to let you down, Rowan. You've put all of your trust in my concepts."

The anxiety in her surprised him. "This is not the perky, confident Dee I know." He gave her a comforting pat on her shoulder. "It's a novel idea and somebody told me it would be a howling success. I have no doubt that she'll be right. We're in this together." There was a quality in his voice that reassured her.

When Dee spoke again, her voice was calmer and, thanks to Rowan, she felt somewhat more in control of the situation. "I think I'm really tired. If you'll excuse me, I'll call it a day."

Chapter Thirteen

Woody and Dee had fallen into the habit of going for coffee after their shift. Tonight they decided on a coffee house along the Thames River. They were becoming good friends and Dee valued their friendship. She didn't have any friends other than Cal.

Her two friends couldn't be more different. Dee cherished the easy companionship she had with Cal. He was someone to explore with or to laugh with over a meal. He was a charmer and a flirt who was honest, open and funny. She liked him immensely and missed him now that he was back in school. Woody, on the other hand, was artistic, serious and compassionate. Everything about him suggested a man of honor, someone you could rely on and trust. Dee appreciated the comfortable relationship she had with him.

Dee tucked her arm through his as they strolled along the crowded boardwalk. They stopped and stood side by side looking out at the river while they listened to the music. It felt natural and comforting when Woody put his arm around her shoulders. They soon moved on and popped into the coffee house. As usual, they talked about the kids, especially Beth. Dee reflected sadly, "I'll never forget the day I met Beth. It was the first day I went to the hospital to see what Evelina's was all about. On the way out I saw her sitting alone staring out the window. For some reason I was drawn to her and I went over and sat down. Within the hour, we'd developed a special bond. It's something I can't explain."

"I've watched you with the kids. They all bond with you."

Dee saw the warmth in his eyes and smiled gratefully. She hadn't expected to connect so deeply with these kids. "I don't think I've done anything as meaningful as volunteering. We share smiles and I brighten my own day in the process. I take these feelings with me and hold on to them all week. I can hardly wait to go back each week."

Woody understood. "Instead of taking their mind off their problems, it's the reverse."

"I know. I leave hoping that at the end of the day I've touched those wonderful souls as deeply as they've touched mine. I draw on their courage that they so bravely demonstrate." There was such passion in her voice. "When I see them my heart fills up. But it also breaks knowing that patients, like Beth, will never go home, never get to grow up. Their lives are cut short because of sickness."

For a moment their eyes met and he looked sad and distant. He understood all too well. "Tomorrow isn't promised to any of us so we all need to make the most of today."

"That's why this Benefit is so important to me. If we can make a difference in any way we'll have achieved our goal. But sadly, it's still only a small step. I'd like to find something special to help raise funds. Oh, Woody, I just had a brilliant idea. Do you remember the day we met and we were talking about Ashton Underwood's art?"

Woody nodded, for he remembered everything about that day. He was drawn to the vibrant lady with the ebony hair that flowed down her back like molten lava. Woody's artistic eye appreciated her face that was etched with beauty and strength. Her face was a painter's dream. She had a timeless beauty and flawless features. Her soulful eyes reflected both innocence and amusement but were always overshadowed by a trace of loneliness. Now that he knew her better, he could also see that even though she laughed freely there was always a veil of sadness in her eyes.

Dee felt as though they'd been friends for a long time. It allowed her to be open with him. "I'd love to have one of his pieces to raffle at our Charity Benefit." Dee sighed heavily, "Forget it. It's a crazy idea. I'm sure a piece of his would be very dear. I let my imagination run and like usual my mouth follows."

Woody couldn't resist asking, "Why one of his pictures?"

Dee responded with passion, "I told you that I was immediately drawn to his paintings in the hospital. Most of his pieces appear whimsical. At first glance they seem to be fanciful and light-hearted. But every time I look at them they draw me in and I lose track of time staring at them. He's able to capture feelings and emotion with his strong emphasis on facial expression." The smile had left her face and a shadow crossed over her eyes. "There's one in particular of a young lady sitting in a garden. A book is open in her lap and she is gazing out at the sunset. There's no mistaking her loneliness and longing. The feeling is so real that it draws you in and you find yourself wondering if she lost her true love or is longing to meet him."

He enjoyed her enthusiasm. "I know the artist. Let's see what I can do on your behalf."

"Keep in mind I have a limited budget and it is a Benefit to raise money."

Woody nodded in understanding. "Maybe, he'll be kind enough to donate."

"That would be awesome but highly unlikely and not expected. But I would appreciate you seeing what you can do."

Woody was utterly intrigued by her, convinced that Dee had some mystery in her life. "Your eyes are often so serious. Perhaps that's why I feel compelled to make you smile."

Dee was sincere when she said, "Not only do you make me smile but I feel I can always talk to you. You're a dear friend."

There was something rare and strange about this woman that touched his heart. He could see in her eyes that there was something buried. Pain, sorrow, loneliness. All were evident. She had a mystery about her that he couldn't penetrate. It made him ask, "What do you long for?"

Dee looked up at Woody. She knew the time had come to explain her unusual circumstances. She swallowed hard, "You'll be surprised. I actually came to London from a hospital in the States. I now live here with my grandmother." And so it began. Dee told him the whole story as Woody listened in sympathy. "I expected my memory to come back in a few days and I'd return to my life in the States. It's been a few months now. I've accepted that I can't make it happen but I haven't given up hope."

Woody cared for this woman with no past. He drew a deep breath, pressed her hand to his lips, and kissed the palm. For Dee, it was a comforting gesture. "I hope you get your memory back soon, Dee. A loss is difficult no matter what it is." Woody felt it was his turn to share. "I lost my sister three years ago. Hannah was sick and died. She had just turned sixteen."

A chill ran down Dee's spine while listening to his words. Once again, she felt her past was presenting itself, but she didn't know the connection.

The conversation changed back to Halloween and quickly moved to Christmas. "It'll be here before we know it. Hyde Park helps everyone get in the spirit with their Winter Wonderland Festival featuring ice sculptures, fairground rides and Christmas markets. Norway always sends a huge Christmas tree that stands in the Square. It's a token of gratitude for Britain's help during World War II. The tree is sixty to seventy feet tall and is decorated with hundreds of white lights. On the first Thursday in December the lights are switched on. It's an epic celebration. We should make a day of it, Dee."

Dee was delighted by the invite. "You have a date. I'll mark my calendar."

"There's an outdoor rink in Hyde Park that circles the Victorian bandstand where the tree will be. We can go ice skating first and then stroll around the park and take in the festivities before we watch the tree lighting."

Dee's eyes widened, "I would love to except for the first part."

Seeing the look of fear on her face, Woody asked, "Don't you skate?"

"I've roller skated." Dee's eyes lit up. Another fact for the memory bank.

"I meant ice skating. It's one of London's favorite pastimes. Where's your sense of adventure?" he asked with increasing amusement.

"I must have left it in the States," Dee said with a giggle.

"You have to give it a go."

Reluctantly, Dee agreed.

Time slipped away unnoticed as the chatted. It was late when Dee returned to the hotel.

Constance was waiting up. "I was worried, you're so late."

Dee winced at the pointed tone and was quick to apologize. "Woody and I lost track of the time. I'm sorry that I worried you."

Constance had to remind herself that adjustments and consideration were required by both of them. Constance was certain that Dee had been very independent before the accident. Her displeasure was quickly gone. "How is the volunteering going?"

A soft smile warmed Dee's face. "When I came back here after my first week of volunteering I had to sit quietly and think about the experience. I was so nervous. I stepped into the music room and there they were, waiting. All eyes were on me and I wasn't sure what to do. Kids are amazing. I knew right away that it didn't matter what we did. They just needed someone to spend time with them. It's fulfilling when you can bring a smile to someone's face as you take them away from their problems for a brief moment. I feel a real strong connection to them and I look forward to going back and seeing them each week."

"They're lucky to have you."

"I'm the lucky one. It's very rewarding to do something for somebody else. The children give me far more than I give them. I began thinking of others instead of just myself."

"You have a kind heart, Dee."

"Today there was a young boy sitting in a wheelchair. One of his legs had been amputated just below the knee. He had a pull toy tied to the back of his chair and was wheeling down the hallway as a toddler with braces ran behind. Both were laughing with pure joy. They were just kids playing and having fun. Neither noticed that the other was disabled. In that brief moment life was so honest and very meaningful."

"The facility is incredible. It's bright, sunny and colorful and presents a happy ambience. Each level of the hospital is named a different part of the natural world from the Ocean on the ground floor to the Sky on the top floor. The floors with wards are named after animals and they overlook a spacious conservatory called the Beach. The Beach is the social heart of the hospital and this is where I spend my time with the kids. We gather together and play musical instruments and sing."

Constance knew that Dee was unknowingly drawing on aspects of her life from before the accident. Constance was happy and sad at the same time. Happy that Dee's subconscious was releasing more than general information. Sad that Dee would have so much more to face when more specific memories returned.

For a moment Dee's eyes clouded over. She told her grandmother about Beth and the special bond that had developed between them. Their friendship allowed Dee to accept life under all circumstances and to accept what she couldn't change. Her voice broke when she told Constance that Beth was dying and had only a few weeks left. "Beth made me realize that my own suffering was minor in comparison to what so many of those children are going through. My life will continue regardless while her short life is nearing the end."

"It's sad but life isn't always fair." Meaningful words that impacts lives again and again.

Dee wiped at her eyes, "I know that Gran. Maybe that's why volunteering is so important to me. It makes me feel good doing something that makes someone else feel good. So I go and share my love for music with the kids. There are a lot of different activities that happen at the Beach besides music. Woody has some of them doing art projects and I've seen giggle doctors who are strange and silly but they make the kids laugh with their magic shows and balloon animals. Their laughter becomes music to our ears."

Constance couldn't resist asking, "So, who is this Woody?"

Dee giggled. "It's late, Gran. We'll save the topic of Woody for another time."

When Dee wasn't thinking about the Benefit her mind was on Beth. The little girl was fading quickly and Dee's heart ached. Dee tried to spend as much time as she could with her because Beth had now been confined to bed. This was becoming more difficult because the upcoming Benefit was also requiring more time as the Event date was fast approaching.

This week was Woody's special craft night with the kids. They were going to carve pumpkins for their rooms. His kindness amazed and astounded Dee when he kindly announced, "I'll carve one for Beth."

Dee appreciated his thoughtfulness. Woody had a kind heart. "It would be nice if we could go together and give it to her." Determined to do it as soon as possible she stated, "I'll come back tomorrow night if that works for you."

"Are you okay?" Woody asked as he saw a flicker of pain cross her face.

Dee quickly averted her face, trying to hide the distress in her eyes. "I'm fine."

Woody knew better for they were both upset about Beth. He felt the same sense of helplessness. With unbelievable gentleness, he gently touched her on the arm. "This is a hospital for sick kids, Dee. Not all of them get better."

Dee only nodded as tears pooled in her eyes. Beth was one of them. She probably wouldn't even see Halloween. It was so unfair. Unable to ignore the jab of pain in her heart, the tears spilled over.

As soon as Dee had finished her shift she went up to Beth's room. When Dee stepped inside the room her breath caught when she saw Beth. Tonight, Dee thought the little girl looked worse and appeared to be more listless. Dee went over and sat beside Beth. She took the little girl's hand in her own. "Hi Beth."

"You can call me Bethie like my mom does." Her eyes were solemn when she said, "I'm not scared to die, Dee, just sad. Mom is going to miss me and Sophie won't have a big sister anymore." Beth's breathing became labored. "I'm really tired. Will you sing me a lullaby?"

Dee was struggling not to cry as she climbed up on the bed and took Beth in her arms. She kissed the child's brow and slowly rocked back and forth. Heartbroken, Dee began to sing, unaware that the lullaby was the one her mom sang to her twins when they needed comforting. Dee lay beside Beth long after the child had fallen asleep and wept.

The next morning Woody called to see if Dee could meet him there right after lunch. He had forgotten about a previous appointment and it was one he couldn't reschedule.

"I'll make it work. Let's meet at the Beach at our usual spot at two o'clock." Dee was unaware that Maeve had stepped into Rowan's office. She overheard the end of Dee's conversation and quickly drew her own conclusion. Thinking of Beth, Dee put aside her unfinished tasks and headed to the hospital.

Dee gently opened the door to Beth's room. "I thought you would like to meet someone new." Dee opened the door wider and Woody stepped in with a pumpkin. "This is my friend, Woody. We thought you needed a jack-o-lantern for your room."

"I like it because it reminds me of you and my mom." Beth looked over and explained to Woody, "Mommy and Dee like to smile but they have sad eyes."

Woody was surprised at the awareness from such a young girl but she was right.

Dee and Woody stayed until Beth fell asleep. They were both speechless as they parted ways. Days like this were difficult.

Maeve was in the lobby when Dee returned from visiting Beth. Maeve intercepted Dee. "You were away all afternoon."

Dee was upset and in no mood for a confrontation. "Observant as usual, Maeve."

"Where were you?"

"It's none of your business. I don't report to you."

Dee couldn't concentrate once she was in in her office. Beth's quaint face was a permanent image in her mind and Dee fought to control her emotions. Dee was glad to see the end of the day.

"What's wrong?" Constance asked when Dee stepped into the flat. Constance always seemed to read her moods.

Dee shared her day including her encounter with Maeve.

"You did what you felt you needed to do. I'm sure you made a little girl very happy."

Not trusting her voice, Dee only nodded. She wanted so badly to believe it. As usual, Dee felt better after talking to her grandmother.

In the morning, Dee headed straight to the kitchen to discuss the dessert menu with the baker. Together, with Sarah, they reviewed the staffing schedule and agreed on who would help them with the table centerpieces. It was mid-morning before she went to her office. She was surprised to see that Constance was in with Rowan. It was evident that she was the topic of conversation and Rowan appeared to be in a foul mood.

Rowan got right to the point. "I heard that you left right after lunch yesterday and you went to meet someone at the beach."

Dee was puzzled by what Rowan just said and was uneasy with his harsh tone. Looking bewildered, she blinked at him. She looked over at her grandmother and knew she would never have said anything. Suddenly, Dee realized that Maeve must have overheard her talking to Woody on the phone. As angry as she was at Maeve's high-handedness, Dee bit her lip before answering. "You authorized open hours," she reminded him evenly.

Dee's thoughts were confirmed when Rowan stated, "I'm sure Maeve felt you shouldn't be taking advantage of time away from work when the hotel has such a significant Event approaching. Were you away on business?"

Dee had never lied to him before. She wouldn't start now. "No." She placed both hands on her hips and glared at him. She refused to defend herself. Instead, she challenged back, "Is the project suffering?"

Rowan had to admit that Dee was putting in a lot of extra hours, including on the weekends. But that wasn't the point.

"Tell me, Rowan, do you have any complaints about my performance?"

"Not until now," Rowan said with a disapproving look.

Yeah, another point for Maeve. Hurt and angry, Dee turned and left without a word. As much as she wanted to slam the door, she didn't give in to her anger. She wouldn't give Rowan the satisfaction of letting him see how much he had upset her.

Reacting to Dee's abrupt exit, Rowan snapped at Constance in frustration, "I thought you said she didn't run away from difficult situations."

Constance stared at him long and hard. "She doesn't. Just difficult people."

Rowan was shocked by Constance. "What do you mean by that?"

"You accepted Maeve's slant on the situation without giving Dee an opportunity to explain. That wasn't fair. I can see why Dee gets upset with you at times."

Like Dee, Constance walked out without saying another word leaving Rowan alone in his office wondering what just happened. Exasperated, Rowan swore under his breath.

Dee managed to stay out of both Rowan and Maeve's way by locking herself in her office. She reviewed her file. Everything was in place with her timeline but she knew there would be unexpected surprises. Just before four o'clock Dee took another call expecting it to be Benefit related. She froze when the voice on the other end said, "Dee, this is Noreen Stone, Beth's mom. Bethie's breathing has changed and it's close to the end. She's asked for you. Is there any way you can come to the hospital?"

All color left Dee's face. She knew it would come to this but it came too soon. She swallowed hard but the lump in her throat remained. Dee sucked in her breath and leaned back in her chair as the tears gathered. She closed her eyes seeking the strength to face the task that lay before her. "I'm on my way." Dee hung up and left.

The door of Beth's room was ajar and the atmosphere in the room was painful. The lights had been dimmed, the curtain drawn. Death itself seemed a tangible part of the sterile room. *This isn't fair. Why is death calling for such a young soul? This little girl hardly had any time to live.* Even though the room was cloaked in darkness, she could see Beth's still form. Dee hovered in the doorway and took a deep breath and somehow managed to compose herself. She would be strong for Beth. Forcing herself to show none of her emotions Dee put a smile on her face and stepped inside.

Noreen Stone rose from a chair on the far side of Beth's bed. She was a slim woman in her early thirty's with a mass of curly red hair. She was too young to look so worn out. "It's so nice to meet you, Dee. Bethie talks about you non-stop." She stepped forward and hugged Dee. When they pulled away, both women had unshed tears in their eyes. "Thank you for coming."

Hearing their voices, Beth opened her eyes. Her little face was drained of all color; her thin arms lay on top of the covers. Dee stood beside the bed and stared down at her unmoving body. Dee pulled another chair to the other side of the bed and took one of Beth's limp hands in her own. She smiled down at Beth and gently caressed her cheek. It took all of Dee's effort to keep her voice steady, "I'm here, honey."

Beth looked up at Dee. Her smile was feeble, her voice was weak, "I knew you'd come."

The atmosphere in the room was painful. Dee willed herself not to cry. Not now. She would be strong. "Isn't this nice, I get to meet your mom."

Beth didn't answer; she just closed her eyes. It wasn't long and Beth was asleep. The ladies kept their voices low as they talked, one on each side of the bed holding Beth's hands.

As Noreen sat across from Dee, she talked about Beth in a strangled voice. "Bethie was first diagnosed when she was four. She was always a happy, healthy child but she had started complaining that she hurt. Her dad and I thought it was growing pains but they didn't go away. It just kept getting worse. In my heart I knew something was wrong."

A wave of anguish washed over Noreen's face as she recalled that moment two years ago like it was yesterday. "I remember every word the doctor said. Our little girl had bone cancer. Treatments began the next day. The next few weeks, then months, became a blur of tests and treatments. We've spent too much time in this place." Bitterness crept into Noreen's voice, "Our family life was turned upside down. My husband couldn't cope. We divorced last year. It's times like this that makes it so much harder being a single parent. I'm lucky though. My mom has been a tremendous help. Sophie is with her now."

Dee wondered how this woman was going to be able to cope once her little girl passed away. She listened as Noreen continued to talk, never letting go of Beth's hand.

"After her initial treatments, Bethie was in remission until this spring. When her cancer returned, they gave her only a few months to live. Bethie is a fighter and she's fought a difficult and courageous battle." She looked down at her daughter. "She has no more fight left in her."

The hours slowly ticked away long into the night. "Do you have to work in the morning?" Noreen sounded so weary.

Without hesitation Dee said, "I'm staying. You won't have to be alone, Noreen."

Just before midnight the nurse came in to check on Beth and shook her head, confirming that Beth had passed away. In that moment in time it was as if all life ceased and no one in the room took a breath. Silence fell over the room. There was nothing the two women could say. No words could eradicate the pain. The two women held hands as released tears streamed down their faces. Dee quietly left the room, giving Beth's mother time alone with her daughter to grieve and say her good-bye.

Dee was exhausted when she got home. As soon as she looked at her grandmother she started to cry. "It's been a difficult day. Beth is gone." Constance took Dee in her arms and held her tight.

CHAPTER FOURTEEN

Dee started in on the pile of mail that Maeve had dropped on her desk. She sorted through it and, to her delight, most of it was replies of attendance for the Benefit. She was flushed with excitement when she joined Rowan and Maeve for their weekly meeting.

Rowan was standing at the window deep in thought. He turned around with a concerned expression. "We've had such a huge response to the Benefit and we're now getting requests from people not on our list asking if they can attend. Can we handle more guests, Dee?"

Maeve updated them further. "Even the Duke and Duchess of Devonshire will be attending the ball. I've already booked them into their usual suite."

Rowan was surprised. "I don't recall them attending in previous years."

Maeve shook her head, "They haven't. When the Duchess called, she said all of Society has been talking about the Masquerade Ball and said no way were they missing it."

Dee opened her file and looked at her guest list and quickly added in the replies. "Fortunately, most have now replied. How many more are you expecting?"

"Another thirty at least," replied Maeve. With a look of exasperation, she glared at Dee before turning to Rowan. "I knew this would get out of control. What did I tell you?"

"Over-reacting won't get us anywhere." After taking a deep breath, Dee did a quick sketch. "We can manage it. We'll have to do some reorganizing but we can accommodate another forty-eight but that is the maximum."

Maeve leaned over and took a look at Dee's sketch. "Why not set up the appetizer table on the wall closer to the kitchen. It can be cleared during dinner and set again with the array of desserts. Due to the higher number of guests we'll have two bars instead of one. It'll be less congested and we eliminate a long line-up at one bar."

Dee had expected more ridicule from Maeve, not practical suggestions. "I think you're right. Then we can put the photo booth on the same wall as the food table."

Maeve looked over at Dee in disbelief. "I still think that's a stupid idea."

Rowan interjected before this discussion could escalate into an argument. "A lot of guests have booked in on the Friday night and are staying for the whole weekend."

Dee's mind was always working. "I've been thinking about that, too."

"Should I be scared?"

His casual teasing had the desired effect and Dee visibly relaxed. "Why don't we offer a buffet brunch Sunday morning in the small banquet room? In the end, it will be easier and a nice closure for the whole Event."

Maeve hated to admit it but the girl did come up with a few good ideas. "The small hall isn't booked so we can certainly do this. There's adequate time to arrange it with the kitchen."

Dee was relieved that Maeve was onboard. "I'll let you arrange taking care of the additional staff since our numbers are considerably higher. As well, you can discuss the Sunday buffet with the kitchen. You can give me an update next week."

Watching Dee, Rowan missed the flash of anger in Maeve's eyes as she left to do Dee's bidding. "You're enjoying this, aren't you? I must say you handled this dilemma smoothly."

"This is what makes life interesting," she replied with a saucy grin.

"A lot of extra work falls back on you. Why don't you have Maeve do more?"

Dee was as honest as she was direct. "That would be an exercise in frustration. It is what it is. My efforts are better spent elsewhere. I know this is the hectic time when unexpected things pop up. So now I'm going to find Andy. The tables for the brunch can be set up early. There'll be enough last minute things that will still have to be done later. And I'll give him the new layout for the amended seating plan and tell him about the second bar. I'll see who he'd suggest as the extra bar tender."

"One of the things I admire about you, Dee, is the way you get things done."

"Only one?" she teased back. Looking at her clipboard Dee sighed. The list was long. She turned to Rowan, "Why are you still standing there. I'm sure you have work to do as well."

"You are aware that you work for me. How many times has someone told you you're pushy and overbearing?"

Dee looked thoughtful for a moment but her eyes twinkled, "This is the first time as far as I can remember."

Rowan knew Dee loved and believed in the project as much as he did. "I did myself a favor the day I hired you."

"You need me. You said so yourself," she reminded him

Rowan turned and shaking his head he walked away in the opposite direction. He realized that Dee had taken total control of the Benefit and she was handling it well.

Maeve and Dee were deep in discussion at the reception desk. The young lady on duty hung up the phone and said, "That was Mr. Ashton Underwood. He said not to bother you as he will talk to you when he gets here. He's on his way and he's bringing something with him."

Maeve recognized the name immediately. "I wonder why he's coming to see me."

The receptionist colored in embarrassment. "I'm sorry, I was talking to Miss Dee."

Dee smiled at her, attempting to make light of the situation. "Please notify me as soon as he arrives. I'll be in my office." She turned and left.

No sooner had she sat down and Maeve flew in. "You know Ashton Underwood? How in the hell do you know someone as famous as Ashton Underwood?"

Rowan, hearing the commotion, joined the two women. Maeve turned in disbelief to Rowan, "Ashton Underwood is coming here to see Dee and she hasn't explained why."

"You never gave me the opportunity." She turned to Rowan. "A friend of mine asked Mr. Underwood if he would allow us to feature one of his paintings at the Benefit as a silent auction item. It seems that Mr. Underwood has agreed and is bringing one of his paintings here."

Maeve spoke with the same haughtiness she'd used before, "You don't have any friends here. Here we go again, Rowan. Another of Dee's brainwave ideas. I told you that she'd turn this Event into a Devon Lock. There's no way our budget extends to this type of an expense. An original Ashton Underwood painting has to cost a fortune. We'd be lucky to break even."

There was disappointment in Rowan's voice, "This seems rather uncharacteristic of you, Dee, and I must say I'm disappointed. What's this going to cost us?"

Dee may have been naive and gullible at first but now she knew better. She appeared to accept defeat and lulled Maeve into thinking she'd won this round. Dee accepted Maeve's contempt for her apparent blunder knowing that Maeve would soon look the fool. She knew Woody wouldn't let her down.

Fortunately, the ringer on her phone interrupted them. "Mr. Underwood is here and I don't want to keep him waiting."

A familiar figure at reception turned. At the sight of Woody her eyes brightened. "This is a wonderful surprise, Woody, but unfortunately now isn't a good time. I'm meeting someone." Dee turned to the receptionist. "I thought you said Mr. Underwood was here."

The receptionist appeared confused. "Miss Dee, this is Mr. Underwood."

Totally astounded, Dee looked at Woody. "You're Aston Underwood?"

"Does that surprise you?"

Dee looked at him carefully. "No," she responded honestly. But she was confused. "So why did you introduce yourself as Woody and why didn't you tell me that you were the artist?"

"I told you my friends call me Woody. I knew we'd be friends. I was right. It was a nice change to have someone comment on my work not knowing that I was the artist. Not to mention the fact that you really like my work. I was afraid if I told you it might change things between us. Sorry, Dee."

Dee quickly regained her composure. "Well, considering we are friends it's easy to forgive you." She gave him her usual hug. "Thank you for bringing a painting. I'm anxious to see what you've chosen. Let's go into the office."

Polite introductions were made. For a change, Maeve seemed lost for words.

Like a child wanting to open a gift, Dee shifted her attention to Woody. She gazed at him, her eyes bright with wonder and anticipation. "I'm anxious to see what you've brought?"

Dee's eyes misted over when Ashton revealed the painting. It sent chills down her spine and unexpectedly her eyes teared up. A young girl, obviously very frail, sat in her bedroom looking at herself in the mirror of her dresser. The reflection in the mirror was a vision of health, rosy red cheeks and the sparkle of life in her eyes. Tears fell softly on Dee's cheeks.

For the moment, it was as if they were the only two people in the room. Woody softly wiped her tears. His expression was sober, his voice low, "The piece is named 'Eternal Hope'. The girl in the picture is my sister." His heart twisted and that familiar ache came over him again, a wound that never quite scarred over. "I started it when Hannah was sick. Thanks to you, I was able to complete it. You opened the door to dormant emotions but it allowed healing back in."

Dee was speechless as she stared at the painting. She knew the feelings that had guided his strokes. "This is beautiful. Thank you," she whispered.

Woody touched his lips to her forehead and then released her as he stepped back. There was no denying that there was something private, even intimate, passing between them. "You don't have to thank me," he whispered back. "I'm donating this in the memory of Hannah. This is my way of honoring her short life. And I also want to show my support for your worthy cause. I felt the need to do something." They stared at each other for a long moment.

Maeve, who hadn't heard their exchange, stepped forward intent on taking control of the situation. "It's a beautiful work of art but I'm sure it's much too dear a price for our Event."

"Mr. Underwood is kindly donating his painting."

Maeve's eyes widened in disbelief. "Did you say that Mr. Underwood is donating his painting?" For a change she actually looked embarrassed.

Every time they were with Rowan, Maeve attempted to make her look like a fool. Dee stood there knowing that today the page had turned. She enjoying watching the Ice Maiden melt right in front of her. "Yes, with a request that the proceeds from the auction go toward the renal unit. Sadly, he lost his sister to kidney failure because she couldn't get a transplant in time. She was only sixteen."

Maeve, flushed with humiliation at being put in her place, quickly excused herself on the pretext of an appointment. Woody, too, took his leave and wished them well on the Benefit.

Rowan, who had remained silent, turned his attention back to Dee. "Okay, young lady. This is the most incredible thing yet. Care to explain how you managed all of this? How were you able to get a renowned artist like Ashton Underwood to donate one of his paintings? He may be young but he's a prominent member of the art world. His last canvas sold for a fortune."

"Woody's a friend. He and I met at the Children's Hospital where we both volunteer."

Rowan gave her a long searching look. "I didn't know you were volunteering."

"You must've quit spying on me. I've been volunteering Wednesday nights for weeks. It's Gran's Bridge night and it's lonely when she's gone. As Maeve pointed out, I don't have any friends and Cal is back at Oxford." Her tone wasn't bitter, just matter-of-fact.

"I've admired the art work by Ashton Underwood in the hospital but I had no idea Woody was the artist. I thought he was an art student who was another volunteer. One day I told him about our Charity Event and, like usual, I got caught up with excitement. I said it would be wonderful to auction an incredible item like one of Ashton Underwood's paintings as a fund-raiser. Woody said he knew the artist and he'd talk to him. So I asked if it would be possible for him to price a small piece."

"Nothing shy about you, is there?" Rowan said frankly.

Dee reminded him, "If you don't ask you don't get. And if you have a good reason, people are usually open to your request."

"This is hardly a small piece, Dee. One day it will be considered to be a priceless piece of art by a very famous artist. And he just donated it?" Rowan was still in awe.

"Yes. You heard him yourself. He donated it in honor of his sister. Woody wishes to help our cause knowing that the proceeds will help others like Hannah. That's what the Benefit is all about, isn't it?" Dee's eyes welled again. "Oh, Rowan, it's such a beautiful piece. His work is unique but this piece is exceptional. I feel so connected to it. I love volunteering. My dad said you always need to give back in life. Our family spent countless hours doing volunteer work. It's very gratifying to do something good." Dee was so caught up in the moment she didn't realize what she was saying about her past.

Rowan did but remained silent. More and more things were coming back to Dee, which she was accepting unknowingly. "Congratulations, Dee. You surprise me over and over. Not to mention the effect it had on Maeve."

Dee gave an expressive shrug. When she smiled, there was as much humor as smugness in the curve of her lips. "I'd be lying if I said I was sorry."

"Not to worry. She'll get over it. Just in case I haven't told you lately, I don't know what I'd do without you."

Dee grinned back. "I planned it that way. It's called job security."

Rowan was surprised with what had just happened. Then he smiled to himself. Why should anything about this exceptional woman surprise him anymore?

Dee was still excited when chatting with Constance after dinner. She told her about the kindness of Woody and the painting and they laughed together over Dee's descriptive recount of Maeve's reaction. "I do believe I've alienated Maeve even more. What's a Devon Lock?"

Constance was mystified, "Where in the world did you hear that?"

"Maeve used it when she was talking about me to Rowan in regards to the Benefit. I think it was meant in a derogatory way."

Constance was quick to enlighten her granddaughter. "Devon Lock was a race horse who collapsed just short of the finish line in a national race. So when someone does a Devon Lock, they suddenly fail when everyone expects them to succeed or they crumble at the last minute."

This information surprised Dee and she lifted her chin defiantly. "Well, we both know it won't come to that. I'll show Maeve just how wrong she is."

After dinner, Dee went out to the terrace. It was still pleasant enough to sit outside in the early evening. She was deep in thought thinking over the last few weeks. Most days she didn't feel like she was going to work. She was busy with the Benefit and the hours flew by. To her this wasn't a job; it was her personal project. It was fulfilling and rejuvenating.

Dee looked up when her grandmother joined her. "You were very pensive just now. Are you still bothered by what Maeve said?"

Dee shook her head, "No, I was thinking about how much I'm enjoying working with this Charity. It's such a wonderful feeling having the personal satisfaction of being part of something that will contribute to making a difference to others. I'm overwhelmed that Rowan put so much faith in me." The thought of Rowan always had a disturbing effect on her. "Rowan still confuses me. One minute he's smug and superior. The next minute he's supportive and helpful. And who knew the man had a sense of humor under that arrogant exterior."

Constance could see that time had altered Dee's negative opinion of Rowan. The tone of Dee's voice had been light with humor. She had mellowed now that she was more settled and less angry. "Rowan is lucky to have you. Being a smart man he knows it. He saw your potential as soon as he hired you and he believed that you'd be up to the demands of organizing the Benefit. So did I."

"Thank you. But you might be a little biased, Gran."

"Maybe a little. You have a brilliant mind like your grandfather did and the driving ambition to go with it. Like him, you always take advantage of an opportunity."

Twilight was fading quickly to dark. Along with it came a chill.

Constance rose, "Let's go inside. We'll get Boris to fix us hot chocolate with marshmallows."

Dee jumped to her feet and put her arm around Constance's shoulders as they went indoors. "Sounds yummy."

Boris had already started a cozy fire and welcoming flames danced invitingly. The ladies had just made themselves comfortable when Rowan walked in. It seemed that since the party it had became a familiar habit for him to stop by for a visit in the evenings. Dee sat on the settee next to Constance while Rowan went and took the chair by the fireplace. Dee enjoyed listening to their stories. She no longer felt like an outsider. Dee studied Rowan over the rim of her cup as he spoke. He looked over and Dee flushed in annoyance aware the she'd been caught staring.

Rowan smiled at Dee. "How is your schedule tomorrow? Is there anything that you can't postpone for a day?"

Dee shook her head. She had everything in control for the time being but knew they were in the lull before the storm.

"I've freed up my calendar until after the Benefit. I thought I'd take tomorrow and drive out to the manor. I need to take some supplies to Emmett. I think you deserve a day of hooky. You deserve it with all those extra hours you've been putting in. It would be a nice break."

When Dee looked into his eyes, she knew he meant it so she was quick to agree.

"There are a few things I want to do at the main house before it gets locked up for the winter. You can explore the house and grounds while I tend to the chores."

Constance agreed with Rowan. "It's obvious that it's been neglected but Rowan has so much planned to restore the manor to its former beauty."

"My intent is to keep as much of the charm and character as I can. I've been sensitive with the restoration, trying to retain the original architectural character and elegance. It was an exquisite and stately home when it was occupied by my grandparents. After my grandmother died, my grandfather moved to London. It's been vacant and neglected since then. Right now it's tired looking. Even though it's difficult to remember my family, I feel a connection when I go there. I only have vague memories of my grandmother and very few of my parents."

Relating to what Rowan had said, Dee's voice softened, "It must have been awful growing up without them." The sadness in her voice was for his loss as much as her own.

"It would have been without Connie." He smiled affectingly at the older woman. "My grandfather was a workaholic and there were times he was so deep in his work he'd forget everything else. He actually forgot my birthday one year."

Dee had never seen this side of Rowan, vulnerable and open. She was surprised at the overwhelming empathy she felt for him. "Were you lonely?"

"Not lonely. Just alone." The tone of his voice sounded forlorn. For a moment Rowan went and stood in front of the hearth. The expression on his face was masked and Dee wondered what he was thinking.

Rowan turned back to the ladies and changed the subject attempting to lighten the mood. He smiled at Dee, "The forecast is for a clear day so I thought we'd make a day of it and drive along the coastal side of our country. There's such a rich variety of landscapes. You'll be treated to breathtaking views of spectacular cliff tops and directly below are imposing waves that continuously break and crash against the rocks."

"The white cliffs of Dover that overlook the English Channel are truly spectacular. It was always one of Oliver's and my favorite drives. There are few houses, just nature as it was intended." Constance excused herself as the phone rang.

Rowan expanded on his plans, "I'd like to get an early start so if it's okay with you we'll leave just after breakfast for Ravencrest."

Raven! Without warning the name escaped from her subconscious. The softly spoken word came out sounding like a scream. As soon as she heard the word, Dee's heart began to beat so loudly that she could hear nothing else. She struggled to fit the word Raven into place. Suddenly, her face became deathly white and she looked like she had drifted into another world.

Dee remembered what was so bad that it had blocked her memory for so many months. The memories that had been pushed to the dark place in her mind were finally allowed their escape. And in that moment she wished she could forget the horror that became real. She was unaware of her surroundings and Rowan's voice couldn't penetrate her mind. It was as if she was outside her body looking in. Her nightmares became her reality. It was Laney who had haunted her nightmares. It was Laney whose soul had floated away into the air. The memory switch had been turned on and the horror was real. The room seemed to close in on her.

She remembered it all, every small detail. The memories evoked a pain so intense and Dee knew it was no dream. It was reality at its cruelest. Even her nightmares were better than this. The pictures that came into her mind now were terrifying. No matter how hard she tried she couldn't erase Laney's frightened face from her mind. She shook her head violently, trying to ward off the memory that erupted from the depths of her soul and her world began to spin. The images kept coming. But this was only the beginning. They tore at her heart in a way she couldn't bear. She remembered. Too much! Dee started to tremble and let out an anguished scream while trying to free herself from this living nightmare. There was more to come, much more. It was endless. It was overpowering. She felt herself slipping into unconsciousness. And then the familiar blackness.

Dee lay on the sofa, her head resting on a pillow. Her face was now as white as paper. An insistent male voice was calling her back to consciousness. The darkness slowly lifted and Dee was back among the living. She stared at Rowan with the empty expression of a person wakened from a terrifying nightmare. The glance she gave him was haunted and it startled him.

In that single moment Rowan knew she had her memory back. The look was one he knew he'd never forget. He looked almost as pale as Dee as he ran a troubled hand through his hair. The look on her face scared Rowan as he stared down at her.

She lay motionless as her mind returned to the present. In a state of shock she sat up and said, "I remember. I know who I am and I know what happened." Dee looked up and simply announced, "I am Desiree Fiona Dare." Then she looked at Rowan with horror in her eyes. "Laney is dead," she whispered in agony.

Her anguished words cut into Rowan like a sharp blade.

Her voice was so fraught with heartbreak that Rowan wrapped her securely in his arms. The pull on his heart was immediate and overwhelming. She clung to him as if she'd never let go. Great sobs wrenched her body as the horror of what happened to her twin overcame her. "Laney can't be dead. She's young and vibrant. She's going to be a super star." Desiree kept crying and crying. She was in a new version of hell.

Rowan held her close, stroking her head. He closed his own eyes and felt the wetness on his cheeks. He paused, hoping and failing to get a grip on his own emotions. Rowan prayed that she'd be able to bear the shock and have the courage required to deal with the recent revelation. "I'm so sorry," he whispered, unable to shake off his own sorrow.

Desiree opened her eyes and caught the look of guilt in his darkened eyes. Desiree sat like a zombie on the sofa, her face bloodless. The numbness was slowly ebbing, harsh reality taking its place. She glared at Rowan, the hurt and bewilderment clear in her eyes. "You and Gran knew what happened? Why didn't anyone tell me?"

"I know this has been a shock. Let me explain." Rowan spoke slowly, choosing his words with care. He had months to think about this moment and now he hoped he could find the right words. "The human psyche is very delicate. It can take only so much pain and when the pain becomes unbearable it escapes into hidden recesses of the mind. You needed time to recover from what you'd been through before you could deal with what you'd lost. The doctors told us not to force any memories. We were to let them come naturally. We were told it would be better to let you discover things for yourself. None of us knew when it would happen. Connie and I were seeing glimpses of it but we didn't know which twin you were."

Desiree's shock and panic turned quickly to resentment. Even knowing they were doing the best thing for her, it still hurt. She was angry at them even knowing she wasn't the only one pained by these revelations.

Rowan had no wish to hurt her, quite the opposite. "In the beginning, it was easier because you were in shock and just floated day to day. Time was giving you a chance to heal and get stronger, both physically and emotionally. The challenge presented itself when you started asking questions. Every day it was getting more and more difficult for us to keep this information from you."

Desiree was too distressed to think beyond her own inner turmoil. She rose and began to pace. Other memories escaped and there was no holding back the tide. Her past returned as random images kept racing through her confused mind. Dozens of scenes poured in and darted back and forth. Past images intertwining with current images but all thoughts returned to the loss of her twin. She remained isolated in her shroud of grief. Rowan watched the blood again drain from her face. Her legs felt weak and she sat back down. Desiree spoke quietly, almost as though she was speaking to herself, "I have to go home. I have to go home for Laney."

Rowan had never seen someone look like that, as though part of her had died in front of him. Circling her shoulder with his arm, he again drew her close. Though she stiffened, she didn't pull away. Rowan felt helpless and he was. "You don't have to go back to America." His voice broke and he had to swallow hard to continue. He lifted Desiree's chin and she looked up at him. His voice was even softer. "Delaney is here. Her ashes were brought with us when I went for you. She's been in the spare room waiting for you to remember. Waiting for you to say good-bye. Come, I'll take you to her." Now all the secrets were out.

Together, Rowan and Desiree entered the spare room. The room was still. Rowan's eyes remained focused on Desiree. She stood there, lost and in shock. Unconsciously, she was whispering, as though afraid to disturb her sister. *"Double dare, pinkie swear. Double dare, pinkie swear. Double Dare..."*

Rowan wanted to hold her, comfort her, make her pain go away. But he knew he couldn't. Desiree needed to be alone with her grief. He knew he was intruding on something very private and he retreated without a word, quietly closing the door behind him. It didn't block out Desiree's anguished chant from the other side. Rowan fought to hold his emotions in check. He went to find Constance. Another person was about to get a shock. He knew he could help his godmother through her sorrow. It hurt him that he couldn't help Desiree with hers.

In a matter of minutes, the life she had as Dee was over. The one to come, again as Desiree, had yet to begin. Desiree stood in limbo struggling to breathe. Laney's urn sat on the dresser. Next to the dresser was a trunk similar to the one that had been delivered to her room. *Our life together is inside.* It could wait.

Desiree collapsed on the floor, her legs having given way, and sat motionless. Every nerve ending in her body was screaming in sorrow, while the world around her remained deadly quiet. Heavy emotions engulfed her. Her grief was so deep. She had never experienced pain at this level. It was so severe it took her breath away.

Like a magnet she was drawn to the dresser. Her hands were shaking as she clasped the urn and held it to her heart. In a trance, she crossed to the bed and lay down. Time passed heartbeat by heartbeat as she lay in the fetal position, the urn clutched tight. Desiree closed her eyes. The moment she did the memory of the accident was back. She again began to sob, raw tears that came straight from her soul. She tried to ward off the memory of those pain-filled moments but the vision wouldn't go away. Desiree didn't want to relive that day. But she knew she had to so she could say good-bye to Delaney Isabel Dare, her twin, her soul mate, her best friend. With darkness enveloping her like a cloak, time ceased to mean anything. Hours passed as she remained frozen in time stunned by her loss. The voice in her head played over and over. *Laney is dead! Laney is gone. She isn't coming back. Laney is dead!*

Even at her worst, her fears had not prepared her for this kind of pain. For a moment she couldn't breathe for the pain was unbearable. *How can you be dead? I can't survive without you. I hate this! I want to die. Oh, God, please let me die.* Her mind fought to come to terms with her reality. Laney was gone. Taking with her the laughter, the love and the dreams. Gone! Forever! Desiree felt the hysteria once again rise to the surface. Her stomach convulsed. Feeling physically sick, she ran to the bathroom. After splashing cold water on her face, she returned to the spare room. *How much more can I take?*

Desiree knelt down and carefully opened the trunk, wondering what treasures had been packed inside. Unlike last time, everything was familiar. With every item she recalled a memory. Desiree became lost in her past. She began to cry again when she saw the tambourine. She remembered being a little girl and Laney and her were playing their tambourines with their daddy. She now knew why the tambourine in the trunk in her room had brought her comfort. *So much for dreams, Laney. You were a shining star who was full of dreams. How can you be dead?*

It seemed that death had been a part of most of her life. First her mom, then her dad. It had been easier to accept their deaths but then she had Laney. This loss went far beyond. Now, it wasn't just Laney she was grieving. It was as if she had lost her family all over again. Desiree began her good-byes one at a time. She started with their mother, who was a beautiful and loving mother but had died too young. She remembered her mom holding them, smiling as the girls played, singing lullabies to them in their bed. Beautiful and happy memories from their childhood. Both girls had been devastated when she died. They were young and missed her all the time. Their dad was always there for them but it wasn't the same. So it was natural that they turned to each other. The bond between the twins only became stronger. And now that had been taken from her. She thought of Laney now, her twin sister who she had shared her life with and loved. All she wanted to do was turn the clock back. She wept for Laney and for all the lost years. She wept for herself, for all the lonely years ahead of her. *It was never just Desiree Dare but Desiree and Delaney Dare. Together. Always we, not I. You and I entwined. We were a magical team, Laney. The two of us, who we were, what we were together, Double Dare. Everything that I was, everything that we were, it's gone.* Laney had always been a part of her life. In fact, the most important part.

Conscious of the void she'd been feeling inside, Desiree now knew the reason why. *Deep inside my voice cried out for you but you never answered. I was so lonely and I couldn't understand why. I didn't know that my soul was missing you. It knew even when I didn't.*

But now everything had changed. Desiree felt a surge of anger replace the pain. She raged at fate and its injustice. Getting mad felt better than being sad. Her anger erupted and she cried out loud, "Maybe if I scream loud enough you can hear me in heaven. How dare you leave me like the others. My life stopped that day, too. I woke up and everything was different. And now my life will never be the same." Her outrage got the better of her. "I hate you for all the years I'll have to live without you." Then she cried harder. "I don't hate you, Laney. I just don't know how I'm going to survive without my best friend? What will I do? How will I live?" Desiree was rambling now, talking to stop herself from thinking about the unthinkable. She was filled with the most conflicting emotions but especially with guilt. "You didn't deserve for this to happen. It isn't fair, it just isn't fair! Oh, Laney, I've betrayed you. I was your protector. If I hadn't been selfish and wanted to venture out on my own, this wouldn't have happened."

Desiree felt forsaken and all alone as she continued to mourn. She knew this wasn't true. She had Gran. But her heart couldn't accept this yet. It didn't matter. Nothing mattered anymore. Emotionally exhausted, Desiree crawled under the covers wanting to end the day. It felt like her life had ended as well. Desiree didn't want a life without Laney. She had no idea how she was going to live without Laney. But she had to, she had no choice. Desiree was again trapped in her own private pain for the memories that lay within her continued to surface. All those tears she had shed had failed to wash away her sorrow. She closed her eyes because sleep was preferable to the memories. She prayed for the strength to get through this. Finally sleep came, but sadly the nightmares returned.

A new day dawned and although the sun shone bright, Desiree was unaware of it. Inside, she lay in absolute darkness, the drapes pulled tight across the windows. The room was eerie quiet, only her own ragged breathing and the frantic beating of her heart disturbing the silence. Her mind was so shattered that she blinked in puzzlement before she realized she wasn't in her own room. Immediately, memories flooded in along with the realization that yesterday was indeed real. She lay there with her heart beating painfully, allowing the misery to return. This nightmare was real. There were no more gaps to fill. There was nowhere to run from the pain. She didn't know what to do. Desiree lay back on the bed and cried some more.

Meanwhile, Constance was just as distressed as her granddaughter. Constance sat staring absently out the window. Although she wanted to check on her, she knew she had to leave Desiree alone. She had to wonder how the poor child was to get through this. She remembered the vulnerability and the fear in her granddaughter's eyes when she had first arrived. Constance had prayed for the day to come when Desiree would remember. Now that she had, Constance prayed for her granddaughter to be able to deal with it. She turned when Rowan entered.

Rowan, too, looked pale and drawn. They were all suffering through their own personal ache. Rowan was concerned not only about Desiree, but for his godmother as well. Constance looked pale and exhausted and he'd never seen her look so fragile. "How is Desiree?" he asked, knowing better than to express his concern for Constance. He'd talk to Boris on his way out.

"I don't know. She hasn't left the spare room. I hear her talking to Laney and in between it's the tambourine. And then the sobbing starts. I prayed this day would come. I thought I was prepared for it. I'm not. I don't know how to help her."

Rowan's eyes darkened with concern as Desiree's image came to mind. She had looked at him with such terror in her eyes. "The poor girl has had another severe shock. No one can help her, not yet. This is her time with her twin. But she will need you when she's ready."

"You're right." Constance knew Rowan was referring to support, compassion and understanding. She recognized that this was why Rowan was here. They all felt helpless in the face of Desiree's overwhelming grief. Constance was grateful to Rowan. He had been there for her granddaughter when she needed him. And even when she didn't.

"She'll be all right," Rowan said, although he didn't know if he was trying to convince Constance or himself. "There's nothing you can do until she's ready." Rowan looked at Constance. He loved her like a son. He wished he knew how to help them both but he was at a loss, a feeling he wasn't familiar with. He didn't know how to deal with the situation either.

Constance's face turned stark white. "What if she wants to go back to the States? Oh, Rowan, I can't lose her. We must find a way to keep Desiree here."

Rowan responded gravely, "When the time comes we'll deal with our own reality. Just as Desiree is now having to accept hers."

After Rowan left Constance went and joined Boris in the kitchen. He quickly turned away to wipe his tears. His voice was grief-stricken when he asked, "What's our poor girl going to do? What if she isn't strong enough to deal with this traumatic shock? What's going to happen to her now?"

Constance searched for the words of reassurance that he longed to hear. None were forthcoming because she was experiencing the same fear, the same uncertainty.

By choice, Desiree continued to confine herself to the spare bedroom for a second day. She stayed in Laney's room refusing to see or talk to anyone. Here she felt protected, insulated from the real world. She knew she was being self-indulgent as she wrapped herself tightly in self-pity. Desiree got up from the bed and began pacing, frowning in thought. Her mind came to terms with her reality. Her expression changed to anguish as she finally accepted it. She was less shocked than she had been at first. She no longer wept. She wished she could ignore this and it would all go away. But she had to exorcise the demons that had haunted her for months. Feeling suffocated, she crossed over and opened the window wide. A biting wind wrapped around her. When she could no longer take the cold, she went and lay on the bed.

Although Desiree's anger had subsided, she couldn't let go of the pain. Not yet. She knew she needed to deal with the reality but her emotions were so confused. Time ceased to exist as she began threading pieces together in her mind, past now trying to intertwine with her present. Desiree would have dearly loved her sister's sense of humor to make light of some of the trials and tribulation she had endured over the last months. Laney had a way of laughing at fate. Desiree would have valued her sister's advice on how to deal with this but she wasn't here. The person who was the reason for it all and who would never be there to answer her. And that was Desiree's dilemma. She spoke in grief and fear of her tomorrows without her twin. "Maybe you're better off than I am. You don't have to feel the terrible pain I'm feeling right now."

Throughout the day she tried to draw strength and hope from past memories but the images of the accident often interfered. Inside her, everything was numb but she knew she couldn't stay locked away. Life wasn't that simple. From somewhere, she found the strength to focus on the matters at hand as she forced her thoughts away from her dark place. She knew she had to continue living despite the terrible emptiness inside her. At nightfall, Dee once again made her escape by falling into a deep sleep.

The next morning Desiree felt emotionally stronger. She had finally achieved a level of resignation. Over the last few days, Desiree had relived the nightmare events in order for her to expel them from her soul. She felt empty of everything. The light had gone out of her life. She rose and while she was pacing she caught sight of her image in the mirror. Stepping closer, she studied her face. It bore the tracks from endless tears. She ran her fingertips along her cheeks. Desiree and Delaney Dare stared at each other. Desiree turned away, went into the bathroom, picked up a pair of scissors and started cutting her hair. *There is no more Double Dare. There is no more Raven. There is no more Laney.* The exorcism was complete. It was time to emerge from her self-imposed exile. Having said her painful good-byes, Desiree left Laney.

The minute Desiree found her grandmother she fell into her arms and sobbed uncontrollably. She so desperately wanted to be held, soothed, to be promised that her world would stop spinning and come back into focus. And she wanted someone to tell her the hurt would go away.

Constance wrapped Desiree in her arms as her granddaughter wept. In support and sympathy, she held Desiree close and let her cry as her own tears streamed down her face. "Shh, my darling child, it's going to be all right." In time, the spasm of sobbing subsided.

Desiree's voice was merely a whisper. "I can't believe this is happening. How can life be so unfair?" She looked up at her grandmother with hollow eyes. "Laney is dead. I don't have a twin anymore." Her tone was flat and empty.

"You will always have a twin. Death doesn't change that. You'll find a way to keep Delaney in your life while at the same time letting her go and moving forward. You'll learn how to live without her. It takes courage to live and we know how brave you are."

"I can't imagine life without Laney. It's hard to lose someone you love. But losing a twin is like losing a part of yourself. I don't feel complete anymore."

"Neither of you deserved for this to happen." Constance's gaze shifted. "I'm going to go and tell Boris you're back with us. He's been so concerned. You know he'll have to pamper you. Will you be okay until I come back?"

Desiree nodded. "I didn't mean to upset either of you. I hope you can understand. I needed to be with Laney. Thank you for giving me the time I needed to find my way through the darkest moments of my life."

Constance stroked her granddaughter's damp cheek before she left to talk to Boris. Desiree took a deep breath and waited. As soon as Constance was back, she took Desiree back into her arms, lifted her chin, and asked, "Are you all right, dear?"

Desiree's reply was candid. "No. I don't think I'll be all right ever again. I feel numb, miserable, petrified, confused. The cruelty of life is that this is what now replaces the fear of being a stranger to myself."

Just then Boris entered with a tray set with the fine china. He looked sadly at Desiree before speaking. "It is good to see you again, Miss Dee." Immediately, his face reddened in embarrassment.

Constance quickly came to his rescue. "What do you want us to call you?"

Desiree looked at their faces etched with confusion. "I thought about that along with so many other things. I was Dee for so long. But my mother named me Desiree. Many shortened it to Des." She touched her hair. "I can change my appearance but I can't change who I am. I am Desiree Fiona Dare."

"I have to ask. Why did you cut your hair?"

Desiree breathed in deeply and Constance could tell she was holding back tears. "It was an act of being reborn and starting over. I had to say good-bye to my past and have the courage to start over." Desiree touched her cropped hair as she asked, "Does it look awful."

Constance approved of the change. "It makes you look chic and mature." In truth, Desiree looked like a ghost, her eyes were darkly rimmed, her face pale.

Desiree focused her gaze on her grandmother. "Without knowing you were here for me I'd still be locked away hanging on to my grief. I'm sorry it took so long. You've been so good to me. When I came here you took me in with open arms. You accepted me for who I was as well as what I was. I wasn't very nice in the beginning but I was so scared. I know that it doesn't excuse my behavior. I'm really scared again, Gran." Tears spilled down her cheeks. "I don't want to feel this way. When will my life get better?"

"I don't know, Desiree. Maybe tomorrow, or the next day, or the day after that. It doesn't go away, but it does get better. I know there's a phase you have to go through, the one where you can't believe anything is ever going to be right again. And then when you think you've gotten through it and you start to heal, you find it still hurts. But you don't let it consume you. You learn to accept the hurt. You let life back in and in time it grows and takes over the hurt. The pain you're feeling right now isn't forever. Nothing is forever. Nothing good and nothing bad. Remind yourself of that every day."

Desiree's eyes were solemn. "At least now there are no forgotten memories, no hidden secrets." But her comforting sense of security had been shattered. "I thought I'd get my memory back and return to my life and everything would go back to the way it was. Life doesn't always work out the way you expect. Sometimes it keeps kicking you in the gut. And you have to dig really deep to find your inner strength." She turned to her grandmother with eyes clear and bright. "I have my life back. I have my name again. For that, I'm grateful. It was unsettling not knowing who I was. But this is unbearably hard. I should feel whole again but how can I when half of me is missing? It isn't fair."

"No, it isn't," Constance agreed.

"Besides saying good-bye to Laney, I spent time thinking about what the rest of my life will be like without her. I'm heartbroken because I'll have to face my future alone. I don't know what to do without Laney." Desiree saw the hurt in her grandmother's face. She turned her apologetic eyes to her, "Oh, Gran. That came out wrong. I love you but now I have to try to find a way to close up this huge hole in my heart."

"Your whole world was turned upside down months ago. It will take time to adjust to this just like you had to adjust when you first arrived here. The important thing to remember is that you know you are strong enough to deal with this as well. But you must put this behind you." Constance knew that in time Desiree would learn to accept this.

There were tears in Desiree's eyes. "I'm sorry. I have so many conflicting emotions." Her life had been deeply shaken. Delaney and Desiree had been one half of each other's whole.

"No need to be sorry, Desiree. The hard part is over."

Yes, for Dee the wondering was over. But for Desiree the future was unclear, even though she'd unknowingly made a new life for herself. One that didn't include Laney.

Seeing the hurt in her granddaughter's eyes made Constance's heart ache. The poor girl was still dazed by what had happened. "You must tell me what triggered your memory."

"When Laney and I lost mom we were at an impressionable age. Dad stepped up with the parenting role but our life still centered around his music. By the time Dad died, Laney and I were strong, independent young ladies capable of taking on the world in our own way. Our world had always been music so Laney and I formed our own band called Double Dare. On stage I went by the name Raven. For some reason when Rowan said Ravencrest it was like a dam burst and a flood of memories came pouring in."

"Laney and I were so excited when we left for the airport to come here to spend time with you. Laney was going back after our visit but I was planning on staying longer in England. I wanted to learn more about our family roots."

Constance listened intently while Desiree managed to tell her everything that had happened leading up to the accident without breaking down. But when she came to the accident words failed her as tears drowned out the words before they reached her lips.

"Desiree, you couldn't change what happened."

Desiree nodded, trying to believe her grandmother, but she couldn't. The look of guilt remained on her face.

Constance stared helplessly while she sat and waited for Desiree to work through her inner struggle. "You can't blame yourself for Delaney's death."

Desiree gazed at her grandmother helplessly. "I know. Do you think things happen because they're meant to or because you make them happen?"

"Both. I think this happened so we could become a family again and together we made that happen."

Desiree's look changed and her tone became more serious. "That's one of the good things that happened as a result of the accident. You brought me into your life and I had family again, not knowing how desperately I would need you. Out of necessity, I learned to trust others. Even Rowan was there for me as I struggled through my new and difficult circumstances. Will he be up later?" Desiree asked, trying without much success to sound indifferent.

"No. He had urgent business to attend to in Manchester. He should be back tomorrow."

"Rowan chose a beautiful urn for Laney's ashes. The gold was perfect. Laney always said to go for the gold when doing anything."

"We'll have a private memorial service when you're ready. We'll lay Delaney to rest next to your mother and grandfather in the family plot."

"I keep thinking this is a horrible dream and I'll wake up any minute." Desiree's voice cracked, "For a minute I wanted to die, too. I didn't think I could live without my twin sister. I can't imagine my world without her. I never want to forget Laney."

Constance smiled, "Like she'd let you. From what you've shared, I'm sure Delaney will make her presence known in many ways."

Desiree smiled as she hadn't in days. "You know I only have to look in the mirror to see her. I'm sure that she'll come back and haunt me." *Think of me and I'll be there.* Dee shivered. *Every day, Laney. Every day.*

Speaking slowly, Constance chose her words carefully, "Whatever you and Delaney were to each other you still are. You have to hold on to the good thoughts, the happy memories, the precious moments that made up your life together and let the rest go. You can move forward without her. Desiree, you have moved forward without her."

Desiree nodded, knowing she had to appreciate that. "I believe her spirit and her energy were with me as I moved forward in my new life here with you. Living here is very different from our life in the States."

"The life you lived with your twin is unchanged. Delaney's memory will live on forever. Never lost, never forgotten, never far from our hearts. Remember her without the shroud of darkness and sadness. Your life still means all that it ever meant. You'll still have dreams. Don't be afraid to live those dreams. Continue to laugh and sing and enjoy life."

Desiree knew her grandmother was right. Life would go on and the bad memories would fade in time. "Everything is going to be so different. I've changed, my life has changed."

Constance took her granddaughter's hand in hers. "Take a moment and think about that, Desiree. You're still who you are, only more. You haven't changed. The difference is that now you know who you are. You can now understand and appreciate why you are who you are. You are an extraordinary woman. Desiree, you have incredible courage, such fire inside of you. Your zest for life inspires others."

Constance listened as her granddaughter shared tales of Laney. Memories were filled with amusement and awe, as well as deep sadness. Whenever Desiree thought of her life before England it was as us, her and Laney. It had always been just the two of them.

"Laney and I were always very protective of each other. That came from losing our parents at a young age. I was always the practical and sensible one. Laney was much more impulsive. She was headstrong and strong-willed enough to bulldoze over anyone who got in our way. She was always the instigator and planner and would often get carried away by her enthusiasm."

Connie laughed and Desiree quickly joined in. They both knew it sounded a lot like Dee. Suddenly Desiree was reluctant to talk about Laney. In time, when the pain dulled, she would share more about Laney.

"I've learned a lot about myself when I didn't know who I was. I know it sounds crazy in a way but I didn't have to be Desiree or compare myself to Laney. I was just me."

Constance looked at Desiree thoughtfully, "Maybe you found yourself by losing Laney."

Desiree's expression remained deeply saddened. "I was always extremely protective of her. I feel like I failed Laney."

Constance patiently corrected her, "You are only responsible for your own life. No one else's. It's impossible to control someone else's life or death. You must put Delaney's accidental death behind you. You have to let it go or you'll never be happy. Don't let what is past interfere with what is now. Sadly, death leaves a heartache that only time can heal." They were both crying as they looked at each other.

Desiree agreed as she wiped the tears from her eyes and faced the reality of her situation once again. She had to remind herself that her life here hadn't changed. And a part of Laney would always be right there with her. *Think of me and I'll be there.*

"I could never have gotten through this without you. I believe this was as difficult for you as it was for me. Perhaps even more difficult. You had to be on guard while you kept sad secrets. Me, on the other hand, had no filter and just reacted. It took awhile but I came to terms with my circumstances. In time, I was able to move forward alone unaware that I was alone. I believe that was God's gift to me to allow me the time to gain the strength I would need to deal with my loss."

Constance was surprised by Desiree's insight as well as her acceptance.

The thought of returning to America and the life she'd lived there filled Desiree with a dull ache. "I love you, Gran. I love London. I don't want to return to the States." It was an easy decision for her to make because this was where she belonged. Her eyes filled with new knowledge and she could no longer deny what her heart already knew. Desiree finally quit trying to fool herself. She loved Rowan.

Desiree was suddenly drained. Although it was early evening she excused herself and went to her own room. She was both physically and emotionally exhausted.

It wasn't long after Desiree retired that Rowan called. "Sorry, I had to leave you alone with this, Connie. Has anything changed?"

Constance filled Rowan in. "I wish I could take her pain away. She didn't deserve this."

"No, she didn't deserve this. How is she handling everything?"

Constance recognized how concerned Rowan was. "Like she does everything. With strength. Now that she has all of the pieces of her puzzle, she will have to pick up the pieces of her life."

Rowan spoke the truth when he said, "Desiree made it through the darkness once. She can do it again."

CHAPTER FIFTEEN

For the next couple of days Constance and Boris hovered over Desiree. She knew they meant well so she accepted their unintended smothering. Desiree gradually worked her way out of her heavy depression. She'd come too far to sink into despair. Nor could she change what happened. It was time to let go and move forward.

When she first regained her memory, Desiree had questioned how she could begin again. She quickly realized that she didn't have to. She only had to continue living with her memory intact with loving family and friends around her. Despite the accident that had taken Laney's life, and shattered her own, she had to keep living. Her life had been spared. For that she had to be thankful and live it with purpose.

Desiree was still finding it hard to accept losing Laney. But the reality was that Laney was gone. She knew she was strong and the new life she'd been building was stable enough to handle the change. She knew who she was and she also knew she had never lost her sense of worth. In the hazy light of dawn, she gazed out at the October sky and knew it was time to go back to work. Keeping busy was the best way not to brood. Desiree decided to continue on as normal even if there was little joy in her life.

Both Constance and Boris were in the morning room. They were a little surprised to see Desiree up so early. Desiree sat down as Boris poured her a coffee. She shifted uncomfortably before stating, "It's time I go back to work." She needed to keep her mind, as well as her body, busy. Besides, there was no way she would give Maeve the satisfaction of seeing her fail. Nor did she want to disappoint Rowan, who had put so much trust in her. She needed to honor her commitment to the Benefit Ball.

Constance paused. "Are you sure you're up to it?"

Desiree looked at her grandmother with a look that begged her to understand. "Don't worry about me. I'm all right."

Constance had prayed for her granddaughter to return to her true self. Now that Desiree had, she had to let her go. Something very gentle tore at her heart. Constance realized that she had to let Dee go just like Desiree was letting Laney go. Ironic how life holds everyone accountable in different ways.

Right after breakfast, Desiree went to change into work attire. Turning slightly, she caught a glimpse of her image in the mirror. It was still a shock seeing herself with shorter hair. Once again, her familiar facial features were marred by dark circles under her eyes. She took the time to apply artificial color. The hollow look in her eyes was gone, now replaced with sadness. She made her way down to Rowan's office. She couldn't help but recall the fear she had the day she asked him for a job. Today there was no fear, just apprehension. She hadn't spoken with him since her memory returned.

Grateful that Rowan wasn't at his desk, Desiree passed through and entered her office. She sat down and took a moment to survey her domain. Everything was the same. Inside her, everything was different. A vital part of her had died. Deciding that a cup of coffee was what she needed to get started, she got up and made a full pot. She had just poured a cup when she sensed his presence.

Rowan was leaning against the door frame studying her. He had never seen her look so empty, so sad, yet so beautiful. He took a careful study of her face, noted the smudges under her eyes, the pallor beneath the carefully applied blush on her cheeks. "Pour another cup and I'll join you." He was anxious to see how she would respond as he sat down at her desk.

Desiree was glad to see him. There was something comforting about his presence. The day became a little more normal. "Who was your slave while I was gone?"

Rowan grinned, appreciating her come back, "It's been really quiet around here."

"Have you missed my sass?" As she said it she began to come alive.

Rowan had missed the spitfire. "You know me. I'm a Bear for punishment," he joked, trying to make her smile.

Desiree smiled weakly. "Rowan I need to work."

Rowan knew it would be a waste of time to argue with her and who was he to question her decision. He smiled at her, realizing he'd missed her. He had to ask, "Are you okay?"

He cared, she realized as she studied his face. It was there in his eyes as they looked into hers. "I'm doing better. Still a little in shock I suppose. I'm trying to put the tragedy behind me. But as far as the Charity Benefit goes, I'm excited to be back."

Rowan felt his heart catch at the anguish in her tormented expression. The look of pain in her eyes was unmistakable. His heart twisted painfully for her. No matter how impossible she was at times he did understand the magnitude of her loss. *Stubborn woman.* But his eyes expressed his admiration. This woman was strong and resilient and obviously determined.

With simple candor Desiree stated, "I don't blame you or Gran for keeping secrets. Or maybe I do, a little. But at least I know I'm being unfair when I do and I'm working through it."

The fact that her look never wavered convinced Rowan that Desiree was telling the truth. It didn't take away his own guilt. Desiree was still dealing with an agonizing loss and he was determined to do everything he could to help her.

The next few days were emotional. Those around her were very kind and supportive. They meant well when they expressed their condolences and she appreciated their concern. But it didn't take long before Desiree felt suffocated with kindness. She went looking for Maeve. A dose of Maeve was just what she needed to bring her life back into reality.

Work once again became her salvation, making her days at least tolerable. Desiree poured her energies, her time and her skills into the project. She did what was needed to be done. Desiree was grateful that her days once again passed quickly. Nights were still long.

There were many times when she questioned if she'd ever find true happiness again. Her grief was still a constant ache. This had changed her life, changed her. *They say change is good. I can hardly wait for the good to start.*

Desiree also returned to her volunteering. She always enjoyed her coffee sessions with Woody afterwards but tonight she was nervous. She needed to tell him she had regained her memories.

The air was heavy, the kind that brewed into thunderstorms and the clouds hinted at rain. A blast of October air hit Desiree in the face. Shivering, Desiree pulled her jacket tighter.

"Cold?"

"It's a little chilly," Desiree admitted as she turned her collar up against the wind.

The rain came without warning and quickly intensified. Woody draped his arm around her shoulders and she leaned into him.

Inside the café, they took a table by the window and ordered.

Woody was concerned about his friend. Leaning back, he sipped his coffee and studied her. He hadn't failed to notice the faint shadows etched below her eyes and her face was drawn. He knew something was wrong because she was preoccupied. He would wait.

Desiree leaned forward and placed her clasped hands on the table. Her eyes went from intense to earnest as she looked at Woody. She was nervous and didn't quite know where to start. Her voice was thick with emotion when she did. "I need to explain why I missed volunteering last week."

Woody heard the slight tremor in her voice, as if she was on the verge of tears. Her sad tone and somber face were almost more than Woody could bear.

Desiree looked up at him, reflecting back to the day he introduced himself to her. She smiled as she said, "I have my memory back. My name is Desiree but my friends call me Des." She told him everything, carefully with every detail. The agonizing grief, the crazy disbelief, her self-imposed withdrawal as she tried to deal with everything.

"Since my arrival in England I came to terms with my memory loss and accepted my life as it was. Now, I have to try to do that all over again now that I have my memory back but knowing that I've lost my twin sister."

As he listened to her, Woody felt sympathy for her tear at his heart. He always knew she had a mystery to her, something she kept buried. Pain, sorrow, loneliness; today she had released it all. His friend's courage and inner strength impressed him. For a moment they sat in silence, sharing the common bond of a loss of a sister. Woody's understanding smile gave her the courage to continue.

"A sister, especially a twin, is special. She's the one person who knows how you feel, how you think, how you laugh, why you laugh, what makes you cry. The person who remembers things from your childhood because she was there to share them. The person who knows it all and is your best friend. She's someone you tell secrets to and even fight with. I don't have that anymore." Desiree's voice broke when she said, "One loses all that is familiar, all that matters. Suddenly you're all alone."

There was an endless pause and then a higher pitch to her voice when she continued, a desperation that Woody didn't recognize. "It was raining the day of the accident." The sentence was punctuated by a clap of thunder. Desiree turned and looked out as the rain drizzled down the window and she listened to another boom of thunder.

Woody leaned over and took her hands in his. She turned back to him, her expression bleak. "You know that I understand having lost Hannah. At first the pain is intolerable and you think you'll die without them. I don't know if you ever get over the feeling that you'll look up and she's back. I used to pretend that Hannah was only away. But I knew better and I'd feel worse than before. In time, you eventually accept that they are never coming back. And you become grateful for what you have because you know how brief that can be and how quickly it can change. In some ways it seems as though Hannah's been gone forever and in some ways it seems like it was yesterday. You can, and you will, get through this time in your life. You're made of strong stuff, Desiree Dare."

Tears fell as Desiree stated, "When Laney died she took a piece of my heart with her. We lived together. We worked together. We played together. We were inseparable. Now all the family I have is Gran. I'm blessed to have her and more than grateful for all she has done."

Woody gave Desiree's hand a gentle squeeze. She'd had so much pain so close together. First Beth, now Laney. "I have such admiration for you considering everything you've had to endure. I like you and I like who you are. You're someone special, Des. That hasn't changed."

Desiree didn't withdraw her hand but with sad eyes she replied, "I'm glad you think so."

"I always did," he confessed. His heart twisted painfully.

"I have a lot to think about. So much has changed now that I have my memory back. I feel like I, Desiree Dare, have been released back into the world. Legally, my life can get back to normal." Normal. Desiree didn't know what that was anymore. "I'm no longer limited by my past situation. But I don't know what to do? Here I am having to decide whether to leave people I love, to leave a place I consider home and leave the work I find fulfilling. I can't imagine my life without Gran. It's bad enough to have to live it without Laney." Leaving would be simple. Staying would be hell. Because she was in love with Rowan.

Woody looked at Desiree thoughtfully. "I want what's best for you but is any change your wisest choice right now? Don't rush into a decision. Don't run away from your problems."

With a gesture of resignation, she replied, "I'm not. I promised Rowan I'd be his Event Coordinator until after New Year's Eve. It's the practical solution for the time being. And it wouldn't be fair to leave my grandmother right now. She's been through a lot, just like me."

Woody admired Desiree's compassion for others. He gave her a long searching look. Desiree appeared to be composed but as he looked closer he saw the heartbreak within. He dared to ask, "Is staying more difficult because you're in love with Rowan?"

Desiree didn't even consider denying it. She knew Rowan had implanted himself in every aspect of her life. "Oh, God, is it that obvious?"

Woody reached over and lovingly caressed her cheek. "I read expressions. I see it when you talk about him, when you look at him."

Desiree didn't take offense because she knew he spoke the truth.

"You deserve to be happy so make the most of your life. Commit to a willingness to take the risk for a chance at happiness. You're being influenced by Maeve and her actions. You've been in her way since the day you arrived. In her mind, you're preventing her from what she believes is rightfully hers and that's Rowan Le Baron. She feels entitled to him and she'll say and do anything to keep him. It could be possible that Rowan doesn't feel the same way. I've seen how he looks at you. As an artist, I read people's faces all the time and, as a result, you get to be a good judge of character. Rowan Le Baron has integrity. You can trust him."

Desiree said nothing as she closed her eyes. She was trying not to place too much significance on what Woody had said. But she couldn't stop herself from feeling a surge of optimism. She felt a greater force pushing her. She could almost hear Laney saying, "Fight for him. Take a chance." She ignored the inner voice that dared her.

Desiree deliberately changed the subject. She considered Woody a valued friend. It was the gentleness in him that she loved along with his compassion, his sound advice, his warm friendship. She needed him now. She needed to laugh again. She smiled at Woody with a glitter of mischief in her eyes. "There's something else I need to talk to you about. I need an assistant. Before I give you the details, you must swear to secrecy." Desiree knew her mind was all too active and it often got her into situations but this time she was willing to run with it. When the thought first came to her, she gave herself a talking to. *You will not lower yourself to Maeve's level.* It didn't work. She got past the feeling of guilt, reminding herself that Maeve deserved this. As soon as the skeleton arrived with the decorations, the idea was implanted.

Woody immediately crossed his heart. He stared suspiciously at Desiree. He detected the sparkle of naughtiness in her eyes and could hardly wait to hear what she had in mind.

With a wicked grin, Desiree quickly got to the point, "I've told you how Maeve is always making barbed comments and tries to make me look inept or puts me at a disadvantage. You saw it for yourself when you brought the painting to my office. I know they say it's better to turn the other cheek but this will be much more fun."

After listening to her plan, Woody chuckled as he agreed without hesitation. He loved her sense of humor. "It's not an assistant you require, it's an accomplice."

"My old accomplice would love this," Desiree informed Woody.

Woody knew she meant Laney. "When do you plan to do this?"

"Tomorrow night. I overheard that Rowan and Maeve have a dinner engagement away from the hotel. We can do it then. Maeve doesn't lock her office. Not only will it be easy to get in, but in reality, anybody could. Although I'm sure I'll be the likely suspect. So I'll stand guard while you position the skeleton." she declared with a conspiratorial smile.

As her accomplice, Woody had to question her strategy, "Why do I have to put the skeleton in her office?"

Desiree blinked her eyes in disbelief. "Because Rowan will immediately assume I did it. So, when he asks if I put the skeleton in Maeve's office, I can honestly say no. I won't have to lie to my boss. We can't have that now can we?"

It was then that Woody realized that behind Desiree's soft, demure look ticked a sharp and devilish brain. "No, of course not. And here I thought you were such a sweet person. I guess there's just no telling about people." Woody tried to be serious but he broke out laughing. Desiree had always impressed Woody with her acts of kindness and her sense of fairness. This was a side of her he hadn't seen.

"It comes from experience," Desiree confessed with a mischievous giggle.

The rain had stopped but by the time they reached the hotel thunder again boomed overhead. Pulling up his collar, Woody said, "I'll head straight home. I hope I make it without getting wet. See you tomorrow. Try to behave until then," he teased as he pressed a good-bye kiss on her cheek.

The next day Desiree did her best to appear normal but she could hardly contain herself as she waited for the end of the work day. All day she was fidgety and she did her best to avoid both Rowan and Maeve.

Rowan knew Desiree was up to something but he didn't have the faintest notion what it was. He decided he'd have to just wait and see. The girl was a challenge but an interesting one.

Desiree managed to keep busy and promptly left at the end of her work day. She quickly escaped upstairs. After dinner she excused herself on the pretext of having to get something from her office. It wasn't unusual for Desiree to be spending extra hours on the Benefit so she didn't have to go into any explanation.

Desiree's eyes were bright with excitement as she met Woody. She started to giggle when she saw him. He had definitely gotten into character and dressed appropriately for his role. He was attired completely in black and wore a baseball cap pulled low over his eyes.

As planned, Woody brought a large duffle bag and they quickly stuffed the skeleton inside. They placed it on the luggage rack that Desiree had brought with her. It was clear sailing as they made a beeline to Maeve's office until they rounded the last corner. Desiree's breath caught when she saw Mrs. Billings, a live-in resident, heading to the lift. She stopped

Woody from proceeding until the door closed. The last thing she wanted was to have a chit-chat with the resident gossip. As soon as it was clear they continued on to Maeve's office. The coast was still clear when they got there.

Woody took the duffle bag and hurried inside so he could position the skeleton at Maeve's desk while Desiree stood outside on guard. With some ingenious maneuvering, he began positioning the skeleton in Maeve's chair while adjusting the blond wig. To his relief it stayed on. Woody was really getting into it. "Her boss must be a real slave driver. The poor woman has worked her fingers to the bone." Desiree was so nervous that Woody's whisperings sounded like he was yelling.

"Woody, come on." Giggling hysterically Desiree pleaded, "Hurry up and get out."

Woody leaned against the desk. It was good to hear her laugh again. He turned and spoke to the skeleton, "Nag, nag, nag. That's all the girl does. You're much more of the quiet type." He leaned over and kissed the skeleton's hand.

Desiree finally went in and grabbed Woody's arm and pulled him out. Neither one of them could stop laughing.

"Congratulations," Woody said, sending Desiree a respectful nod. "That was one of the smoothest capers I've witnessed."

Desiree beamed and tucked her arm through his as they strolled away.

Maeve was immersed in conversation with reception when Desiree came down the next morning. Desiree hustled past, wanting to get into her own office before Maeve went into hers.

Rowan was already at his desk. With no more than a very quick, "Good morning," Desiree rushed into her office and closed her door.

Rowan eyed her suspiciously. He knew her well enough to know she was avoiding him.

Desiree sat at her desk unable to work. She waited, wishing she could be there to see Maeve's reaction. It was only a matter of minutes before Desiree heard Maeve's shriek. "Rowan, get in here."

Desiree bit her lip to prevent herself from laughing out loud. Within minutes Rowan buzzed her to come to his office. Her breath caught in her throat. Desiree took a deep breath to regain her composure.

"Sit down." Rowan's voice was firm.

Desiree did as she was ordered and looked him straight in the eyes. Her heart hammered a bit but her face was the picture of innocence.

"Did you put that skeleton in Maeve's office?"

Desiree managed to suppress a smile but her eyes were alive with obvious pleasure. "No. But I wish I'd been there to see it."

Rowan eyed her doubtfully. "Did you have one of the staff put it in her office?"

Her response maintained the tone of innocence. "No." Desiree didn't appreciate his snort of disbelief. Rowan waited, the pause obviously designed for Desiree to comment. She continued to sit calmly with her hands clasped in her lap.

Rowan tried a different approach. "Are you responsible for this incident?"

Without flinching, her eyes met his. Her answer was the truth, "Yes. Obviously I am the person responsible for the Halloween theme and it's evident that both staff and guests have gotten caught up in the theme. It might be surprising who really did it. *Like you'd ever guess.* Believe it or not, I may not be the only person here who doesn't like Maeve Spencer."

Desiree didn't look the least bit contrite, nor did Rowan believe she'd given him the whole truth. Yes, it was probably true that she personally didn't put the skeleton in Maeve's office but there was no doubt in his mind that she was the instigator. "Well, based on your answers, I guess there's nothing further to discuss unless there's something more you want to add." There was a definite smile in his voice.

"No. Unless you still have a bone to pick with me?"

Desiree was relieved when she heard the thread of amusement in Rowan's voice, "Off you go. Do you think you might have a use for our unexplained visitor?"

Desiree could tell that Rowan was more amused than annoyed. She smiled at him, "Well, we might as well make the best of this. I'll find a more suitable place for him." Before she could stop herself she asked, "May I have a key to Maeve's suite?"

Rowan looked at Desiree, glad to see the fire of life in her eyes again. His smile matched hers. "You're still a brat."

CHAPTER SIXTEEN

Now that her days were less pressured, Desiree could once again spend more time with her grandmother. Desiree found it was getting easier to talk about Laney. The fact that Desiree could talk about her had become part of her healing process, slowly filling the hole in her heart. "I wish you had met her and seen her determination and her zest for life. Together, Laney and I had a wicked sense of humor. But we were never destructive or hurtful."

"You still do. That skeleton episode was a novel idea and executed brilliantly."

"It was so much fun, Gran." As soon as the words were out her mouth dropped open. "But how did you know?" And then she started to giggle. "Does Rowan know it was me?"

"Of course he does. But he doesn't know how you accomplished it. He knows you didn't lie to him when you said it wasn't you who put the skeleton in Maeve's office. Rowan couldn't quit laughing when he told me about it. I guess the expression on Maeve's' face was priceless and he said her scream was bone-chilling. He seems to have more of a sense of humor since you arrived. You're a good influence on him in many ways."

Desiree quickly changed the subject, "The Benefit is coming fast. I think it's time to order our costumes. Have you thought about your costume, Gran?"

Constance shook her head, still bewildered at how Desiree had talked Rowan into the Halloween theme. The Conlyn Grand Hotel had never hosted a Masquerade Ball.

Desiree's face brightened, "Well, I have. What do you think about being the Queen of Hearts? You have the gift of love that comes straight from your heart. And you are definitely the Queen of this castle."

"Well, how can I say no to that," Constance said, displaying an endearing enthusiasm.

Boris, who had just walked in with tea, stated in his dry humor, "It's a good thing you don't expect me to attend. You'd have me dressed as the court jester." Both women smothered their need to laugh at his deadpan delivery.

"What about you, Desiree?"

"Honestly, with everything else that's been happening, I haven't thought much about it."

Constance looked at Desiree and her heart hurt for a moment. "With your new haircut, being Cleopatra is the obvious choice. Your haircut completely changed your look."

Desiree agreed and was relieved knowing she'd crossed another item off her list.

It was hard to believe it was only a week until the Benefit. Everything had come together nicely but this last week would be intense. Rowan was gone by the time Desiree went downstairs. She'd forgot that he had an early appointment. Maeve was civil, even friendly as she was coming out of Desiree's office. Desiree was instantly suspicious and wondered why Maeve was even in her office. Being busy, she didn't contemplate it for long.

It was mid-afternoon when Desiree returned to her office. She went to grab her Project Orange folder. When it wasn't where she always put it, she felt a stab of panic. She knew she was tired and had been distracted the last few days but she couldn't see herself misplacing her folder. She was quickly becoming flustered.

She was so busy rummaging through her papers on her desk that she failed to realize that Rowan had walked in. "What are you looking for?"

"My Project folder which has all my lists, modified notes, contact numbers and floor plan," Desiree said as she crossed over to the file cabinet and started rifling through it.

Rowan realized that she was truly rattled. "It has to be here. You probably misplaced it." At Desiree's scowling look, even he knew that was highly unlikely. No one was more organized than she was.

"Thank God, here it is," Desiree exclaimed as she pulled it out from behind the filing cabinet. There was no way it could have fallen there. She felt a sudden chill that started at the base of her spine. *Even Maeve can't be that malicious.* A warning bell began to ring in her head. *I'm an idiot. That's why Maeve was in my office.* She couldn't forget Maeve's smirky smile as she glanced over her shoulder on her way out. Desiree recalled Cal telling her to watch her back and not to trust Maeve. Desiree had put it out of her mind. But it sure made sense now. *I wonder what else she did?*

Desiree refrained from saying anything as she forced her thoughts back to the task at hand. It would've been so easy to march right into Maeve's office and shout her anger but she knew she had to handle it in a different way. Her old way always got her in trouble. Desiree would bide her time for now. But this did nothing to improve her cranky disposition. There were still too many things left to do.

Rowan knew there was more to this than met the eye. Much more. He quickly addressed the reason for being in her office. He surprised Desiree when he said, "I would like you to give the speech after the meal." This was not a demand but a request.

"Will you want to approve it first?" She enjoyed giving him a hard time.

He couldn't resist teasing her back. "I don't believe that's necessary. You're never at a loss for words and you're very gifted in using them." Before she could voice any objections, he added, "From day one this has been your vision. I have complete confidence in you."

Desiree was more than honored and quickly agreed.

Later in the day, when she knew Rowan wasn't around, Desiree decided to confront her enemy. She marched down the hall in a controlled fury. With folder in hand and fire in her eyes she entered Maeve's office without knocking.

Maeve's face paled when she saw the folder.

Today Desiree was going to impart a few unadorned facts to this woman who badly needed to hear them. She erupted, "You're contemptible but your spiteful games are pointless."

Maeve looked at the folder. With a skill Desiree had to admire, Maeve recovered immediately. "I have no idea what you're talking about."

Desiree glared at her in disbelief. "Don't be obtuse. Did you think I wouldn't find my folder you hid?" Desiree lifted her head with a look of power. If Maeve thought she'd simply ignore this she was wrong. She and Laney had learned to fight for what they wanted along with what they believed in. Desiree could hold her own with Maeve or anyone else.

Maeve's expression remained unchanged. "How dare you stand there flinging accusations? I resent your insinuation."

"But you can't deny it, can you? You wasted your time and mine and all it did was make you look petty. I didn't think you'd stoop so low. What do you think Rowan would say?"

"Rowan and I understand each other. I've been an important part of his life for years. I don't appreciate all the time you've been spending with him, Des. I did warn you to keep your distance." Her tone matched the coldness in her eyes.

"It's Desiree. Only my friends get to call me Des."

"You haven't been in England long. Why don't you go back to the United States where you belong? The old lady bought it all. The big innocent eyes, the helpless granddaughter looking for her forgotten past. She thinks she has her daughter back. But you're not her. You're nothing more than a long lost relative that was taken in out of pity."

Desiree knew Maeve could be vicious but this was a truth she couldn't deny. Her face paled as the words hit her.

Maeve knew she had hit a nerve and continued. "Rowan's been diverted because of his devotion to Constance. Since I'm going to marry Rowan, it's time for him to refocus."

"You've never once said that you love Rowan." The calculated look on Maeve's face told Desiree she wasn't wrong.

"That's a minor price to pay for a man of his stature and wealth." An evil look came over Maeve's face. "Oh, my God! Tweedle Dee fell in love with the Bear. How pathetic." There was something frightening and determined about the way Maeve now looked at Desiree. Her eyes narrowed, "I've read up on the Dare twins and how demanding Delaney was and that she used people to get ahead in business. They say she'd do anything to get what she wanted. It appears that you've morphed into your evil twin."

Desiree felt her blood run cold. It was no secret that Maeve didn't like her and she resented her position as co-chair of the Benefit but now it had become personal. Without hesitation, Desiree slapped Maeve across her face. The sound of flesh on flesh echoed through the room. Both women stared at each other in shock. Maeve could say what she wanted about her but Laney was off limits. "Stay out of my life." Desiree turned and left the room.

Desiree knew she had to put what just happened out of her mind and refocus on the Event. Still distraught, she almost ran into Rowan. The episode between her and Maeve had upset her more than she realized. Her shoulders were tense and she had a headache. She stared at Rowan while she continued to struggle with her temper. But for once, Desiree held her tongue. Instead she said, "Sorry, I was distracted. There's still so much to do for the Benefit. Every time I think I'm in control something else pops up." She rubbed her tense neck in frustration.

"You know you have everything in control. The little things will take care of themselves or they won't matter." Rowan could tell that Desiree's nerves were frayed and her body was fatigued. All week she'd put in endless hours. Not to mention her personal struggles. Without a word, he headed off to the spa. Desiree headed off in the opposite direction.

It was the day before the Ball and Desiree knew it would be a busy one. There was still a lot to do. Just before eight o'clock she stepped into the hall to meet with the display company's representative. After a brief conversation, he quickly had his crew working. Desiree looked around the hall with a thoughtful eye and went to muster her own troops. She turned to Andy, "I will trust you to keep an eye on everything throughout the evening. You've been such a big help right from the start. Let me say thanks now. I appreciate everything you've done, sometimes twice. Sarah, bring Jayne and follow me. I'm going to show you how to arrange the table centerpieces. Then I'll leave you to do the rest." Once she knew they understood her design, she left them on their own. Desiree had to admit the centerpieces looked amazing.

When Rowan walked into the hall he had no trouble finding Desiree. She was up on the ladder trying to secure a string of lights that had come loose. Avoiding the decorating crew that was bustling around, he crossed the floor. He raked a hand through his hair as he looked up at her in disbelief. "Are you out of you mind? Get down from there. Why didn't you get one of the boys to do that?"

There was amusement in Desiree's eyes as she climbed down. "Don't take that tone of voice with me, Rowan. Sometimes it's quicker to do it yourself than explain it to someone else. Laney and I did this stuff all the time to help the boys set up the stage. I am more than capable of helping. I'm not your ordinary office girl, you know."

Constance, who had come down to take a look, smiled. "Are you two fighting again?"

"No," Rowan replied.

"Yes," Desiree replied at the same time.

The arguing continued. "Are you trying to be difficult?"

"No, I can be difficult without trying."

"You really are stubborn."

"Adamant, definitely determined," she corrected. Desiree enjoyed the verbal sparring.

"More like pig-headed," he said bluntly, but his eyes smiled back at her.

Constance laughed as she interrupted the two of them, "I just had to come for a quick peak. The ballroom looks wonderful. I can't believe the transformation."

"Despite what you just heard Rowan and I are in complete agreement that everything is going to look marvelous. I knew this was a good idea." She said it smugly.

"You're awfully young to be a know-it-all," Rowan said, before turning to Constance. "Your granddaughter can be awfully stubborn."

"You're every bit as stubborn as she is, Rowan Le Baron. I'm so proud of what you both have done. I can't believe how excited I am." Constance grinned, "I feel like a kid again."

No sooner had Constance and Rowan left and Maeve strolled over, fashionably attired in a charcoal gray dress and black patent heels. "Can I help?"

The ill-timed offer tried Desiree's patience, which she had no problem admitting she had a short supply of. She knew that Maeve was only offering because Rowan was within earshot. "You're hardly dressed to help,

Maeve. Mind you, you've had no trouble climbing the ladder of success in high heels."

Maeve chose to ignore Dee's comment. "I've never understood what possessed Rowan to trust you with this project. You'll never get this set up in time. You're totally disorganized and out of your league on this. It looks like a circus."

"That's why I'm running this Event. You can't even tell the difference between a circus and a Halloween party."

Because Rowan was watching carefully, he saw Desiree's eyes darken. He knew her temper was winning and from the few times he'd seen it fly he knew Maeve was in for it. But to Rowan's surprise, Desiree quickly composed herself and simply shook her head.

Desiree decided to put aside her negative thoughts and not let Maeve get to her. She was disappointed that Maeve could never see her vision. She had worked hard and knew it would all come together.

Rowan was quick to return to her side before she could race off somewhere else. "I've booked a massage for you."

Desiree felt tears fill her eyes and felt foolish because she could have hugged him. "What a wonderful surprise, Rowan." Desiree looked down at the papers on her clipboard. "But there are still things to do." She went and sat down on the stage steps, fighting exhaustion and the pain in the small of her back. "I need to be here helping with the mayhem. I need to see if everything is under control. There are things that need my attention."

He could see how drawn and tired she looked and dropped down beside her. "You've been overdoing it. Go have your massage and call it a day." Rowan flashed a wide grin knowing she was struggling with giving up control. "Don't like taking orders do you? You're much too used to giving them. Tell me what's left to do?" His tone was firm.

Desiree glanced at her clipboard. She removed a piece of paper with a scribbled list and with a weary gesture she reluctantly handed it to Rowan. "See, I told you lists were useful."

Rowan grabbed her list and sauntered off whistling.

Desiree realized that Rowan understood how trying and difficult these last few weeks had been on her. Her tired features brightened. She was looking forward to the massage.

Thanks to the massage, Desiree felt like a new woman. Refreshed, she returned to the ballroom after dinner. She knew she wouldn't be able to sleep until she'd checked everything out one last time. Thinking she was alone, she wandered around the room. Desiree saw the fulfillment of her vision and felt the excitement as she anticipated tomorrow.

To her surprise, she came face to face with Rowan when she got back to the doorway. He smiled knowingly, "Checking up on me?"

Desiree looked a little sheepish. "I want everything to be perfect." The two of them surveyed the hall, both proud of their accomplishments. She smiled, satisfied.

"Tired?"

"Yes, but in a good way."

"Well, head off to bed and get your beauty sleep. It will be a big day tomorrow."

Desiree woke early filled with excitement. It had been an intense week and now the long awaited day had arrived. Thanks to the massage, Desiree felt refreshed and ready to take on the day. The warm rays of the morning sun drew her to the window. Taking a few minutes for herself, Desiree took her usual seat. Out of habit she turned to her twin. *Oh, Laney, I wish you were here. You would enjoy this so much.* It was still strange not having her here.

After breakfast Desiree headed downstairs. Today, there were no pressures other than the last minute details that had to be attended to. She could feel the anticipation like a hum in the air and knew it would only intensify throughout the day. The hotel was buzzing like a beehive. Staff was caught peeking into the ballroom and giggled when they were caught. The hall had been transformed and was ready for the Spooktacular Masquerade Ball.

Rowan saw Desiree in the hall and was greeted with a quick hello as she passed by. Gauging by the degree of determination in her step he knew she was on a mission. Throughout the morning he watched Desiree race around, solving problems, checking and rechecking every detail. He was no longer amazed at what she did. It was organized chaos but also exhilarating.

Rowan was drawn by the sound of laughter drifting from the kitchen where frenzied preparations were still taking place. As he entered, Desiree was licking orange frosting from her fingers. On the table in front of her was an assortment of themed cupcakes. A staff member was putting black licorice legs on the ones that were spiders.

Desiree took another bite of her cupcake and now had orange icing on her fingers and all around her mouth. "Taste test," she said with her mouth full. Rowan grabbed hers and took a huge bite. He nodded his approval, his mouth too full to speak.

Desiree gave him a quick update. "Everything is ready in here except for final touches and setting out the food. Sarah has that covered when the time comes. And I don't know what I'd do without Andy. He's setting up the bars. He laughed when he saw the boxes of fangs under the counter. I believe we're ready."

"Then off you go, young lady. It's time to go and get ready for tonight."

Desiree took the opportunity to slip outside for a breath of air before heading upstairs. Rowan saw her leave and sensed that she needed to be alone. The trees that were shades of vivid greens only weeks ago were now bare. Warm copper, gold and russet red leaves had been shed and now blanketed the ground below. Desiree strolled along the leaf-strewn pathway. Fall had definitely arrived but fortunately the mild weather remained much to Desiree's delight. The sun shone bright and the temperature was warm for fall. She knew that when the sun went down the air would chill but it wouldn't have the bite of winter. It was a perfect day. It was good; it was all good. She glanced at her watch and smiled. It was time to go upstairs and get ready.

Desiree slipped quietly back into the hotel and headed to the private lift. The door opened and to her surprise Rowan was standing inside. She looked up and her smile brightened her face. "I took a moment and went out to the garden to clear my head. A little fresh air can do wonders." She blushed, recalling the night of her dance.

Rowan laughed out loud knowing why she blushed. He held the door for her as he stepped out. "We better hurry and change. We have a party to attend and we'll want to greet our guests when they start to arrive."

Boris and Constance were both flitting around the flat. Constance was already in her costume and looked regal in every way. Desiree hugged her grandmother. "I'm so excited. I hope everyone enjoys themselves. I want the Benefit to be a success for our Charity. Oh, Boris, doesn't Gran look magnificent?"

"Indeed she does," he said as he bowed in jest.

In her bedroom the nerves surfaced. Unconcerned, Desiree knew that once she put on her costume her inner Raven would kick in and she'd be fine. On her way to the bathroom she noticed the flowers on the dresser. Smiling, Desiree reached for the card thinking how thoughtful her grandmother was. She was shocked when she opened the card. Recognizing the bold handwriting, the card read, *Glad you took on the challenge. GREAT JOB! Rowan.* The words made her heart swell for she appreciated the praise.

Once Desiree had changed into her costume the nerves were gone. This was like performing. It was now time to embrace her role and take center stage. She took one last look in the mirror. She looked calm and composed. Desiree closed her eyes and in her mind she could hear Laney say, "Showtime."

Rowan greeted Constance and Desiree when they arrived downstairs. He knew Desiree well enough to recognize both her excitement and her anticipation. He took a moment to look around, seeing it all through her eyes. The full effect was breathtaking. "It really is magical, isn't it? You more than met the challenge, Desiree."

Desiree smiled up at Rowan as he stood at her side. A flush warmed her cheeks. "The flowers are beautiful."

Overhearing Desiree's last comment, Maeve, who had just arrived, scanned the room failing to see flowers anywhere.

Always observant, Rowan winked at Desiree as she mouthed, "Thank you."

Desiree gazed around making sure everything was in order. The ballroom looked spectacular. Flickering light from lit candles in tall candelabras danced beautifully on the black curtains draped around the room, undeniably setting the ambiance for a haunted evening. Rowan leaned in closer to Desiree's ear. "We've done all we can. Now is the time to stop worrying and enjoy the evening. This is your party."

"Don't remind me. I pray everything goes well."

"You know it never does. But together we'll deal with the little things." Rowan smiled and turned to greet a guest.

Maeve, who was out of earshot of Rowan, turned to Desiree. "I thought for sure you'd come as Tweedle Dee," she said spitefully. At one time Desiree would have cringed but now the painful nickname had no power to hurt her.

Ignoring Maeve, she turned to welcome Cal who had just arrived totally in character as Dracula. Desiree shook her head in amusement. Cal was never one to disappoint.

Cal looked at her in awe. "Blimey, Dee, you cut your hair. Shocking, but stunning."

Desiree flashed a pleased smile. She'd have to tell Cal how so much more had changed.

Rowan, dressed as Robin Hood, greeted Cal. Both men looked impressive in their attire.

Cal couldn't resist, "Here to steal from the rich?" Desiree recognized the mischief in Cal's voice. He turned to Maeve, who as usual, was at Rowan's side. "And you must be Old Maid Marion," he mocked.

Everyone nearby laughed, except Maeve, who found his humor less than amusing. Her eyes flashed with daggers as her face reddened. "You should've dressed as the devil."

Infuriating Maeve more, he grabbed her tight. "Come closer, I vant to bite your neck."

"I really don't appreciate your caustic wit," Maeve snapped.

"Have a positive attitude, Maeve, and try to look like you're enjoying yourself," he whispered in her ear before letting her go.

Desiree turned to Cal. "You're wicked."

"I know. That's why you love me. I told you that it amuses me to annoy Maeve."

Desiree excused herself and took on the role of hostess as she'd seen Maeve do on several occasions. The hum of excited chatter took away her fears. Guests began to form small groups at tables and in corners. Others flitted from group to group. She moved through the noise and excitement as she greeted their guests and spoke gracefully to as many as she could.

A gentle tap on her shoulder drew her attention. The friendly eyes were familiar and held a sparkle of humor. "Woody?"

The street urchin bowed in acknowledgement. "A lot of people know me so I'd like to remain incognito. This is your night and nothing should distract from it. But I had to come. Someone told me it would be an Event like no other. You're right. Great job, Des."

Desiree's eyes were swimming with mirth and there was unmistakable affection in her voice as she promised, "Your secret is safe with me. By the way your costume is great."

"Yours is spectacular. Perfect costume with your new haircut. You're so beautiful. One day you must let me paint your portrait."

Desiree beamed with pleasure. "You always flatter me. Thanks."

"Save me a dance?" Woody asked, his voice a gentle whisper.

Desiree nodded as more guests arrived and she left to greet them. Bright-colored costumes were everywhere. Every era was represented, from caveman to futuristic. And there was no end of super heroes.

Rowan waved at Desiree and she knew it was time to join him at the head table. With confidence, she crossed the room to take her place. He watched in awe as Desiree made her way through the crowded room, taking the time to chat with guests at their tables. Rowan was struck by her natural ease with people. As soon as Desiree reached his side at the head table Rowan, as co-owner of the Hotel and co-chair of the Benefit, welcomed everyone. Desiree was impressed by his ease. "I'm so honored to be standing here tonight with my co-chair, Desiree Dare. We're touched by the incredible turnout for this evening."

Desiree observed the curiosity in Cal's eyes when Rowan introduced her as Desiree Dare. Cal still had no idea that she had regained her memory. She'd have to find time later to explain. Sitting at a table in front of the head table was a young lady beautifully dressed as a gypsy. How many times had the twins been called gypsies growing up? At that moment, Desiree knew Laney was watching over her and was there in spirit.

The atmosphere in the ballroom of the Conlyn Grand Hotel was electric as laughter and music floated everywhere. After the meal was over, the dessert table became as big a success as the appetizer table had been. When friends came over to talk to Constance, Desiree took the opportunity to slip outside. She needed to focus her thoughts before she had to give her speech. Desiree made her way through the guests as she headed to the exit. Conversation followed her. "What a fun idea. Wait until the grandkids see our photos. How creative was that desert table? I hope they do this again next year."

Desiree's smile was wide as she sat in the garden. The first part of the evening was a huge success but the fund raising itself lay ahead. She hoped it would be the success she envisioned. This was such an important cause.

Rowan approached her when she returned. "Are you ready? It's time for your speech."

Desiree nodded as she felt her stomach clench with anxiety but she forced her expression to remain composed. Rowan squeezed her hand. "Off you go, young lady. Work your charm."

Desiree had spent countless hours preparing her speech. At first, she struggled trying to decide what to say. In the end, she knew her only option was to be genuine and speak from her heart. She had practiced her speech over and over in her room for the last week but she was still a little nervous.

Appreciative of Rowan's encouraging smile, she took the stage. His physical presence brought her reassurance. The music stopped and seconds later she could hear the ballroom go quiet. Looking out at the crowd her eyes came to rest on the gypsy. *Thanks for being here, Laney.* Desiree was completely composed when she took the microphone; it was like holding hands with an old friend. "On behalf of Constance Malone, Rowan Le Baron and the family here at the Conlyn Grand Hotel we want to thank all of you for attending our Spooktacular Soiree. This was definitely a change from the traditional gala of previous years and we hope that you all enjoy the rest of the evening. As much fun as the evening has been with the dramatic change from our traditional past, the goal of this Event is still the same."

With inherent ease and confidence she continued, "Constance and Rowan are of one belief, you always give back and giving to charity is a large part of the Conlyn Grand Hotel philosophy. I have been blessed to see this first hand more than once during the short time that I've been living here with my grandmother, Constance."

Desiree paused dramatically and her tone changed. "Having spent time recently in the hospital I relate to the fear of the unknown. It's very frightening not knowing what's going to happen the day after today. No child should have to struggle through such a trauma. We are asking you to help take away that fear and give the gift of hope."

"In preparation for this Event I went and spent time at Evelina Children's Hospital and I was so impressed with the facility and with the staff who provide high quality, compassionate and innovative care. It is a world-class hospital with the latest technology and the best specialists, scientists and health professionals. There are many wonderful things that help to make it feel like the patients aren't in a hospital. Their rooms are bright; the halls are filled with cheerful art work. They have a cinema and they bring in special visitors who spend time with the children. Specialty toys, like Charlie Doll or Cathy Doll, are instrumental in helping children as well as their parents, understand what is being done to their bodies. These special dolls are anatomically correct and are used every day to help hundreds of children a year cope easier with their time in the hospital. The hospital would not be able to buy these without the help of donations so it relies heavily on people's kind generosity. Support from wonderful donors through fundraisers is what helps buy specialist items like these dolls plus so much more."

"That first day that I went to Evelina Children's Hospital I met Beth, a six year old girl who had cancer." Desiree faltered just thinking of Beth. She continued, trying to keep her voice steady, "This unfortunate child had spent extended periods of her young life in the hospital, receiving all kinds of treatment and procedures. Sadly, she passed away." To Desiree's distress, tears began to gather in her eyes as she continued telling Beth's heartbreaking story. When she was done, Desiree took a moment to compose herself.

Desiree smiled at everyone through her tears. "There is still a child in every one of us. This evening's event allowed that inner child to come out. I know everyone here is having a good time. Don't our children deserve the same? We hope you will find it in your hearts to donate to our cause so that today's children can have every opportunity to become tomorrow's adults. That opportunity shouldn't be taken from them because there isn't money for research, technology and specialty equipment. Or for a special doll that brings comfort when it's needed most." Rowan nodded in agreement. Desiree was right and he was proud of her.

A heartfelt sigh escaped Desiree's lips. "I'm so glad you were all able to grace us with your presence this evening. In hopes of making this evening a true success please open your hearts and wallets for today's children. It has been an evening of trick-or-treat fun so let's give these kids the treat of another tomorrow."

It wasn't only the women who were wiping tears from their eyes as thunderous applause broke out. Flushed with a mixture of pride and embarrassment, she thanked everyone.

Rowan's chest swelled with pride as she walked gracefully back to the table. "What an unbelievable evening. You were amazing. Your speech had everyone reaching for their pocketbooks and wallets. Well done. You did a wonderful job, Dee."

"I'm Desiree," she corrected.

"I know, but it was Dee who sparked the idea for tonight's soiree. She just passed the baton. I'm very proud of you both."

Desiree's face was radiant. "I had the best time of my life working on this Event. I must admit that there's definite satisfaction in succeeding. More than anything I wanted to prove myself to you and I'm proud that I did that. But it became much more than that when I realized I wanted to succeed for the Benefit more than for myself."

This woman never ceased to amaze him. Rowan continued standing there regarding Desiree in a thoughtful silence that she found even more disturbing than his conversation.

Maeve walked over and extended her hand to Desiree. "I have to congratulate you. You pulled off a very successful Event." Desiree could see she meant it. "I must confess, I didn't think you had it in you."

"Thank you, Maeve. The efforts of everyone contributed to its success."

Later in the evening, Rowan went looking for Desiree. He found her in the kitchen thanking the staff for all their hard work and congratulating them on a job well done.

Returning to the hall together, they were passing by Maeve as she was talking to a couple dressed as Raggedy Ann and Raggedy Andy. "My husband and I are having a wonderful time. What a novel idea."

"Thank you. Rowan and I thought it was time for a change from the usual black and white affair."

Typical Maeve, thought Desiree. Unfortunately, some people never change.

Before Maeve could continue, Rowan interjected, "Actually it was Desiree's idea and her hard work that made this evening so successful." He held Desiree firmly by the elbow so she couldn't escape.

"Brilliant idea, young lady. This will be remembered as one of the best parties of the season. I hope it becomes an annual event."

Desiree smiled politely and excused herself to mingle with other guests. Many were gathered around the dessert table and the bars. The largest crowd was gathered at the photo booth. She knew it would be a hit. Laughter and music filled the room.

Rowan sought out Desiree when the DJ announced the first dance. She knew as co-chairs it was their duty to take the floor first. Her nerves jumped at the thought of waltzing with Rowan again. She was sure he could hear her heart beating when he took her in his arms. He smiled down at Desiree, "I lost count how many times I heard someone say what a wonderful evening this is. Thank you for all you've done. This evening far exceeded my expectations. It has been fantastic and I couldn't be more pleased."

"Sometimes the hard things in life are the most rewarding," Desiree said sincerely.

"You're the one who had the vision and followed it through every step of the way." Rowan's eyes twinkled. "I hold you entirely responsible for the evening's success. The Charity is lucky and so am I."

Desiree laughed when she saw a drunken sailor dancing with the skeleton. Rowan and Desiree shared a knowing glance. There was enough humor in Rowan's eyes to tell her he knew where her mind had gone. She also knew full well that he knew that she was involved in its appearance in Maeve's office.

The entire evening flew by. All too soon the party was over and the last of the guests had finally gone. Desiree knew she wouldn't be able to sleep if she went up to the flat. Instead, she snuck into the lounge for a moment of solitude. She sat down at the piano and began to play. Aware that someone else had come into the room, she looked up and smiled. Rowan stood there with two flutes of champagne. Without a word, Desiree accepted the glass he handed her. He sat next to her on the piano stool. It was the perfect ending to a magical evening.

Chapter Seventeen

Now that the Benefit was over, Desiree knew it was time to think about Christmas. She went looking for Maeve hoping to discuss decorating the hotel for Christmas and begin planning the New Year's Eve gala. Desiree's attention was drawn to the commotion at the reception desk. The concierge was talking to a tall man whose waste-length hair had been secured behind his neck with a leather thong. As he stood there in ripped jeans and well-worn denim jacket, it was evident that he came from a totally different world. Desiree couldn't believe her eyes. The man's rakish features were familiar. Desiree stood frozen, her eyes wide when she realized who the visitor was.

Just then he turned and looked over. Cash Bentley's grin added interest to his rugged looks. Bronzed skin confirmed he still spent his time in the California sun.

Desiree stared wide-eyed at Cash realizing that he really was here in the flesh. Unable to contain her pleasure, she cried out and ran into his arms. His arms around her brought comfort and with it a familiarity of something they shared with no other.

Cash held her longer than he should have but he didn't want to let her go. Feeling a lump in his throat, in a strangled whisper he simply said, "Hello, Des."

Their eyes met and held, hers wide and haunted, his narrow and troubled. Neither said a word for several moments. They fought back tears as they looked at each other, momentarily clinging onto the past.

Cash blinked first knowing he saw a more mature looking Desiree. "It's wonderful to see you," he said, flashing her a genuine smile. He had an amazing voice, deep and distinctive.

"How did you know where to find me?" she asked in astonishment.

Before Cash could answer, Rowan appeared. The two men stood staring at each other for a long moment. Two dynamically different men, one in tattered jeans, the other in a custom tailored suit. "Nice to see you again, Cash," Rowan said as they shook hands.

"You, too." Cash was a man of few words when he was in an uncomfortable situation.

Desiree responded in shock, "You two know each other?"

Cash nodded, "We've met."

Rowan explained, "We met when you were in the hospital. Cash was kind enough to keep what happened to you and Laney out of the papers. With his help we let the public think you and Laney had extended your holiday for personal reasons. The band's response to any gossip was always 'no comment'. I'm not excusing what we did. We did it to protect you."

Cash turned to Desiree. "Mr. Le Baron invited me here as his guest. I'll be staying for a couple of days."

Rowan could see that Desiree was in shock. It was a look he'd seen not that long ago. All the color had left her face. "Take the next few days off so you can spend time catching up with Cash." Knowing she was about to refuse, Rowan insisted, "You need this time together."

Rowan's gentleness was almost her undoing. Desiree struggled to compose herself. "Thank you, Rowan." She tucked her arm around Cash's arm. "Why don't you get settled and I'll come up once I clear my calendar and straighten my desk." Suddenly it was all too much for her. Desiree left the two men staring intently at each other and went to her office.

Once inside, Desiree eased into her chair. She started to shake as she tried to make sense of what just happened. Desiree had adjusted to the reality of regaining her memory and losing Laney. Not a day went by that she didn't think about Laney but she'd worked through the panic and pity, the anger and denial. This was an unexpected shock. Seeing Cash again intensified her loss. Double Dare had been the center of her life up until a few months ago. Visions of Laney and the band flashed through her mind.

Faded memories were now a kaleidoscope of brilliant images. It was like Laney was in the room with her. Grief resurfaced.

After composing herself, Desiree left her office. Hoping no one would see her, she headed up to the flat. She ran past her grandmother, rushed into her room, shut the door and burst into tears.

Constance knocked on her door and entered. "What in the world has upset you?"

Desiree was curled up on her bed. "I don't know how much more I can take. It's been one shock after another. I finally start to feel normal and I get hit with another one. Cash Bentley, one of our band members, just checked in. It was like seeing a ghost from my past."

Constance sat down next to Desiree and stroked her hair. She didn't know how to react to this so she just waited. But Desiree was right. Another shock to deal with and for Constance there was the fear that Desiree would want to go back with this man.

After several minutes Desiree sat up. "I'm all right now. Seeing Cash, I suddenly felt very homesick for my old life, for what was, for Laney. Rowan has given me time off so that I can spend time with Cash while he's here. I'm going down to visit in his room. There are a lot of things he and I have to talk about. Cash was only able to grieve a loss. Now, he too, is saying good-bye to Laney. I have someone who, in a way, can bring Laney back to me even if it's only for a little while. He's the only person who knows her like I did, good and bad. I believe this is what I need to really let go of my past." Seeing the worried look on her grandmother's face she added, "Don't worry, Gran. I'm not going anywhere and I'm going to be okay. You and Boris are stuck with me." She gave her grandmother an extra big hug as she left.

Up in Cash's room, they looked at each other for a few seconds without speaking. Neither of them looked the same; neither of them were the same.

Cash's eyes were still moody and deep, they seemed to reflect his soul. Everything about him was rough and rugged but now there were lines around his mouth and eyes that hadn't been there before. They weren't marks of age but of pain.

Desiree's eyes, though sad, were clear and bright. She carried with her an air of casual sophistication that wasn't evident before. With her shorter hair she looked older and more mature. She was. Life could have that effect on a person.

"It's good to see you again, Des. You were obviously shocked when I showed up so I guess no one told you I was coming?"

All Desiree could do was shake her head.

"We've shared so much, haven't we? And now this." Cash pulled her into his arms and they both broke down and cried.

Wanting both quality and undisturbed time together they stayed in the room. This time was for the three of them; Desiree, Cash and Laney. Together they shared old memories, good and bad. They recalled the highs and lows with the band, the early missteps and foolish mistakes. Some of the emptiness within Desiree was filled thanks to Cash.

Cash got up and began to pace. He was afraid that what he was going to say would cause a wave of pain that threatened to dim the pleasure of their visit. "I have something to tell you." He faltered between words as though what he had to say was very difficult for him and the look in his eyes told Desiree it was. "The boys and I are forming our own band. I'm going to be the lead singer. I'm sorry if this hurts you, Des. We all loved Double Dare as much as you and Laney did. After the accident we were lost and miserable but we had to move on."

Desiree was grateful for his openness and honesty. She was happy for him and relieved. "You're all so talented. You're gifted with your song writing, Cash. I understand that you had to move on. Laney would understand, too."

Cash could see that she meant it. He sat back down beside her and dropped his face into his hands. He looked so defeated. "I missed what we had. You and Laney, the band, the lifestyle we lived. I felt completely lost and devastated and I couldn't grieve like I wanted to."

At that moment, Desiree realized just how much Cash had loved her twin sister. She took his hand in hers. "You were special to Laney. Other than me, she felt closer to you than anyone else in the world. Laney was in love with you. She just hadn't admitted it to herself."

"Does it hurt to talk about Laney?" Cash asked, revealing his own hurt.

Not a day passed without Desiree longing for her twin sister. "Not anymore. It did at first. Now I find it's good to remember. It hurts that

Laney was taken from us too soon. But I'm learning to live without her." The tears began their familiar flow down Desiree's cheeks.

"Please don't cry," Cash pleaded, his own face pinched with misery.

"I miss her terribly, Cash. I miss her annoying teasing, her genuine laughter and her spontaneity. I even miss our arguments. I miss her with all my heart."

Cash could understand. "I know, I miss her too. It's almost like our world isn't as bright as it used to be but the sky has one more shining star. Our universe isn't in balance anymore."

Once the death of Laney had been addressed and Cash had shared his news about his new band, things returned to normal between them. Time passed quickly as they reminisced. "We've been friends for a long time. I don't want to lose that."

Absently, Cash reached out and caressed her cheek. "Then come back to the States. We could use a female singer."

His offer was touching and Desiree felt comforted. "I've moved on, Cash. There's nothing there for me anymore."

Cash knew they had all changed. His voice became serious, "Even though both of you embraced Double Dare and loved to perform, Laney thrived on the lifestyle. You let Laney be the boss because you were willing to compromise and swing with her moods."

Desiree smiled as she confessed, "It made my life easier. Laney had so much ambition and a love for the business. She was bold and strong with total confidence. She had such innovative ideas and was always so sure about the direction the band should take." Her eyes suddenly filled with tears as she spoke in soft memory, "Laney was passionate about what she did. She wasn't fickle, just flighty at times."

Cash agreed. "You knew how to keep her grounded. You have a gift of listening to people with understanding and compassion and making them feel you care."

"That's part of the reason I fit in so well here at the hotel. I feel like I'm home and I belong here. I hope you can understand."

Cash understood.

The hours flew by all too quickly. Together they laughed and cried. It had been a very emotional day.

"It's late, I should go."

"Do you have to?" Cash asked in a husky voice.

Desiree smiled knowingly, "I'll stay." Neither of them was ready to let Laney go. The two of them talked long into the night and in the early hours of the morning Desiree fell asleep on his couch.

Just after dawn Desiree went up to the flat. Constance greeted her with a raised eyebrow. The look didn't need words. Desiree quickly explained how she'd fallen asleep on Cash's couch. Then she went to her room to shower and change.

Over breakfast, the conversation was centered on Cash. "We talked endlessly about Laney and the old days. It's crazy. Part of me wants to forget and part of me wants to remember. I can tell you about Laney and share stories with you. But you didn't know her. Cash did and I realize I need this time with him. I don't know what Rowan's motives were for bringing Cash here but I'm grateful that he did."

Constance looked at Desiree thoughtfully, "I would like to meet your friend."

Desiree smiled warmly, "I would like that too, Gran. How about lunch up here before we head out for the day?"

After a pleasant lunch upstairs, Desiree and Cash were ready to take in the sights. Cash wore his faded denim jacket and worn jeans. Since Desiree was off the clock, she resorted back to her casual attire. She, too, was dressed in jeans and the denim jacket that she wore the day she arrived. Cash had his arm draped casually around her shoulders as they entered the lobby. It felt like the old days. It felt good.

Maeve walked by and glared at them in disgust. It didn't go unnoticed by Cash. Desiree just laughed. "Pay no attention to Maeve. She's often gobby." At Cash's questioning look Desiree enlightened him, "Sorry, gobby means rude."

"Picking up the British slang, Des? You act like you've settled in nicely."

Desiree nodded, "It was a struggle at first with both the unknown and the changes. I was so scared and angry. After a while I got tired of fighting. Once I did, life got easier."

As he looked around, Cash slipped his hands into his pockets. "This is quite the place." He suddenly looked uncomfortable. It was a whole other life than what he was used to.

Desiree understood and confessed, "I was overwhelmed at first. I didn't have any memory but I knew I had never lived in this kind of luxury. Now I love the Conlyn. It's been home since I arrived. It's a far cry from the tour bus, isn't it?"

Together, they spent the rest of the day walking around, relaxing over dinner on the boardwalk and talking. On their return to the hotel, they were making plans to meet for breakfast as they were crossing through the lobby. Cash was leaving in the morning. He gave Desiree a quick kiss and entered the lift.

When Desiree turned around, Rowan was directly behind her. Without a word, he grabbed her elbow and pulled her into his office. His manner was so unexpected that Desiree had no time to react. After firmly closing the door, Rowan verbally pounced on her. "I've been told that you were seen coming out of Cash's room at daybreak. You may have lived a promiscuous lifestyle in the States but I can't believe that you'd jump into bed with Cash Bentley the minute he gets here."

If Desiree hadn't been so shocked at his anger she would have told him nothing happened and explained. Instead she resorted back to her old habit and attacked back. "Are you back to spying on me?" she hurled at him.

Rowan was hurt by her accusation and by the fact that she didn't deny his comment. "I guess I owe Maeve an apology. I refused to believe her when she said she heard you were staying in Cash's room."

"Just like she overheard I was going to the beach with Woody. You should get your facts straight. For your information that's what they call the main floor at Evelina Children's Hospital where Woody and I volunteer. Maeve ran to you and blew an overheard conversation out of context. Like usual, Maeve is being a conniving trouble maker. Why else would she feel it necessary to report to you other than to cause trouble? And, I don't know how this concerns you. It's nobody's business what I do. I go where I please and with whom I please."

"Our hotel maintains a strict moral code among our staff."

Desiree's face went dead white. She was hurt and insulted by his comment so her voice trembled with emotion, "I didn't realize I was considered staff."

"Did you stay in Cash's room?" Rowan demanded to know.

Desiree looked at him and said fiercely, "The fact that you give credence to whatever Maeve says tells me that you and I have nothing further to say to each other."

Rowan continued, ignoring the effect of his words. "I asked you a question." His mouth had thinned and his eyes clearly showed disappointment as he glared at her.

Desiree felt she had nothing to apologize for. Besides, seeing Rowan's clenched jaw, she knew it would be pointless. "I don't owe you any explanation in regards to Cash. Besides, you were the one who invited him here, not me," she threw back in his face.

"It was actually Maeve's idea." Rowan defended Maeve's behavior. "She said you were missing your boyfriend and your old life and it was only a matter of time before you'd be returning to him in the States. I'm surprised you didn't contact him yourself."

Desiree was sure Maeve's real motive was jealousy. She looked at Rowan defiantly, "Maeve was hoping Cash would persuade me to go back with him. Am I right?"

"That's not for me to say." Rowan couldn't stop himself from asking, "Did he?"

"I'm tired of explaining myself to you because of Maeve. I don't know where she came up with that notion. Probably wishful thinking. Now, if you'll excuse me I'm going up to Cash's room where I'll be welcomed."

"I don't know what to think about you anymore. You're not who I thought you were. How can you be so disrespectful to your grandmother after all she's done for you? Desiree, I told you if you hurt Connie I'd make your life miserable. So clean up your act."

Tight-lipped, Desiree strolled blindly out of the room.

Desiree couldn't believe Cash's short stay at the hotel was over. They were in the lobby saying their good-byes. "You'll survive, Des. We've had plenty of experience in surviving."

The best Desiree could manage was a nod.

"Are you sure I can't talk you into coming back with me? It'll be like old times."

Not quite. Everything had changed and they both knew it. That was a very different time in their lives and there was no Laney. Her eyes filled with sentimental tears. "The past is the past. I'll never forget what we all had, you, me and Laney. Nor will you. But that part of my life is over. Nothing is forever. I'll never forget you Cash and I'll always remember the good times that we all had together. But I wouldn't be happy going back."

Cash took her face in both of his hands, "You don't look happy now." Desiree didn't answer him. Cash understood better than she thought. He saw the sadness in her eyes. "Is Rowan the reason you're staying?"

"No. I may not be firmly settled in my new life here but this is home for me. You don't just walk away from family; they're everything. I can't walk away from here, this hotel, the work I've come to love." Desiree finally realized that she'd been looking for commitment and stability even before the accident. No matter what her future would be, Desiree had made her decision. There would be no regrets.

Cash took Desiree in his arms. It wasn't the embrace of a lover, but one given to a caring, loyal friend. "Call me anytime you need me or if you change your mind. I love you, Des," he added as he kissed her, knowing Rowan was listening from the doorway of his office.

Desiree hugged him tightly, not wanting to let him go. Rowan walked over as Desiree declared, "I love you too, Cash."

"I'm sorry to intrude but the car is ready to take you to the airport." Although Rowan spoke to Cash, his attention was centered on Desiree.

Cash captured Desiree's hands in his. "Everything is going to be all right." The look on her face told him she didn't believe him. He turned to Rowan. "Take care of this girl, she's special." Desiree could see the two men measure each other up. Then Cash walked away. He turned and glanced over his shoulder at her one more time and winked.

Watching Cash go out the door, Desiree never felt lonelier in her life. She closed her eyes as she experienced another sense of loss. This was the last ghost she had to let go of. Desiree looked away and mentally closed the door to her past.

She turned and encountered Rowan's cold stare. "Do you thrive on making all of the men in your life fall in love with you?" Not expecting an answer, he turned and walked away.

Not all. Why can't you love me? Tears welled in her eyes. Desiree's eyes followed Rowan, knowing he didn't have any idea that he was shattering an already broken heart. She brushed away the tear that had sneaked past her guard.

Chapter Eighteen

Desiree was nervously waiting for Woody. They were spending the day at Hyde Park. Today was the annual tree lighting and their ice skating date.

Woody was grinning in anticipation when he entered the lobby and caught sight of Desiree. She looked adorable in her knee-length quilted coat with fur-lined hood. A wool scarf hung loosely around her neck and she was holding a pair of matching mittens. They were both excited as they left the hotel.

The air was crisp with a hint of frost in the air and snow was forecast for later in the day. The streets along the way were festive and store windows were beautifully decorated with spectacular Christmas displays. Desiree enjoyed the window displays and appreciated the artistry that had gone into creating them. She was feeling the spirit of the season and was quickly absorbed in the scenes around her.

At the park, they rented their ice skates. Woody sat down next to Desiree. He laced his own skates while she put hers on. He then kneeled down to tighten her laces.

"Aren't you gallant," she teased nervously.

Woody looked up, a hint of amusement in his eyes. "Not really. I can hardly wait to get you out on the ice. Time to stand up."

Desiree made a face. "Do I have to?"

Woody reached out and pulled her up.

Hanging onto Woody's hand for dear life, she allowed him to lead her to the rink. As soon as her skates hit the ice, her feet seemed to slide out from under her. She immediately let go of Woody and grabbed the railing with both hands. She caught it just before she lost her balance. "Don't think I don't know that you're laughing at me."

Woody's dark eyes danced with amusement. "I'm smiling out loud. Let go of the rail."

Desiree shook her head. "I really like this railing."

Woody laughed. "You don't need it. Come on." Woody lifted her hands away from the rail. He held them in his own and skated backwards slowly, helping her move forward. She held on tight, feeling awkward. "Good job, you're doing great," Woody said as he let go.

Suddenly a cry escaped from Desiree as her skates slid out from under her. She lay there, flat on her back, astonished that she didn't hurt. It took a moment to catch her breath.

Woody bent over her. "Are you okay?"

"How graceful was that?" Desiree said, caught between embarrassment and giggling.

On impulse, Woody leaned over and kissed her forehead.

"Our mom always kissed the part that hurt. I didn't fall on my face." She giggled again as Woody helped her up. Desiree clasped his hands tighter as Woody once again started to skate backwards while pulling her along. Once she gained more control, her feet began to glide. With new confidence, she held his hands more loosely. Every once in a while he let go, still keeping his hands where she could reach them if she wanted to.

With a great deal more ease than she was feeling, Desiree let go longer and longer. Soon her glides became more fluid. When Desiree realized she was skating, she beamed up at him in amazement. Woody was excited for her. "You've got it, Des. You're ice skating." There was a soft disbelieving laugh of pure joy from Desiree. It filled the air as well as Woody's heart.

When they returned the skates, Desiree's legs ached and felt a little wobbly but she was glowing with triumph. Woody turned to her, "Would you like a coffee?"

"I'd rather have hot chocolate."

Woody ordered two cocoas and they went over and sat on a park bench and watched the other skaters. Desiree drank her hot chocolate while holding the cup in both hands to warm them. She giggled, "Even the little kids are better than I was."

It felt natural when Woody put his arm around her. "You enjoy children."

"I do. They never cease to amaze you."

Twilight had fallen, bringing with it the forecasted snow. Light flakes began to fall adding magic to the evening. The hubbub in the park had increased throughout the day. They meandered throughout the park along with a throng of sightseers. Hand in hand, they strolled their way through a wonderland of thousands of lights that lit up the darkened sky. The winter air made everything sparkle. There was already a massive crowd surrounding the tall Christmas tree. Woody skillfully maneuvered their way through the crowd toward the front of the stage. Towering in front of them was the great tree that had been strung with delicate white lights from top to bottom. It began to snow heavier and big fluffy flakes stuck to Desiree's long lashes. The crowd around them began the countdown. As soon as the tree lit up there was a thunderous cheer. Kids and adults alike marveled at such a magical sight.

Desiree's eyes got all misty. This would be her first Christmas without Laney. When a group of joyful Christmas carolers began to sing "Hark the Herald Angels Sing" the tears began to flow. Woody understood. For Desiree, Laney had been a part of every single Christmas memory. He knew that in time those memories would only become more precious as she created new ones without her. He stood behind Desiree, wrapped his arms around her and held her tight. His feelings for her went much deeper than he cared to admit.

"Christmas memories are some of the most precious. Thank you for helping me to create new ones. This is a perfect ending to a perfect day."

It was late and the winter air now had a bite so Woody and Desiree took a taxi home. Desiree realized this was the first time she'd been in a taxi since the accident. She grabbed Woody's hand tight. Woody, recognizing her fear, laced his fingers in hers and pulled her close. So many memories to relive and conquer.

"Thank you for a wonderful day, Woody. It was all you promised and more." Expecting his usual kiss on the cheek, she was surprised when he took her in his arms and kissed her on the lips. There was no catch in the area of her heart, no erratic heartbeat. She liked Woody but only as a friend. Nothing like what she felt for Rowan.

Desiree was still shocked by Woody's goodnight kiss when she entered the flat. She was distracted as she took off her coat. It was just a kiss. It didn't mean anything.

Constance was still up reading. The fire in the hearth was inviting and Desiree went and stood close to the dancing flames. Within a few minutes she began to feel toasty warm. "Did you have a nice day with Woody?"

Desiree smiled as she went and sat next to her grandmother and she shared the festive events with her. Constance had to laugh when she told her about her fall. Desiree hesitated before telling her about the goodnight kiss. She wasn't angry at Woody, just confused. "I care very much for him." It was easy to be with Woody and he made her happy.

The look in her granddaughter's eyes revealed more than she intended. "Woody is a wonderful person, Desiree, but don't confuse gratitude for love."

Desiree felt amazingly close to Woody as a friend. "I'm not in love with Woody." No one could compare to Rowan.

"Are you in love with Cash?"

Desiree shook her head. "Laney was but she was afraid to admit it. Oh, Gran, what am I going to do? I can't deny it any longer. I love Rowan."

The anguish in Desiree's voice tugged at Constance's heart. "I know you do. You have for a long time. You were just too stubborn to admit it to yourself."

"Please don't tell him."

The look in her granddaughter's eyes told her something else was troubling her. "What else has you so upset?"

Desiree was reluctant to share her plans with her grandmother but it was time. She'd spent days agonizing over her dilemma, trying to sort out her future. She had made painful decisions that would force her to confront realities she'd rather not face. They were reasonable, logical and adult but it didn't make it easier to say what she was about to say. There was no point in prolonging the pain for either of them. There had been entirely too much of that. She reached over and took her grandmother's hands in hers. "I've reached the point in my life where I need to put down firm roots. I was thinking that I should start looking for a place."

"A place to what?" Constance asked, totally confused.

"A place to move to."

Her grandmother had always been understanding and patient. Until now. "What on earth are you talking about? Is there something wrong with this place?"

"Of course not. I love living here. But I know that despite your generosity and your hospitality, you're a very private person. It's time you have your home back."

"This is your home as much as it is mine. On a purely selfish level, I want you here. You're the family I've been missing. I didn't realize how much until now. Please don't rush into anything. Has this anything to do with the fact that you love Rowan?"

"Yes. You don't stop loving someone just because they hurt you. But you have to figure out how to move on without that person." Desiree's mind argued with her heart. Did she leave because of Rowan? Or did she stay because of Rowan? Desiree wasn't sure which prospect was more distressing. Desiree knew she loved Rowan desperately but she'd have to be strong enough to find a way to live without him.

Constance knew that something had transpired between Desiree and Rowan. Things had been strained between them. Whatever it was had hurt her granddaughter deeply.

Desiree let out a heavy sigh, "I don't want to leave here, Gran. I really don't. But I can't stay living here. I don't even know if I can continue working here. Especially once Rowan and Maeve are married." Leaving would be simple. Staying would be hell.

"Running away isn't the answer. What do you think Delany would do?"

"I don't know," was all Desiree could bring herself to say.

"From what you've told me about her, she would be fighting tooth and nail for Rowan. There comes a time when you have to take chances."

Desiree decided to change the subject, "I always envied how outgoing and confident Laney was. As young as we were, Laney had a dynamic personality and persuasive powers to match. Without her drive, our band would never have been as successful as we were."

"If I didn't know you were talking about Delany, I'd have thought you were talking about yourself. Look at your accomplishments with the Benefit Ball. You're special on your own. I wonder if you sold yourself short because of Delaney. It's not that you weren't capable but why would you have to do certain things when you knew she would?"

Her grandmother's uncanny insight surprised her. "I've come to realize that there's a lot more Laney in me than I thought. The Halloween Benefit was a blast, wasn't it? Laney would've been impressed. Before my memory returned I was surprised at how good I was at delegating. I thought that I'd learned it from Maeve. But Laney and I did everything in regards to our band. Because we had so many years alone, we only trusted each other. Sometimes things happen to you, or around you, that you can't control. When that happens, you pull yourself together and go on. That's what I'm trying to do. Memories of my last moments with Laney still continue to haunt me. It happens less often and when it does I think of something positive. That's easy, because Laney and I had so many good times together. But even better, I think of our times together as well, Gran. The good times continued after I got here and I know there are good times ahead."

CHAPTER NINETEEN

Desiree had the apartment to herself. Both Constance and Boris were out having dinner with friends. When she heard the knock on the door she wished she could ignore it, knowing it was Rowan. The persistence of his second knock pulled her off the settee. She opened the door. "Gran isn't here and I really don't have anything to say to you."

"Good, I'll do the talking." Rowan gently pushed the door open further.

"I don't believe I invited you in."

"I don't believe I asked." Rowan leaned over, reached for the package he had in the hall beside the door and stepped inside. He folded his arms across his chest and stood with his broad shoulders against the door. "I brought you a present."

"It isn't Christmas yet."

"This isn't a Christmas present."

"I don't want it."

Desiree Fiona Dare was the most frustrating woman he'd ever met. She was a complicated woman who constantly tried his patience. Yet she was also the woman who had captured his heart. "Open your present."

Desiree knew it would be useless to argue. She removed the wrapping paper and her eyes grew wide with disbelief. It was Woody's painting that he donated for the Benefit. The look in her eyes changed in the space of a heartbeat. Her heart fluttered and she had to swallow as she forced her words past the lump of emotion lodged in her throat. "But how?"

"I was the one who bought it with help from Ashton. You're not the only one who can have an accomplice help to do a deed."

Desiree gave him a sideways glance. She knew he was referring to the skeleton in Maeve's office and smiled reluctantly.

This was the greatest gesture of love Rowan had ever made in his life. "I knew it had a very special meaning to you and no one else should have it." *I know how you feel when you look at this picture because I know how I feel when I look at you.* So much could be read in his dark eyes; passion, desperation, regret, love. How could he tell her that he wanted her so badly he could hardly breathe? Instead, he said, "Ashton is a true friend to you. You do realize that he's in love with you?"

Desiree smiled sadly, "Maybe a little. Woody is, and always will be, my friend."

"Despite the fact that he's in love with you, Ashton said he knew that you were in love with someone else. Is it Cal? He's awfully smitten with you."

"Cal will fall in and out of love many times before he finds his true love. Right now he loves life and everyone in it." Desiree smiled wickedly, "The boy tolerates Maeve for God's sake. He's a saint." She became more serious. "Cal helped me through the transition from the United States to here and he helped me to accept the person called Dee. You and Gran had expectations from me because of my past. With Cal there was no past. Time with him was fun and easy. He made me laugh."

"It seemed that every time I turned around there was another man in your life that I thought you were in love with. I heard you tell Cash that you love him. And Maeve said you were in love with him and it was only a matter of time before you left us to be with him."

"I do love Cash. The same way I love Gran. But I'm not in love with him. Cash loved Laney. Both Cash and I had to say good-bye to Laney, good-bye to our band and good-bye to each other. There's nothing and no one for me in the States."

Desiree turned and walked across the room. She needed to put distance between them so she could think. She realized it was time to be honest with herself as well as with Rowan. It was time to face her truth without reservation. It was time to take a chance.

Rowan walked slowly toward her. She remained still. He gently turned her to face him and lifted her chin so he could look into her eyes.

Desiree let out a long, slow breath as she looked up at Rowan. "Woody was right." They were eye to eye, barely a breath apart. She was moved by the flicker of pain that crossed Rowan's face, for he had misunderstood. Desiree smiled, a look that always made his breath catch in his throat. Her look didn't waver. "He knows I'm in love with you."

"Desiree." He breathed her name softly. "I've been waiting for you all my life. You've changed my life. You've changed me."

"I thought you were in love with Maeve. You've been seeing each other for years. She told me you're going to get married in the New Year."

"That's what Maeve wanted to believe. Maeve and I had a comfortable and satisfying relationship that worked well. Maeve fit into my plans as I did hers. That is until you arrived and knocked me off course. I was always in control of my emotions but you kept challenging me with those intense gray eyes. You challenged me on everything. Suddenly, my life was in chaos. Maeve knew before I did that I had fallen in love with you. She has accepted a promotion. She'll be moving to Manchester next week where she'll be managing our hotel there. Once Maeve realized that she no longer had a place here at the Conlyn she admitted she was looking forward to the transfer."

It took all of Desiree's effort to maintain control of her emotions. Her heart lightened with every word he spoke.

"I never gave much thought to falling in love. Then I met you. I think it happened the first day I saw you laying in that hospital bed. You were so defenseless. Nothing has been the same for me since that day. You were so frightened. You kept looking at me with those large sad eyes silently pleading for help. Other times, you would look at me so outraged and tell me how much you hated me."

Rowan continued to watch her carefully, measuring every gesture, every expression. "You arrived as raw as a human can be. But you weren't going to let anyone mold you. You molded yourself with inner strength and personal beliefs. I once called you unique. You're more than that, Desiree. You are extraordinary. The first few days you were here I'm sure Connie felt she had her daughter back. You'd occasionally take her back in time because you were so much like Phoebe. But she loves you for who you are."

Desiree knew this was true. Her grandmother had welcomed her and accepted her unconditionally. Whereas, Rowan had put her on the defensive. "You felt protective of Gran. Your loyalty was with my grandmother. I resented your relationship with her. I felt I had to fight you for her love."

Regret cut through him. He had made his share of mistakes dealing with Desiree. He was sorry for the things he'd said and done when she'd been frightened and vulnerable. "I believe my frustration was due to not understanding you that caused me to appear insensitive. But your strength and courage kept drawing me to you. You weren't the only one who was confused and guarded. You were so tangled up in my thoughts all day long that you wound up in my dreams at night. I couldn't escape you." Rowan wrapped his arms around Desiree, "Do you know how hard it was for me to let you go every time I had you in my arms?" Lowering his head he touched his lips to hers. They were gentle and tender.

Rowan's kiss felt so good, so right. Her fingers locked behind his neck, their eyes met and held. Desiree could see the truth in his eyes. She surrendered. Her smile was radiant as she touched her lips to his. Her kiss was demanding and wild with all the locked-up longing she'd kept hidden within her these long lonely months. Her passion quickly took his breath away. As his mouth slipped from hers, she let out a long, pleased sigh, opening her eyes slowly. She felt alive, aware of every beat of her heart.

Rowan could see her joy and her love, the same emotions he was expressing.

Desiree gave a silent prayer of gratitude. This was life; this was real. She had lost family and found family, remembered her forgotten past, confronted fate and found love. A vital part of her had died with Laney but she was coming back to life and living her own life for the first time. She'd never get over Laney's death but she was ready to move forward and live her own life to the fullest. She knew that was what Laney would want for her. Desiree sighed with pleasure. It was time to live for the future.

Rowan's steady gaze stayed on her. "I hope the worst thing that ever happens to you is in your past and the best thing that happens to you is in your future. I'll be there for the good times, the bad times and all the times in between. The nightmares will not return. We'll replace them with happy memories." Rowan released her slowly as if he was reluctant to let her go. When he spoke his voice was husky with emotion. "I'm in love with you and I want to be part of your future. Never doubt my love for you, Desiree Fiona Dare."

Desiree would not look back in sorrow. "The past is gone and nothing will change it. It's the future I'm interested in. I love you, Rowan Le Baron." Desiree knew her life was here. In her heart she knew she was home.

Thank you for reading my book!

If you enjoyed it, please post your review on Amazon.ca. For more information about the author and upcoming events, check out Facebook & Instagram.

 LindaRakosAuthor   LindaRakos

CPSIA information can be obtained
at www.ICGtesting.com
Printed in the USA
LVHW030229031219
639137LV00001B/1/P